Best of British Fantasy 2018

Best of British Fantasy 2018

Edited by Jared Shurin

NewCon Press
England

First edition, published in the UK May 2019 by NewCon Press

NCP 190 (hardback)
NCP 191 (softback)

10 9 8 7 6 5 4 3 2 1

ISBN: 978-1-912950-17-1 (hardback)
978-1-912950-18-8 (softback)

Cover art by Matty Long
Cover design by Ian Whates
Text layout by Storm Constantine

Contents

Introduction:
We All Fall Together

Jared Shurin

When starting a new tradition - and I sincerely hope this inaugural volume of *The Best of British Fantasy* becomes one - the respectful thing to do is study what came before. And then promptly do the opposite.

In the case of the "year's best" subgenre, introductions tend to take one of two forms. The first approach is that of the annual overview. The editor heroically attempts to catalogue all things related to the genre that occurred in the calendar year. Some of these introductions can run into the hundreds of pages: an annual index of trend-spotting that captures publications, movies, comics, awards, theatre, and beyond.

I suspect the reasoning behind this approach stems from the sub-genre's distant origins – that is, 'before the internet'. It is flattering to be part of a tradition this ancient, but, in 2019, I think these details are best captured elsewhere. There are a host of formal and informal resources that capture this data for posterity far better than I ever could.

The second approach found in *Year's Best* volumes is the imposition of thematic consistency. The editor stares at the year's fantasy outputs until the void stares back - and then helpfully whispers a single, unifying truth. Future readers then learn that 2018 was entirely about *the apocalypse.* Or *nostalgia.* Or any other themes that could, with the appropriate amount of pruning or plumping, define the historical record. As a fan of brutal simplicity - and of sweeping statements - I can't help but appreciate this approach.

However, as much as I admire the ambition, I'm not comfortable with how the thematic approach deceives when it comes to chronology. All of the stories enclosed in this volume, for example, were definitely published in 2018. They were *not* all written in 2018. Some were written and published that same day: the miracle of self-publishing. Others were written in the interminable past, then sent forth to run the submissions gauntlet: the vagaries of traditional publishing. Some were inspired years before being written; some were constructed on the spot in workshops. Nor can we even ascribe 'publisher intent'. The websites, anthologies and magazines that published these stories all began their own selection and publication processes at various times.

As much as I would love to declare 2018 to be the year of the *apocalypse*, *nostalgia*, or *anxiety*, that would be a false imposition not only of my own perspective, but of what even constituted '2018'.

What unites both approaches, the fact-collecting and the theme-building, is the sense of writing for posterity. These are introductions not for readers in 2018 (or even 2019), but in 2028, 2038 and beyond. They are attempts to provide valuable context for future readers of the collection. To explain not only that these are the best stories of the year, but to provide a 'why': what it is about the stories that makes them so very 2018ish. But if the 'facts' are best provided elsewhere, and the 'theme' is chronologically suspect, what else is there?

Only the most important thing of all: the reader.

Whenever they were written, commissioned or conceived, all of these storis were first *read* in 2018. The reader is therefore the ultimate context. Who are the people who read these stories? And how would the stories have reflected their attitudes, or their perceptions?

This is a vast question, and hopefully the readers of 2028 will turn to more than the introduction of *The Best of British Fantasy* when it comes to understanding the many nuances of British life in 2018. But, for the sake of the attempt, I've relied heavily on the massive database that is YouGov Profiles. The December 30, 2018 updates contains within it an audience of over 15,000 people who agree with the statement "I enjoy fantasy fiction". This is a large enough pool to allow us substantial numbers for analysis, even as we dive into some of the database's more esoteric statements.

To set the scene: fantasy readers are, demographically, representative of the UK as a whole. Fantasy readers do skew a bit younger (only 30% are 55+, compared to 38% of the overall population), and very slightly more male (51% to 49%), but, for the avoidance of doubt, they are statistically distributed across all shapes and sizes. They're also distributed across the UK, although fantasy readers are over-represented in Scotland (much like this book's list contributors). But, like the characters in this book, British fantasy readers come from every possible background - urban millennial renters, middle class village dwellers, second-generation immigrants, and much more. Fantasy readership, like the genre itself, knows no bounds.

Given this diversity, all the attitudinal statements should be taken with a grain of salt. However, there are some clear trends. Over a quarter (27%) of fantasy readers, for example, say that "life is more uncertain than previous generations". This is a significantly higher proportion than the rest of the population. Aliya Whiteley's "Dark Shells", for example, captures the bridge between generations – the "then" and the "now"- with a poetically hazy confidence in the former. As is befitting in a genre well-rooted in its traditions, many of the other stories in *Best of British Fantasy* also capture the weight of history. Tade Thompson's "Yard Dog" harkens to a different era (and country), but similarly captures a sense of the oral tradition, the importance of storytelling, and a certain glamour that comes from a bygone era. Even Adam Roberts' "Godzilliad": an elegant concoction that uses the formal mode to elevate a giant stompy lizard from pop culture to something even more significant.

Fantasy readers also revealed themselves to be cautious folk. 53% said they were not risk-takers, not only a majority, but also, a significant difference from the rest of the population. (It is hard not to blame our active imaginations.) But throughout *Best of British Fantasy*, the risk-takers are lionised. Lizzie Hudson's "Boys" features a young woman taking a risk: a plunge from the safe into the true unknown. Ian McDonald's "The Guile" is an improbable heist in an impossible setting; a feat of daring and deceit that can only leave you smiling. Lisa Fransson's "The Moss Child" features a young woman of incredible courage: brave enough even to defy those who love her. None of these stories are pure escapism: everything comes with its price. Indeed, Matthew Hughes' "The Prevaricator" serves as a sorcerous parable in a secondary-world setting. The story's cunning anti-hero reaps the rewards of deceit, but eventually pushes his luck just the tiniest bit too far.

Fantasy readers have a distinct view of social mobility as well. 39% believe success stems from "good fortune", while only 24% believe it comes from "effort": both clear departures from the national average. Fantasy readers understand the "Chosen One" trope well, and the stories within *Best of British Fantasy* play with the tension between what's destiny and what's due. Liam Hogan's "The Dance of a Thousand Cuts" is centred around a duel for the ages; a story packed with stunning swordplay. But it is also a discussion of privilege, both magical and political. R.J. Barker's "To Look Upon His Works" is an aggressively rebellious, if gruesome, piece, in which an artist strikes back against tyranny in the only way he knows how. Steph Swainston's "Velocity" is an exciting return to her world of Castle. It features an Immortal - a man honoured as the very, *very* best at what he does - and his ignominious homecoming. It is also a tale of with frustration at its heart. No much our hero has earned, he is perpetually at a disadvantage. Reggie Oliver's "Coruvorn" has the tone and style of a classic 'Club' story, but the author turns this narrative tradition on its head. The title character has managed to fail upwards, lifted by his class, gender, contacts and the warm air of social standing. But when he finally brushes against real achievement, he finds himself challenged - in two worlds - by a new social order.

Fantasy readers are also more likely than the population as a whole to feel like there's no sense of community in their local area - and over a third agree that they feel "a bit alienated" by modern life. This sense of being out of place is present in stories such as Heather Parry's "The Small Island" and Priya Sharma's "A Son of the Sea". In the former, there is a literal separation that neatly fits alongside the figurative. In the latter, a young man roves around the world looking for a sense of belonging. Paul McQuade's "A Gift of Tongues" contains a physical metaphor for alienation, and the story's protagonist sacrifices herself, and her voice, in the quest to fit in. Harkiran Dhindsa's "The Woman Who Turned Into Soap" features another sacrifice - slower, but no less tortuous. By dipping into fantasy, the stories are able to express alienation both symbolically and physically, with effective results.

The vast majority - almost two-thirds - of fantasy readers say they are disengaged from politics and politicians. And they are more likely than the rest of the population to *disagree* with the statement that "it is important to find their place in society". Accordingly, several of the stories in *Best of British Fantasy* express an compellingly absurdist view of the world. Beth Goddard's "The Councillor's Visit" features a Very Nice Couple who, having been briefly inspired to Get Involved, now find themselves in an incredibly awkward situation. Rhys Hughes' "Counting the Pennies" gleefully pokes fun at the maxims of capitalism, while James Warner's "12 Answers Only You Can Question" is a Kafkaesque romp centred around a standardised test. Kirsty Logan's "We can make something grow between the mushrooms and the snow" takes a fantastical approach to a quintessentially British horror: the housing market. For those reading the hardcover edition, Archie Black's "Underground" is a similarly grim exploration of public transport. Fantasy allows us new perspective on British culture and society - even allowing us to laugh at it.

Perhaps most the upsetting revelation from the data: 28% of fantasy readers say that they are unhappy with their lives, significantly more than the 21% national average. Many of the stories within resonate with varieties of sadness and strain. In Ben Reynold's brief and glorious "Mushroom Speed Boosts", a young man uses a video game to come to terms with loss (or, possibly, not). Helen McClory's "The Farm at the World's End" reveals another way of coming to terms with loss; acknowledging that "an apocalypse can be as small as a palm." Malcolm Devlin's "We Are Now Beginning Our Descent" - from which the title of this introduction is lifted - features a man so out of place, so out of sorts, that he deliberately courts death time and time again. Jenni Fagan's opening poem, "There's a Witch in the World Machine" channels a furious frustration into an incantation. These stories use fantasy as an emotional sandbox, using the freedom of the genre to find creative ways to express deeply internalised challenges.

In an interview with the Arts Council (given in 2019, forgive me), Syima Aslam, Director of the Bradford Literature Festival referred to stories as "magical portals, through which you can explore different emotions, realities, and ideas". Good fantasy has always been capable of the latter two: imaginative worlds and impossible ideas are the genre's bread and butter. Great fantasy - dare I say it, the *best* fantasy - can do the former. Stories can help us grapple with, come to terms with, or simply recognise how we feel. Fantasy can be inspiring, but it can also be therapeutic.

Lest the reader of 2028 worry too much about the readers of 2018, please note that I've used my editorial prerogative to select the most dramatic attitudes. The database reveals many positive and optimistic trends as well. The most impressive is this: despite the unhappiness and alienation, fantasy readers are also significantly more likely to participate in volunteering, activism, and charitable donation. Fantasy stands long accused of being the genre of escapism, but here we see it as the genre of hope. The fantasy readers of 2018 are not only able to imagine a better future, they are willing to work hard to make it happen.

Within this book, you'll find mermaids, rogues and magic swords; monsters, ghosts and local councillors. If you need further context for the stories, imagine yourself one of the diverse, unorthodox, slightly grumpy, and secretly-willing initial readers. Or, better yet, enjoy them for yourself.

Jared Shurin, London
April 2019

There's a Witch in the Word Machine

Jenni Fagan

There's a witch in the word
    machine
spell-casting:

dots, particles, atoms

elemental, bodiless,

a typing shell!

The nothing sky has no good
    intentions.
Go beyond it.

Timber wolves bay in testimony
as fingertips trail light:
argot idiom, double-grave, slash-
    through

words have no pure notions…
they are flesh

strong and ventricle –
poison tipped arrows,

gouge them out

with a sharpened athame.
This is no thaumaturgy

Jenni Fagan

(she can't leave the word machine)
astral lovers (as they are)

cannot be parted by logic or
    reason,

she brings no betrayal,
only incantations, divination,
sex magic
and a desire to crash the pro-
    gramme

rewrite it as it should have
been.

We Are Now Beginning Our Descent

Malcolm Devlin

I have always dreamed I would die in an aeroplane crash. It will be a big plane. A commercial flight. I will be seated in economy as normal, I have never had an upgrade and I have never expected to deserve one. On this flight, the dice will have rolled against me and I will be trapped in the middle of a row. There will be a businessman on my left: he will be portly, balding, busy with a briefcase. His tie will have been loosened with a nervous tug of a crooked finger, and beads of sweat will have started pebbling his forehead before the cabin doors have even closed. To my right, there will be an elderly woman who will spend the majority of the flight tottering up and down the aisle to the bathroom and chewing the teeth that do not quite fit. Reading her complimentary tabloid, she will tut over the stories of benefit frauds and immigrants; she will linger over the nudity with a mournful fascination.

We will attend to the ritual incantations of the air stewardesses as they perform the hallowed sign of the emergency exits and direct our wandering attention to the airline safety catechism located in the rear pocket of the seats in front of us.

In the unlikely event of loss of cabin pressure, oxygen masks will fall from the overhead compartments. You use them like this, like this, like this.

It will be too late for all of us, and I'd like to think that somehow, we will know all of this in advance. Terrible events don't need portents, we retrofit them afterwards as though by making them inevitable, we can make them digestible. Accidents have always been a part of the world, we will tell each other. This is unavoidable. This is *written*.

As we fall, we will see the engines blossom into fire, lighting the cabin with a private sunset. Our heads will be pressed deep into the foam of the seats and even without looking through the windows we will know the plane is pointing downwards. We will give ourselves to gravity and the rush of it will be delicious. Together, we will cast ourselves at the brittle sea with such force it will make salt of us all.

A dream, then. One I have had many times during my life, since before I ever stepped foot on an aeroplane in person. As a child, I would cast my toys down the stairs or into the bath, until they fell apart and were confiscated from me. It was not because I was tired of them, as my parents believed, but because it seemed a more fitting conclusion to the games I played. It would end with fire, with twisted metal, with broken parts skittering across the kitchen floor.

Through my dream, I have always known how to fly. Because I knew it would be the end of me, there was peace in that understanding.

My wife always promised me she understood.

"Sometimes we only appreciate the places we are," she said, "once we've determined the manner by which we can escape them."

My first flight was a shuttle from London to Edinburgh, barely an hour in the air. I was fifteen and we could have taken the train, but I had begged for the opportunity to fly for the very first time. My father had agreed, because he believed he might be the one to show me something new.

I let him pretend the experience was his to teach. Even at that young age, it felt known and unsurprising. The ritual of it reassured me while my father tried to mask his fear. He had been born soon after the war and had grown up amongst the ruins of the cities the enemy's aircraft had razed. He flew infrequently if at all.

For me, the plane was as warm and familiar as the womb. The dip in the gut as the plane lifted its nose from the runway, the thick, granular roar in the ears, the sharp and sinus-scratching coolness of the processed air. I had dreamed all of it, and even as the plane bucked in turbulence prior to landing, making my father clutch at the arms of his chair, I was never afraid.

I should be clear. My dream has never been a nightmare.

There is comfort in the perception of five hundred people enacting the exact same emotions at the exact same time. There is comfort in being part of something greater than yourself.

There is comfort in dying in company rather than alone.

Those who die in aeroplane accidents are granted famous deaths, but also anonymous ones. For a brief time, your flight number will be on the front page of every newspaper back home, and there won't be one member of the informed public who will not have been touched by the news. But your face will be lost in a grid of casualties and no one will see it unless they are looking. No one will see you unless they know who they're looking for. Tracing their fingers over the matrix of blurry portraits like an old woman working her way through the Sunday word search. There you'd be, surrounded by strangers. A smile intended for someone else, a photograph you'd have been too embarrassed to share when you had been alive, but one that someone, somewhere, thinks represents you in the way they want to remember. Perhaps there'll be a memorial? That must be a consolation. Who hasn't dreamed of leaving their name carved in stone in a public square, open letters weathering the human years, outlasting us all?

I grew up and flew up as much as I could. Business and pleasure, long weekends away. My wife was first flattered by my extravagance, then frustrated by my excess. We flew too much, she would tell me. Think of how much it's costing us. Think of the environmental impact.

She was a patient flyer. She would sit in the light of the cabin window and read one of her paperbacks, unmoved by the alien tilt of the horizon beyond the glass. She would smile flintily at the security staff and avoid eye contact with the passport officials. She would sigh with impatience by the baggage carousel and check her watch as though it might hasten our belongings. Air flight was never more than transport to her. For a time she would humour me, but that did not last.

"Perhaps we should take the ferry next time," she would say, or, "How about the train?"

This was after she had read the newspapers, covers blackened with the photographs of remains. She would cluck her tongue at the outrage and when she had gone to bed, I would find the grid of casualties within the paper and, using scissors and glue, add myself to their number. Just so I could see.

I followed the exploits of terrorists in the news with an enthusiast's interest. Please don't misunderstand, I did not support their causes. For the most part, I didn't quite understand them, but their appreciation of the aeroplane as a form of sacrifice, a burning Viking vessel to bring down an empire? Well there, perhaps I admired their invention.

It was never about ethos. I mourned those they murdered as everyone did, but somewhere deep and private and buried, their atrocities *excited* me at a personal level. By making air travel more dangerous, they made my dream more achievable. I could remain apathetic to their wars and their casualties, because their atrocities glimmered with a self-serving light.

"You're more likely to die in the home than in an aeroplane accident," my wife told me once, while outside in the world, other people's crusades fought to redress the balance.

A bomb would be no good. There would be no beauty there, because a bomb would be too quick to *know*. How would any of us appreciate our final moments in the sulphurous seconds between trigger and release? I longed instead for the cruel longueur of an accident. A crack in the hubris of rocket science, the laws of physics snatching us from the air.

A bomb was a fruit plucked too soon, an accident had ripened on the vine. It deserved to be relished.

Nevertheless, as the bombs sang their baritone chorus, and the airports darkened one by one, I flew more than I ever had. Seeking out the remaining flights that criss-crossed the globe, intersecting with the news feeds and column inches with spots of brilliant light.

When the news cycle quietened, I learned that budget airlines often fly with only limited fuel. Enough to get them from one location to another and no reserve to keep them in a holding pattern. It's a dangerous practice but it means they have to land on time or risk the safety of the passengers and the ground crews. I mortgaged the house when I learned that, I booked every flight I could find. It felt like a promise.

My wife flew less frequently. I would call her before each flight I took and tell her I loved her. I did this because it was true, but also so that, after the accident, she would have a story to tell the paper when they called.

"My husband called me before he boarded the flight," she would say. "It was almost as though he knew."

The media adored that sort of thing: love stories cut short, last words delivered in tears before the final curtain. A perfect bittersweet ending. They weren't interested in sequels. They didn't care how the loved ones were left behind at the departure gates, playing their messages over and over again.

I was spending more and more of my time in the air, wondering on each occasion if the next flight would be the one that would take me. I would reserve seats in the middle of rows and wait for the businessman and the old woman to join me. Every time I landed, the plane thump-thumping onto the tarmac, the shriek and holler of shredded atmosphere outside, I felt disappointment that the flight had done only what was supposed to do. It was upsetting that the pilots had done their job; that the journey had been routine. Amongst the clatter of released seatbelts and the whistle of mobile phones returning from blackout, I would sit back in my seat, dejected until the plane had cleared. This time, at least, the journey had not transcended its purpose.

My wife left me somewhere between flights. One moment she was by my side by the check-in desk, the next she was gone. I don't remember where that was. I don't remember when.

The phone rang and rang and rang. The papers wanted to know if she'd told me she loved me.

"Do you know why they make you wear seatbelts on planes?" I told them instead. "They won't save your life. It's so they can identify the bodies if something goes wrong."

I won't bore you with the particulars of how I died. Only that it wasn't what I had in mind. There was no aeroplane crash for me. No glorious company, no memorials or front pages. My death was an embarrassment. It was rushed and incomplete, and if you'll forgive me, I intend to leave it at that.

My days are now spent in transit, hurriedly moving westwards down the concourse, my hand luggage rattling behind me on its tiny little wheels, my coat draped over my arm, my passport in my hand.

The airport is familiar as all airports are. An international space, culture shaved down to the basics so it has become something bland and palatable. The signs are written in international glyphs. Stick men and symbols, yellows and blacks. The windows to my right show a tarmac ground and a matching tarmac sky, each punctured with red and yellow lights moving in preordained lines.

I don't remember landing here. I don't really know where I'm going, but I know I should head westerly, always westerly. The signage indicating the boarding gates clocks upwards one by one as I walk.

Double figures, treble figures. More. I know that despite the fact I have been walking for days, months, years, I have a flight I must not miss under any circumstances. The concourse stretches onwards to a distant point, my bag clatters behind me. I feel the tug of the weight it at my shoulder, a roughly drawn stress line, thick across the muscles of my back.

Everyone is rushing to go somewhere else, I have the sense that no one really sees each other. We are all trapped within the borders of our discrete groups. There are businessmen, families, couples linked arm in arm. Sometimes they jog past me, sometimes they're heading the opposite way, sometimes they're lingering by the concession stalls and the duty free. They talk idly in languages I don't recognise, let alone understand. This too, is comforting in a way.

Sometimes the gates I pass are full, with great crowds of people sitting together under storm clouds of impatience and exhaustion. I know it's impossible to get comfortable on those seats and my heart goes out to them. People pace back and forth. They lie on the cold thin carpet as though it might let them sleep.

I see the way they look at the information boards for updates about their progress. A child cries, a couple argue. I walk on.

Every now and then I see someone I recognise, sitting alone in the ranks of seating beside an otherwise empty gate. I never remember their names, I don't seem to remember anyone's names and they don't look up as I pass by; they stare into the middle distance instead, preoccupied by something private I have no wish to interrupt.

There is one woman in particular. I have seen her before, but I couldn't tell you where from. She always sits at the end of the row of seats, closest to the aisle. Her coat is arranged neatly on the chair beside her and a small cabin bag is tucked between her feet. She has a paperback open in her lap before her which she reads intermittently as though she is saving it for the journey ahead. She seems to know I'm coming because she always looks up from her book as I approach and she smiles at me.

I don't know how she moves from one gate to another. She's always getting there before me. I have come to look forward to seeing her again. I look forward to her smile lighting the path as I go on my way.

I have spoken to her only once. She smiled at me as she always did and this time I stopped beside her. She lifted her coat and set it on her lap, her hand touching the seat alongside, inviting me to join her.

We talked mostly about air travel, but I have always found remarkable how it's a subject that can connect to nearly everything else. Politics, culture, love. Its roots stretch broad and deep, touching all of us in some way.

We talked for hours as though we had only just met. There was so much we had missed.

She told me how she had always dreamed she might have a family, and I told her about my dream in turn. I told her how I always expected to die in an aeroplane collision but how I was disappointed.

"I died in an aeroplane crash." She said this simply as though it was a fact of little or no consequence. It meant nothing to her. Not any more.

"Was it beautiful?" I said.

She smiled at me again and there wasn't judgement there, nor pity, nor anger.

"I don't remember," she said.

She glanced at my luggage.

"They're not going to allow all of that on your flight," she said. "They have restrictions."

I told her I wasn't ready to leave any of it behind and she nodded as though she understood. I checked my watch, even though I couldn't read the time on it. I told her I should be on my way if I was going to catch my flight.

I haven't spoken to her again but she still smiles at me when I pass. She lowers her paperback and moves the coat from the chair beside her and I smile back, I wave and pass by.

Some time ago, I thought I saw the businessman. The portly gentleman I dreamed sat to my left as our plane crashed into the sea.

I saw him disappear into the lavatories outside one of the gates, and I waited outside for three days expecting him to come out again.

I haven't seen him since. I haven't seen the old woman at all, but I find it reassuring to think that they're both here somewhere. It gives me a certain purpose I might otherwise have lacked. It was my first sense that things were moving forward, the first time I understood I wasn't simply going round in circles after all.

I hurry down the concourse, my luggage skittering and skuttering behind me. The gate numbers clock up but now I know they're converging to a point. The woman with the paperback smiles at me and

I salute her as I pass. My flight is ahead of me. They will call my name and I will be there.

We will take off, launching expansively into the night. How arrogant it is to fly! How beautiful! How absurd! And when it is time, we will all fall together, unified and exhilarated and finally complete.

The Dance of a Thousand Cuts

Liam Hogan

If the sword Ellie found tucked into the blackened trunk of a lightning-struck oak hadn't been magical, this story would have a different ending.

If it had been a normal sword, she'd never have mastered it. Those thousand cuts would have as likely been hers, not her opponents. If it had been a normal, dumb sword, it would have been taken off the young village leader's daughter and certainly no one would have bothered to teach her.

The *sword* taught her.

That was what it was, this is what it did. A training sword designed to teach an ancient art from an age long since passed. From the vantage point of its venerable creators, its powers weren't magical. The same technology that coaxed Ellie's hand to hold it right, that made her flex her arm just *so*, also kept the sword's edge pristine through the eons, if deliberately rather blunt.

It had done this before, for others. But not for a while. It hadn't been hidden in the blasted trunk where Ellie found it. Rather, it had been lost centuries earlier, had lain underground and undisturbed while men lived and died and returned to dust, before being lifted back to the surface and absorbed into a sapling. A sapling that grew into a mighty oak, that lived for many hundreds of years before lightning struck and liberated the sword contained within, long after the civilisation that forged it had fallen into fable and myth.

An hour with this sword would teach even the clumsiest dolt the twelve basic forms. A week would lead to utter mastery.

Ellie had it for nearly two years.

True, this was not time she could fully devote to swordplay. She stole an hour here and an hour there, while supposedly collecting firewood, or wild garlic, or acorns.

Still, it was enough.

The woods whistled to the sound of the blade turning and twisting in her supple hands. In autumn, no leaves were allowed to fall that were

23

not struck in their twisting descent.

Though never cut in two. The sword was blunt, remember?

In Ellie's fourteenth year, a tournament was announced, to select the new King's new champion. Each town, each village in the land, was requested to send their best swordsman to the Capital.

When Ellie stepped forward to represent her village, everyone laughed, even her father, even her brother, Billy. Especially her brother; a strapping man five years Ellie's senior, with visions of fame, of glory.

"But father!" he protested, when the one-sided contest was over, when none were found to stand against her flashing blade.

"But Billy nothing," grunted his father, her father; the village leader. "Can *you* best her?"

His sullen silence was answer enough.

"Then it is clear. She goes in your place. Remember, son, honour at the King's tourney reflects back on this village. Pray she does well."

In the Capital, surrounded by Knights and men-at-arms from all corners of the Kingdom, she had every right to feel nervous. Even more so when it was explained that no, she couldn't use her training sword. Handed a poorly balanced replacement, she danced the dance of a thousand cuts as a warm up. Flawlessly, elegantly, the blade a blur of light and whispered sound. The training sword had long since stopped having to correct her movements, even for a dance as complicated as this one.

And, just like that, the tournament was over.

Her open-mouthed opposition sidled away into the crowds, sheathing their swords or just letting them fall, never to dare pick one up again for fear of facing an opponent such as she. It didn't take much imagination to feel those one thousand cuts and the slow death caused by that keen edge.

A Courtier escorted Ellie into the Castle. In a private chamber, he told her the true nature of her uncontested victory: she was to fight the heir to the throne.

"It is tradition," the Courtier explained. "The Prince proves himself worthy by besting the greatest swordsman--or woman--in the land."

"And if he loses?" Ellie asked, wide-eyed.

"Then he is not worthy."

Ellie frowned, toyed with the frayed rope belt that cinched her faded dress. "It's not a *fair* contest, is it?"

The Courtier smiled thinly. This was breaking his heart. He had a daughter Ellie's age. He was thankful this would be his last Royal duty.

"No, child; it is not."

Ellie nodded, thoughtful. "Then I wish to fight the Prince with my own sword."

"But it is blunt!" the Courtier exclaimed.

"I may leave my mark upon the future King, but I will not dishonour my father or my village by drawing Royal blood."

The Courtier stifled a sob, blinked away tears. Screwed his courage to perform one last betrayal. "We will respect your wishes, bravest of girls. But, in order to satisfy the... um, protocols, we must prepare your sword for its place in the Arena's weapon rack."

The Prince stood before Ellie and bowed deeply. Uncertain of the 'protocols', she bowed back. The audience of nobles and visiting dignitaries arrayed in the steep fencing arena tittered in astonishment, drawing a blush from both young contestants.

The Prince raised his jewelled rapier in salute and adopted the first form.

Ellie blinked. He performed the manoeuvre well enough. But surely this was child's play? Was she merely to trade forms with this handsome young Prince, rather than crossing blades?

She mimicked the move, right down to the slight hesitation in his final flourish.

The audience murmured its approval. Here were two equally matched opponents. They had suspected a fraud. A girl, that young? Even though the Prince was a mere lad, the supposed contest insulted the intelligence of the assembled spectators. But the swordplay put paid to such fears. How many of the forms would these two complete, they wondered? And who would emerge victorious?

The Prince perhaps had entertained similar doubts--it was difficult to believe that this slip of a girl had scared away the best swordsmen in his army. And the rumour that she had performed the legendary dance of a thousand cuts--ridiculous!

He too had feared he faced an innocent plucked from the crowd. Perhaps as an attempt to discredit him. After all, besting a girl not yet grown into a woman; where was the honour in that?

More confident, he performed the second form, his steel drawing smoothly through the unresisting air, remembering his lessons from those exotic foreigners his father employed for the purpose. Remembering their admonishments not to overextend his elbows; to let the weight of the sword do the work.

Exhilarated, he took a pace back, to watch Ellie attempt to follow his lead.

She smiled up at him. Cocked her head and *danced* through the form.

Connoisseurs in the galleried stands gasped and rose to their feet in admiration.

On they performed. As the stations increased in difficulty, the Prince's supple body gleamed with perspiration. But while each successfully completed form brought him yet more to life, Ellie felt oddly leaden. Not only did it seem that her trusty sword no longer responded when she fumbled a move, but she felt it was actively sucking the feeling from the fingers of her right hand.

For the seventh move, she switched the blade to her left, and the audience gasped as the thrilling perfection returned once again.

The Prince shook the sweat from his brow. He had thought he had reached and surmounted Ellie's abilities. Had she been toying with him? Was she left-handed all along? The way she performed the difficult eighth move--now it was *he* who was out of his depth.

On the ninth form, muscles straining, he made his first mistake. A thrust where a parry was required. An error that left him overextended, vulnerable. He could almost hear the accented curse of his fencing tutor.

Embarrassed, he hardly dared watch as Ellie took flight, her young face strained with concentration. He assumed it was because of the difficulty of the level and not because she could no longer feel the grip of her sword with either hand.

As in a perfect mirror, though, her left to his right, she copied his mistake. The Prince narrowed his eyes. Was this a compliment, or an insult?

The audience bubbled with excitement. This was swordplay of the highest order. Few attained such ranks as these and none so young.

Halfway through the eleventh form, Ellie's sight dimmed, the images separating, her eyes seemingly losing their ability to work together. The doubled vision almost made her falter and only muscle memory allowed her to complete the complicated sequence.

Blinking, she watched the Prince hesitate. He thought--for the first time--that he might have edged the manoeuvre; that her positioning and execution was not as accomplished as his, that not only did she not, on this occasion, copy his faults, but had made some of her own. She had obviously reached her limits.

The problem was, so had he. He had never completed the twelfth form successfully. It was an order of magnitude more difficult than its predecessors. Though he had been coaxed through its individual steps, the whole had always defeated him.

Still. He had long since exceeded his own expectations, as had this waif of a girl before him. Gone were his worries that the contest was fixed, that his opponent was deliberately inexperienced, or had in some way been weakened. The comments and glances of his courtiers had made him fear so. It was shameful and his protestations that this must be a fair fight had only encouraged insincere avowals that it *was* fair.

And indeed, the fight had been fought on merit. More: if he was to win, he needed to complete--for the first time--the twelfth form; an achievement that would automatically qualify him as a sword master. Nail that and there was no way Ellie could follow.

The young Prince summoned his nerve, calling upon his long line of Royal ancestors to help.

Ellie stood, panting, squinting. It was hard to tell through her blurred vision, but it seemed the Prince had completed the final form. All she had to do was match him and then the contest could begin in earnest.

She had wondered how the duel was to be fixed. Had assumed the judges would not be impartial, would favour the Prince. But they'd been more subtle than that, hadn't they?

Her limbs were leaden and she could not see.

She could have laughed, had she the energy. She'd been prepared to cross her blunt sword with the Prince's sharp one. Prepared, if need be, to let him strike home a blow, to receive a cut that her blade could not inflict.

The poison had not been necessary. Yes, poison: it was obvious. Poison that sapped her strength and her skill. That would surely kill her, if the Prince's sword did not; once they were through with the trivialities of the twelve forms.

Somehow she knew there was no cure, no antidote. Such a terrible, pointless waste! Anger battled with her tiredness, lost out to the sapping toxin in her veins.

So be it. In her final actions she would at least bestow honour on her village, on her father, on her brother.

She closed her eyes. Felt the hushed silence of the Royal arena. And *danced*.

Despite the numb feeling, the tunnel vision, the lump in her throat that made swallowing difficult and had begun to hamper her breathing. Despite her young heart pounding like it had never pounded before. Despite all of this, Ellie's dance was faultless.

It was, after all, a form she had danced hundreds of times.

The watching crowd erupted into rapturous applause. No contest fought in this hallowed arena had ever reached this point before.

If it had been independently judged, Ellie would have won. The twelfth form alone would have guaranteed it. But no such independent judge could be found, not on the Prince's Coronation day, not for an opponent who had no right to still be standing, let alone flashing her sword.

With solemn reverence, the announcement was made: a draw. The winner would be decided by the drawing of first blood.

Even before the Prince had a chance to process this, while he stood, staring slack-jawed up at the Courtier who had made the announcement, Ellie summoned up the last of her nerve and stumbled forward onto his outstretched sword. She felt its cold tip pierce her stuttering heart and gasped her final breath.

The Prince was crowned an hour later, tears still wet on his cheeks. The following day he issued his first Royal Decree. The Courtier and the Royal Physician were arrested on charges of treason.

The Physician died by his own hand; swallowing poison from a hollowed out pearl button on his jerkin, the same poison that had been smeared on the hilt of Ellie's magical training sword.

As for the loyal Courtier he was hung, drawn and quartered. Who knows? Perhaps he would have suffered the legendary dance of the thousand cuts, were there anyone alive who could perform it.

A Son of the Sea

Priya Sharma

Cadogan stood at the end of the bed.

"Feeling better? Good. Now, ground rules. Scream and I'll stuff rags in your mouth and break your legs. And you eat and drink or I'll make you." He pulled a funnel and a hose from a bag to demonstrate.

After we talked I lay on my side trying to get comfortable, and eventually fell asleep. I dreamt of the sea.

I stood on the shore, the rim of the aquatic world. Its shallows were pale and translucent. I wanted to be further out, in its dark depths. The surf rushed up to me, covered my feet and ankles in welcome, then rushed off again. I waded in until I was waist deep. A wave broke against the underwater slope, sending up spray that looked like a fan of molten glass.

In my dream, as in life, just looking in the water, just knowing I was going in was enough. My body readied itself. It relaxed. I took three deep breaths, working the muscles in my stomach and chest. Then I started packing, the act of gulping air, forcing it into my lungs.

The housemaster at one of my boarding schools once said to me, "Leave before you're expelled, you lanky streak of piss."

He wasn't to know the ways in which I'm made for water.

All the wonders that have blessed my eyes, they were there in my dream, when I needed them most.

I've always sought the ocean. Rivers are insufficient. I need water in the thrall of the moon. I need tides not just currents.

I'd spent six months working as a barman in Greece when Cadogan found me.

"Mick's Shack" was a concrete box with plastic tables and chairs but I liked it because it was on the beach. I had a sea view as I poured drinks.

We were getting ready to open for the evening. In an hour we'd be heaving with island hoppers, pumped up on pheromones and their own immortality. It never occurred to me that I wasn't that much older than them but I'd never had a night of drinking, pill popping, and fucking, followed by a day lying on the beach cooking a melanoma.

I was bringing up crates of beer from the cellar. I could see Suzie's flip flops as I came up the steps, her feet skimmed by her thin, long skirt. She was talking to someone. One look told me he wasn't looking for work. He was in his fifties and his hands were spread on the bar in a proprietorial manner that made me dislike him straight away.

"Thomas Briggs." It was a statement, not a question.

"Who's asking?" I felt as if he was about to arrest me.

"I'm Paul Cadogan. I need to talk to you."

"Do I need to talk to you?"

"It's important."

"Still not interested." I picked up a cloth and wiped down the bar, making him move his hands.

"In that case, I'll have a beer."

Suzie went to the fridge but I pulled a warm bottle from the crate I'd just brought up and levered it against the bottle opener on the bar. The cap dropped into the bin beneath with a tinkling sound.

"Ten euros."

His laugh was sour. He shook his head as he pulled out his wallet. "It's all on expenses anyway."

Knowing what I do now I would've made that beer ice cold and gratis but I was thorny because I suspected he had something to do with my father.

"You were difficult to locate. Why don't you get a bloody mobile and a Facebook page like the rest of the world?"

"Because nobody gives a fuck where I am."

"Poor little lost boy."

"I'm not lost."

"If you say so. You're certainly not poor any more." Cadogan took a long deliberate pull from the bottle. "That got your attention, didn't it? Why don't we go outside?"

I followed him out to the chairs and tables under the canopy, not because of the prospect of a fortune but because I thought I might as well get it over with.

"Your father's solicitor has been anxious to find you. Your father's dead."

"How?"

"Diving in Mauritius. He had a heart attack. It happened two months ago. We couldn't find you in time for the funeral."

I looked towards the sparkling, dark blue waves. The Mediterranean is relatively placid, being a landlocked sea. It calmed me. "How did you find me now?"

"You cashed one of your father's cheques."

"Oh, right."

"You're wealthy." He couldn't keep all his bitterness from his voice, not entirely. All he saw was a twenty-five-year-old who'd piss a fortune he hadn't made up the wall.

He slid something across the table at me.

"What's this?" I picked up the business card.

"It's how you cash in. She's your father's solicitor."

"Where was Dad buried?"

"In Sussex."

"Did many people go?"

"A lot."

"Did you know him?" I tried to sound casual.

"Never met him but I did a lot of research about you two when I was trying to find you. Did you know that he kept the apartment in Hong Kong where you both lived? Perhaps you should go. You might find out more about him."

I made a non-committal sound. Cadogan had done his homework. He knew Dad and I barely spoke.

"It's on Ma Wan, the island where your mother was from."

I stared at the card, turning it over in my fingers, angry that I'd learnt more about my mother from an ape like Cadogan than my father had ever told me.

"You're leaving, aren't you?"

Suzie threw her bag down on the sand and sat beside me. The bar had closed and the punters had taken the party out onto the beach. They gathered in the firelight. I sat apart, where I could hear the waves.

"How do you know?"

"I can just tell. Are you in trouble?"

"My father died."

"I'm so sorry." Suzie meant it.

"It's okay. I didn't know him."

She didn't press me. I liked that about her. She knew when to leave things alone. She clutched at the rough grass that pushed up through the sand in clumps, pulling the coarse blades through her fingers.

"I'm sorry you're going. This is going to sound selfish but you're the only person here that I'm comfortable with. Everyone else thinks I'm bossy and stuck up."

By everyone, she meant the other staff.

"I reckon we're a lot alike."

"Are we?" I tried not to frown. I didn't want to hurt her.

"I was carted about as a kid," she said. "Army brat. Never settling makes you seem more self-reliant than you are. What's your story?"

"Boarding schools. Lots of them." I didn't elaborate.

"I knew it. I could tell. You're different to all the others."

I *was* different but not in the way she thought. "We're all misfits, Suzie. We can't outrun ourselves."

"No, I suppose not." She sounded disappointed at that. "You don't care what people think of you, do you?"

I shrugged. I had no idea if I cared whether people liked me or not any more.

Loneliness was a constant friend. I nurtured it.

Suzie poured sand from palm to palm. "I envy you. You're comfortable in your own skin."

There was always one in the group, wherever I went. I was a blank canvas on which they projected their own desires and hopes. Suzie dusted the sand off her hands and reached for my beer bottle. She drained it.

Her face told me everything she wanted from me. I envied her ability to make herself that plain. She pulled her t-shirt over her head, revealing her bikini top. Her skirt sat low on her hips and she leant back, forming a long curve from her ribcage to her waistband.

I reached out and touched the tattoo on her side, tracing it with my forefinger. It was perfectly formed from its coronet to its curled tail. Suzie had spent proper money on it. The fins were picked out in fine lines and the shape of the armour beneath the skin gave it substance. Its colours were delicate yellows. Seahorses give me heartache. Little fishes of surreal grace. Ground up for medicine as a panacea for asthma, skin issues, heart disease, and erectile dysfunction. Taken from the wild and sold as pets only to die within a few weeks without expert care. Weight for weight, they command the same price as gold in some quarters.

"Do you like it?"

"It's beautiful."

She thought I meant her, in a roundabout way. I hadn't noticed how she'd closed the gap between us. She mistook my concentration for sexual tension, letting out a gasp as her mouth found mine. My hand drifted to her waistband. I could smell the monoi oil on her neck. Her hands crept inside my t-shirt and examined the hard edges of my shoulder blades.

I envied Suzie's hunger. It stoked something inside me. I wanted her sex, her seahorse tattoo. I wanted relief from the sudden ache that had sprung up in my groin.

Maybe, just maybe, this time will be different, I thought.

I undid her bikini top and ran my fingertip around one areolar and then the other. I sucked each nipple until she stifled a cry, her hand in her mouth. Her skirt was tangled around her legs and I pushed it up around her waist. Suzie fumbled with the buttons of my fly. She reached into her bag and pulled out a packet of condoms. I recognised the brand from the vending machine in the bar's toilets.

"I don't want you to think that I do this all the time. I got them for us. Not that I assumed..."

"I know." I kissed her, just to shut her up. Talking would make things more likely to go wrong.

I pulled at the side tie of her bikini bottoms. Suzie pressed her lips together as I ripped the packet open and rolled on the condom. The smell of the lubricant and the oily texture made me feel sick. I didn't want to be distracted. I needed to stay in the moment. I pushed her down and she opened her legs. We moved against each other, mouths and groin joined. I nudged my way into her, towards the heat within her.

Instead of the mounting excitement I was overcome by the feeling that something was wrong. Something was missing. So it was, yet again, that I failed to make a success of sex. I wilted with each thrust, getting rougher as I got softer until I lay flaccid against her thigh.

"It's okay." Suzie kissed my cheek. "Just lie here with me. Let's just be together."

"It's not okay."

What would've happened if I'd stayed there, in her arms? Instead, I got up and ran to the water, plunging into the safety of the waves.

I was dreaming of the sea.

The average person can stay underwater for forty seconds. The best free divers can manage six minutes.

I can stay under for half an hour.

In my dream, I felt my heart beating; one slow boom after another. My diaphragm twitched. It was just a reflex, my body trying to make me breathe but I ignored it.

My dreaming seabed was a drowned land with hills and valleys. It was punctuated by ship wrecks reclaimed by coral and anemones, by eels and fishes.

I crossed a field of moon jelly fish. They numbered in millions. These ethereal, pulsing creatures were a dense carpet of alien blooms. There shouldn't have be so many. They thrive on pollution. It's our fault, not theirs. Like all living things, they procreate while they may.

Cadogan had made all the arrangements for my trip to Hong Kong. He handed me a wallet containing ticket and instructions.

"It's first class all the way for you." His grin revealed yellowed teeth.

Cadogan had even arranged someone to collect me from the airport. The driver wore a black suit, cut like something from GQ magazine. The man insisted on carrying my rucksack and opened the rear passenger seat of the Mercedes for me. People kept looking at my jeans and scruffy boots, wondering if I was a film star or singer they should recognise.

I sank back into the leather seats. We emerged from an underpass. Hong Kong's islands arose from the South China Sea. High rises clung to their lower slopes and green covered the peaks. It was beautiful but I wanted more. I wanted the frisson of recognition.

"Tsing Ma bridge." The driver was embarrassed by his lack of English. He needn't have been. I knew no Cantonese. Not even *please* or *thank you*.

It was a suspension bridge, stretching out across the water with graceful arcs and angles. A tanker passed under us, a floating monolith shepherded along by smaller tugs.

There was another island to our left. I could see wooden houses on stilts along the shoreline and boats stacked up beneath them.

"Ma Wan." I didn't know if the driver had noticed my interest or was just announcing that we were close. Then he added, "Old part. Here is new part. Park Island."

Park Island Apartment Complex came into view. Tower block after tower block. We took the slip road down towards it.

"What's that?"

"It's a —" he paused, searching for the correct word, "Noah's Ark. For tourists."

A theme park for the evangelical, with the Ark beached in the bridge's shadow. Life sized model animals poured from its hull in pairs, into the garden below.

At least it wasn't the crucifixion

"No cars allowed beyond this." He pulled up by an escalator.

I refused his help with my rucksack and he refused payment, not even a tip.

Cadogan had dealt with everything.

The escalator came out onto a plaza. This was something familiar. The suspension bridge bisected the sea and sky. Tsing Yi Island rose ahead of me. A ferry was docked at the terminal, topped by a clock tower. Suddenly, the small child inside me was turning circles in the sun. I had run around the plaza on a day like this.

I found the right apartment block and rang the buzzer. The man at the desk gave me a toothy smile and let me in. He wore the concierge uniform; grey trousers, white shirt, and a blue and orange striped tie. I showed him my passport, as instructed by Cadogan, and in return received a set of keys. I was trembling as he called the lift for me. I looked at the man's shoes while we waited. They were polished to a high shine. He took pride in his work.

The hall of my father's apartment. The walls were white, marked with nails where pictures had once hung. I put down my rucksack and pulled off my boots. There was a stillness and I had the oddest idea that someone was waiting for me. I expected to go into the lounge and find Dad there, the same distant look on his face as when I'd last seen him in a restaurant in Barcelona. We'd both been passing through.

He wasn't there, of course. There was a dark grey L-shaped sofa, the minimalist sort that always looks modern and uncomfortable. The coffee table was glass-topped. The bookshelves were empty. Each surface was polished, which made me feel sadder, somehow. I went through the kitchen cupboards. They'd been fully stocked. Fresh milk was in the fridge. Cadogan's efficiency.

The cleaner had made up the master bedroom for me. The wardrobes and bedside tables were empty. I slammed the doors shut, seething at the fruitlessness of travelling halfway around the world because of a throwaway comment from Cadogan. Stupid.

There was a second bedroom. A nautical-themed frieze ran around the walls. Sea creatures bobbed along with the boats. An orange octopus smiled despite being sun-faded. A purple octopus wore a sailor's hat at a jaunty angle. It was a child's room. My room.

I was exhausted. I pulled a cushion from the rattan chair, lay down on the rug of thick, blue pile, and feel asleep in the square of sun.

I went out for breakfast, even though there was plenty of food in the apartment. The coffee was strong, covered in a layer of foam, coated with cocoa dust. I ate a croissant and then a second, realising that I was hungry.

Park Island had a manicured, artificial feel. The pathways between the buildings were covered so you could walk the length of the complex without being bothered by rain or sun. Gardeners tended the borders and cleaners emptied litter bins.

I read the notices regarding the consultation on the ferry fees while I waited for the lift. The concierge bowed to someone. As the lift doors opened the mirrored walls reflected the woman behind me. She followed me in and turned on her heel. I leant over and pressed the button, looking at her enquiringly.

"Same floor."

She was stylish in tight khaki trousers and a well cut white shirt. She looked at me with unconcealed curiosity. I looked right back. She was in her late sixties and from Hong Kong, I thought. Her hair was bobbed and she had flat cheekbones.

On impulse I reached out and touched the charms on her bracelet. Each one was marine – a sea urchin, a manta ray, a starfish, and a seahorse.

"I'm sorry."

"Don't be."

She wasn't unnerved by my breach of her personal space.

"I love it," she said. Do you love it?"

"Yes."

As the lift doors opened at our floor I extended an arm. *After you.* She turned right and then left. We found ourselves outside neighbouring doors. She burst out laughing. I didn't understand why.

"You're Jonathan Brigg's son, Thomas."

She took my face in her hands. I could hardly object. The charms tinkled as she moved. I got a waft of whatever perfume she wore. There were notes of brine, algae and dry driftwood. I resisted rubbing my nose against her wrist.

"You don't remember me, do you? I'm Darla."

"No, I'm sorry."

"You're handsome. You have your dad's jaw." Her face changed as if she just remembered Dad was dead. "Should I be saying how sorry I am for your loss?"

"You can't mourn what you didn't know."

"You have the look of someone who's been mourning his entire life."

My smile was the bitter curve of being understood far too late in life for it to make a difference.

"Are you in a rush? Why don't you come in and tell me what you've been doing all these years?"

Darla's apartment mirrored Dad's but it had been remodelled. One of the bedrooms had been removed to make the lounge larger. The white walls were covered in swathes of blue canvas.

"What do you think of them?"

"They're wonderful."

"I did them."

Darla went off to fix us a drink without asking what I wanted. I admired her work while I waited. Blue, the most nuanced colour. All her paintings were abstracts, ranging from stormy greys, through brooding indigos and onto playful aquamarines and greens. The movement of the oil paint reflected the moods of each shade.

There were gallery catalogues and monographs on the coffee table. Darla wasn't an amateur dauber. Each one was about her work.

She put a tray down and passed me a chunky glass tumbler. I took a sip. Whisky and soda.

"What's with Noah's Ark?" I asked. We looked down on it from her window.

"One of the brothers who developed the island built it when he found God."

"It doesn't look like it could save a pair of everything."

"Token atonement for his sins. I say we need a great flood. Wouldn't that be a good thing?" Such a strange thing to say but before I could ask her more she went on, "I tried to find you. I know Jonathan went to Germany but what about you?"

"I was sent to boarding school in England. Lots of them. I kept getting expelled. When I was twelve I went to Texas. One of Dad's cousins offered to take me in. Did you keep in touch with Dad?"

"No. He was a busy man. Very in demand. Brilliant engineer from what I gathered. Good business brain too. He made a lot of clever investments. The family you lived with, were they good to you?"

"It was just Uncle Paul and Aunty Jean. And yes, they were. Why do you care?"

"You were such a lonely, sad little boy. I like to think that someone was kind to you. Do you still see them?"

"No. I'm not a very good human being."

"That's okay. Neither am I."

I didn't want to remember my last conversation with Paul and Jean. I called them before I left for Hong Kong. It was the first time in over a year. *We've been so worried about you.* Not a single reproach for missing Dad's funeral, just concern and sympathy.

Paul and Jean didn't deserve my shoddy treatment. They put our awkward interactions down to their inexperience with children and adolescents and to my rootless, unloved state. The real issue was that I was strange. It wasn't their fault. They weren't to know what the problem was when I barely knew myself. The arid vista outside my window unsettled me. There was no water to salve the endless land.

"Did you see much of your dad?"

"No. He used to phone once a month but the time between calls got longer and longer, and the calls themselves got shorter and shorter."

"What happened to you after Texas?"

"I left when I was eighteen. I worked in bars and restaurants. Between what I made and Dad's allowance, I managed."

I didn't use much of what Dad sent me but I wanted my lack of ambition and education to piss Dad off. If Darla judged me, she gave no sign.

I tried to explore the city.

I queued with the commuters at the ferry terminal on Ma Wan island. There were people dressed for city jobs. Children in a variety of different school uniforms that looked like something from 1940s Britain. The younger ones were shepherded along by helpers, the maids-of-all-work imported from Bangladesh and the Philippines.

Water sprayed the window as we headed into choppy straights, crossed by a tanker that made us bob up and down like a toy in a tub. Most of the passengers didn't even look up, intent on their phones or tablets.

After fifteen minutes the ferry curved around the islands and Central came into view. This was the financial heart of Hong Kong; The Bank of China, HSBC, Standard Chartered, all sought to dominate one another. Their success was manifest in steel and glass. Its wealth was crushing. People teemed along the waterfront.

I stayed on the ferry and went back to Ma Wan.

I was dreaming of the sea.

Except everything was mixed up, as if one ocean had run into another. Sea creatures that should never meet swam alongside one another. Many were out of their normal depths.

The dolphins were puzzled. They didn't know whether I was fish or mammal. They were frustrated when I didn't join in with their chatter so they abandoned me.

I dove deeper. That far down my lungs were compressed to the size of clenched fists. Below thirty metres my eardrums should burst but they never do. I'm made of more pliable stuff. My concavities and my long, spidery limbs give me negative buoyancy.

Fishes followed me. The water was dense with them. There were silver sardines, open-mouthed. Tropical colours and spots darted around me, in the most electric of blues, the yellows neon. Tuna and swordfish cut through them.

The human view of beauty is arbitrary. The Atlantic seabass was a joy, muscular in its velvet grey, its light smattering of gold scales elegant and tasteful.

And rays. Finally, the rays. They covered me with the friendly flap of their wings. They looped-the-loop for me, revealing smiling white undersides. They're an amiable sort. They have grinding plates, not teeth.

Eels that lurked in holes revealed themselves. They came rippling out like black ribbons. Their secret is extra-terrestrial in its nature. A second set of jaws complete with teeth, as if one isn't enough.

In my dream, I felt the shift, my blood moving inward to prevent my organs collapsing. The familiar feeling was like a balm. It comforted me. I accepted the ocean's pressure and its depths in a kind of meditation.

Darla is the closest I've ever had to a real friend.

She cooked me delicacies for purists, not the standard fare dished up for tourists. We trekked the dragon's back, a ridge running around Shek O Country Park. We followed the dragon's undulating spine, the sea on one side of us and the hills on the others, covered in blazing azaleas. The heat and the humidity were stifling but it was worth it to plunge into the cool waters of Big Wave Bay at the end.

There weren't any big waves but it was a proper beach, not like the artificial one on Ma Wan which was a strip of sand that had to be raked each morning.

Darla was a strong and graceful swimmer. I fought the urge to overtake her, to go far out and then dive until I reached the bottom. To stay there until I was sated. I resolved to return alone, when the beach was quieter.

Afterwards we stretched out on towels. Darla was striking in a navy halter- neck swimsuit and cherry red nail varnish on her finger and toenails. We drew looks from people who strolled by, curious about the nature of our relationship.

A group of young women unfurled a blanket nearby and started laying out a feast. They seemed happy in a way I'd never known, attractive because everything was ahead of them.

Darla's careless sophistication drew them, just as it had drawn me. One of the women came over and offered her a fancy pastry from a carton. Darla refused with a wave of the hand but gave her a big smile. I followed suit. The young woman nodded, suddenly shy at her own forwardness, but her gaze sought me again when she'd returned to her circle of friends.

"Shall I get her back for you?" Darla asked. She sensed my hesitation. "Do you prefer men?"

"Women might as well be a different species to me. Men are no better." I'd tried both without success.

"Darla, are you my mother?"

"No, silly boy, I'm far too old."

"You don't look it." I rolled onto my back, shielding my eyes from the sun with my forearm. "I'm disappointed."

"I'm not sure whether I'm flattered or not."

"Do you have any family?"

"Not children. But I'm responsible for a large extended family. Totally self-appointed, of course, because somebody has to make the difficult decisions."

"You make it sound like a military operation."

"It's about survival."

I'd never seen her so serious. It added years to her face. "Darla, do you know anything about my mother?"

"Very little." She sighed.

"Am I being tiresome?

"No, never. You might not like what you hear, though. She left you at reception in a cardboard box with strict instructions to call your father's apartment. Except he was at a meeting with investors. It was for his land reclamation project."

Land is king. Kowloon waterfront, which sits across the bay from Central, was once submerged.

"They heard you squalling and called me instead. I looked after you until he came back."

"What was her name?"

"I don't know. I only ever saw her at a distance. I think your father met her on one of his evening walks. She lived in the fishing village on the other side of the island. She was from one of the old families."

"I saw it from the bridge on my way here."

"You should take a closer look. Not many people live there now. Most of them have relocated. It'll get knocked down eventually to build luxury apartments. That's progress."

"Tell me about the old families."

Darla sat up and put sun cream on her arms. I watched as she rubbed it in. "They were a different breed, those fishermen and women. Some of their daughters became pearl divers." She chuckled. "I don't know if they were people who adapted to the sea or fish that had learnt to live on land. I swear, they'd stay underwater for quarter of an hour in one go. I used to time them."

It was only then that I realised I'd been holding my breath.

I needed to be outside the confines of the apartment. I was staying in a space that would normally house an extended family in Hong Kong and yet it chafed.

I headed for the service road that circumnavigated the island. It was lined with letting agents, hairdressers, and low-rise flats. Darla had said this was where many of the villagers had moved to.

Does my mother live there?

I doubt it. I never saw her again after she left you.

I crossed over and kept going. There was a path that led into the trees. I stepped aside to let a runner pass. He was breathing hard as he took the incline towards me. Sweat marked his top. He was what people here called *gweilo*. A term for foreigners, literally translated as *foreign devil*. Only mad dogs and Englishmen go out in the midday sun.

I was a *gweilo* too, only it didn't matter where I was. In Britain and in the States it had been the same. Even when people didn't give a damn where I was from I felt like an outsider. Here in Hong Kong I looked like a native but it didn't take long for people to realise that I wasn't when they tried to talk to me in Cantonese.

The path forked and I had an overwhelming urge to follow the left one. It led into the narrow corridors of trees.

I emerged into the light. There it was, Ma Wan proper, laid out before me. I walked along abandoned streets. Weeds pushed up through the cracks in the concrete to reclaim the land. Some of the houses were blocked off with chain link fences. Others were accessible. I went into a few of them. Faded imprints of life remained within. Torn wallpaper. A rotting mattress. Piles of cardboard boxes and bags covered in dust and rubble. There were empty shops and open-fronted sheds. Washing hung on lines, stiff from continual cycles of being rain-drenched and then sun-dried. Litter gathered where the wind had left it.

Slogans had been painted on walls in red. Banners were hung over doors. I didn't need to be able to read them to know that they were protest calls. Not everyone wanted to leave here. Some had remained. Somebody had left vases of chrysanthemums and incense sticks burning in pots of sand. Little gifts for silent gods.

One side of the village overlooked the water. There was everything a community needed. I looked through the window of a building marked as the 'Ma Wan Rural Committee'. Chairs were stacked up in the hall. On one wall there were photographs and yellowed notices. There was a school house further along and a playground that comprised a slide and a frame missing its swings.

Along the shoreline were stacks of plastic pipes. The suspension bridge loomed over me. I'd reached the houses on stilts. They were rotten. The rooves had collapsed in on some of them. Struts had given way.

I followed the shore to the very edge of Ma Wan. A house stood alone on a promontory and it looked out onto the South China Sea. It was close to the water. Perfect.

The front door and window frames were missing. The building was unrendered. The concrete floor had been swept clean but it was stained. The plastered walls were unpainted. There wasn't a stick of furniture inside but I couldn't see beyond the tattered, yellow curtain that divided the room. Somebody had planned a life here that never materialised.

I could be happy here, I thought.

I stepped inside. It was as though I'd stepped into a vacuum. The roaring in my ears wasn't the rush of blood. It sounded like the sea. It was so loud that I crumpled to the floor. Shadow rushed at me and then receded. It was too much. I panicked, as I never had at open sea. My chest was tight. I couldn't breathe.

Then the world went black.

I was dreaming of the sea.

Great white sharks circled me. Thousands of years of unthinking history looked out from eyes that offered neither pity nor remorse. Their smiles were serrated. They're psychopaths, designed for survival. The sand shark will eat its siblings in utero. Their personality issues are no excuse for what we do to them. I've seen them hauled onto boats, fins hacked off while they're still alive, then they're thrown back in. Rudderless, they fall through the water. Death comes slowly by suffocation, exsanguination, or they're eaten alive by other fishes.

Man must consume a small part of the mighty and discard the major portion like it's garbage. We will have dominion over everything.

We will have soup.

When I woke, I was on the other side of the yellow curtain. It was cool. I heard a woman humming. The metal bedframe creaked as I sat up. I could feel its springs through the cheap mattress. This end of the room had been tiled in white. It felt oddly clinical. Cupboards ran along one wall and a sink was set in the worktop at one end.

"You scared me. You took quite a turn."

A woman sat down at one end of the bed. She was a pearl. Luminous. "Drink." She handed me a bottle of water.

"How long have I been here?"

"Half an hour." Her accent was French.

She wore shorts and a t-shirt. Her hair was black and straight, her irises so dark that I couldn't make out her pupils. She shifted, pulling a bag onto the bed between us.

"Here," she rummaged inside and pulled out a bar of chocolate. "You should eat something."

The first bite made me realise that I was ravenous. The chocolate was bitter and restorative. She leant back on the head of the bed and watched me eat. There were bottles of water lined up on the worktop and a bag of apples. A red dress and coat hung on a peg. A suitcase lay open on one corner of the floor. "Feeling better?" she asked.

"Much. Do you live here?"

"I'm squatting."

She pulled her hair into a loose knot and fixed it with a hairband from her wrist. The dark strands were matted, as if she'd been swimming in the sea and not rinsed it out with freshwater afterwards.

"I'm Tom."

"Simone."

I held out my hand to shake hers but it was really an excuse to touch her. I'd never felt the need to do that before, not with anyone. Her hand lingered in mine as if in answer to a question that I didn't know I'd asked.

Simone took the water from me and tipped her head back to drain what remained in the bottle. I could see the muscles of her throat working. It reminded me of Suzie, just before she kissed me.

I didn't want to be reminded of the disappointments of that night.

"Where are you from?"

"Paris." She tossed the empty bottle on the floor. "My father was a diplomat so we travelled a lot. My mother died when I was six. She was from Hong Kong so I always wanted to see it."

"I see you're doing so in style."

"I do everything with style," she laughed. "My father disagrees about what style is. I inherited some money from my aunt. It's not a huge amount, so I'm economising. To be honest, I don't need posh hotels. It's more important for me to be by the sea. I die inside if I can't see it."

"Me too. I lived in Texas when I was younger, near the desert. I couldn't breathe."

"What about you?"

"My father died recently. My mum was from Ma Wan. I never knew her. I came here to find out who I am."

I'd never said that aloud before.

"I've no idea who I am either, or where I belong." She made it sound inconsequential. Funny, even. "My father stopped loving me when my mother died."

"*My* father *never* loved me. He never wanted me. Apparently he had me tested to check I was actually his."

We laughed, incredulous at how our fathers had scarred us.

"Have you found anything worthwhile here?" The sound of my own voice shocked me. I realised I was flirting with her.

She responded with an honesty that floored me, as if she'd misunderstood the question.

"That I can't escape myself. Wherever I go, I'm already there."

My heart leapt and twisted, like a fish with a hook in its mouth. She had me with that line.

"I can't make friends, Tom, not the way other people do." She shrugged, embarrassed. "There's always someone who singles me out, who thinks that I need saving or that I can save them. Fellow freaks, maybe."

"And they scare you because you're not like them and you don't know how to be what they want —"

"— because I have no idea how to be myself." The hairs on my arms stood on end.

"Tom, I need to be in the water. Naked. Will you swim with me?"

Her lips were parted. I was acutely aware of the rise and fall of her chest. It was the most earnest and erotic invitation of my life, made sweeter by our sudden empathy.

"Yes."

Simone stood on the rocks, not caring about the spray from the waves or who saw her. She stripped off her t-shirt and shorts. Then her underwear. Naked, she was made anew. Every muscle tensed as she stood on tip-toe, arms stretched out. She was tanned and sleek with a slight belly. She dived, a knife that sliced the surface.

I tore off my clothes as I followed her. My heart was hammering. The ocean enveloped me. Water filled by vision. Simone's hair floated around her like seaweed as she rolled onto her back, baring her neck and chest to the sun like a basking seal. I trod water beside her.

"I'm happiest here. So are you." She didn't look at me to gauge my reaction. She knew she was right. Then she kissed me. I kissed her back. When I held her there was no softness beneath her skin, as if she were armoured underneath it. I was so hard that I thought I'd burst.

"Shall we?"

I nodded, already knowing what she was asking. My breathing was slowing and deepening. Down we went.

We twisted around one another, sometimes only an inch apart but never touching. Drifting out with the current, we went closer to the sea bed. A shoal of tiny fishes moved around us like slivers of silver. I could see the crab crawling along the bottom. I could sense the microscopic plankton that fuels the world.

We broke the surface in unison. Here she was, the person that wouldn't find me wanting. For once, I was in the moment, not trying to guess at what was required of me. Thought could be suspended and everything would be right. All those unsatisfied nights. I thought the joy of Simone would break me, right then.

We floated further out. Ma Wan looked miniature. I packed my lungs as much as I could. *Let her see. Let her know the man I really am.*

We spiralled back down, corkscrewing around one another. My breathing was controlled enough, my exhalations deep enough to give me the negative buoyancy to make giant strides along the sea bed.

Simone matched me, step for step until she wrapped her ankle around a drift of sea weed to anchor herself. I did the same. She put her forehead to mine. Her hands were on my shoulders. Mine were at her hips. She shifted to let me inside her.

There it was. The great mystery. We were synchronised. Our rhythm was primal. Tidal. Something in me rose. I could feel Simone tightening around me. I was clamped, the tip of my penis sucked and messaged by her cervix. I was so close to coming that it was painful. She gripped me tighter. My own orgasm was a dry spasm as she ejaculated inside me.

It was like breaking up and dissolving, every particle of Thomas Briggs dispersed on the currents.

Simone and I walked back to the house, naked and dripping, carrying our clothes in bundles.

I reached for her hand but she moved away.

We dressed in silence, me into what I'd been wearing and Simone into the red dress on the peg. I watched, throat clogged, as it slipped over her slight, bare breasts and then over the triangle of dark hair between her legs.

"Simone."

"You should leave."

She sounded angry. I reached out to touch her shoulder but she stepped back. "Please, Simone. I've been waiting for you my whole life."

"Then you're stupid."

"What have I done? What's wrong?"

"Don't you get it?" She pushed me away, both hands on my chest, not hard, but it hurt all the same. "I don't want you. It was a mistake. Get out. Go on, go."

I didn't want to sit alone in my father's apartment. I knocked on Darla's door. Cadogan answered. I stared at him, taking a moment to register it was really him.

"What have you done with Darla?" I pushed him out of the way. The lounge was empty. Nothing was out of place.

I was angry. I wanted to fight with someone who'd fight back. Let him kick the shit out of me. It didn't matter.

"Where's Darla?" I pushed him again. "Darla?"

"She's in there." He pointed to the bedroom. "I'll wait here, if it's all the same to you. And she said to shut the door after you."

I'd never been in Darla's bedroom.

There wasn't a bed in there. A footed bath occupied the space where a bed should've been. It was giant, with clawed feet. The floor was marble and ornate drains were set into the floor at regular intervals. It was a giant wet room. The tap dripped at regular intervals. It landed in the water below with a heavy splash.

One wall was covered in a huge canvas, just like the lounge. This was an angry, swirling blue, as if from an abyss.

A strangled, sucking sound came from the depths of the bathtub.

What was in there was at least eight feet long. Its skin was like hide, a mottled brown colour. Its gills moved as it squirmed with pleasure, its underbelly revealed. I could see patches of human skin.

The eel was thick around the jaw. It had Darla's face and when she opened her mouth to speak I could see the thick spikes that she had for teeth and the second set further down her throat.

The sea within the canvas writhed in fury.

"Thomas," Darla said and all the pounding water came pouring out.

I woke on the bed in the little house on the promontory. Simone was dabbing at my face with a cool, damp cloth.

"Darla, she's..."

Simone shook her head. Her lips pinched together, leeching them of colour. Her eyes were pink and tear-stung.

Fever raised beads of sweat on my head and neck. A sudden chill went through me and my teeth started to chatter. I didn't trust that Simone was there after all. I reached for her but a chain rattled, restraining me. I was tethered to the bed frame.

"Simone." My voice was hoarse. I followed her gaze to the corner of the room.

It was Darla. Darla as I'd always known her, dressed in linen and looking refined.

"Let me go."

"I can't. Not now." Darla was the one in charge.

"I want to go home."

"You *are* home. I've been calling you all back here, one by one."

I tried to sit up but slumped back, exhausted. My every joint ached. Every muscle felt weak.

"He looks really sick. I think we should get a doctor."

"And say what?" Darla asked sharply. All I could hear was their breathing. "Good." Darla had taken Simone's silence for acquiescence.

"I can't do this anymore." Simone was trembling.

"You've done it before and you'll do it again because it's what you were born for. You can't help yourself. Like draws like. Something in your father found something in your mother. It was the same for him." Darla motioned to me. "A recessive gene, to be sure, but mixed together and becoming more manifest with each generation. You're a daughter of the sea, just like Thomas is a son. And you're all coming back to replenish what's been lost."

I was dreaming of the sea.

I reached a coral reef. Sea horses were on the ocean floor, a grazing herd. They anchored themselves where they could; on coral, sea grass.

One wrapped its tail around another's neck. Elsewhere they were knotted together in what looked like an orgy. Their prehensile tails were sinuous.

They rose to greet me when they saw me. They varied in size, some as long as my hand.

Their translucent fins were like delicate propellers. All they could manage was a drunken canter but they danced for me. A chorus line of prancing seahorses.

Emboldened, they came closer. Close enough for me to see their eyes moving independently of one another. That their snouts made a constant sucking motion. Lacking a stomach means that they must feed perpetually.

I pity their poor cousins, pipe fish, who lack the seahorse's equine angles. Such elegance. They bowed to me, even though they were the ones with coronets.

I felt as if my chest would burst with their sweetness.

Darla and Simone left. My fever settled as I slept.

Cadogan stood at the end of the bed.

"Feeling better? Good. Now, ground rules. Scream and I'll stuff rags in your mouth and break your legs. And you eat and drink or I'll make you." He pulled a funnel and a hose from a bag to demonstrate.

"I thought you worked for Dad's solicitor."

"I work for lots of people. That's the fun of being freelance."

"Conflict of interest doesn't bother you, then?"

"Clearly not. You're mixed up in some weird crap here, aren't you?"

"Can I have a drink?" Talking hurt. My mouth was dry.

He smiled as he handed me a plastic bottle of tepid water. What I wouldn't have given for a glass of cold beer, cold enough to make my teeth ache.

I looked at the curtain, moving in the breeze. Simone's things were gone. He pulled back the yellow curtain a fraction so I could see the water.

"Was Simone worth it?" He didn't wait for an answer. "My dad used to say killing and fucking are what makes a man."

"What about parenthood?" The thought surprised me.

"He knew bugger all about that and never bothered to learn. Any idiot can father a child."

"Yes, it takes a real man to raise one." I was thinking of my own father as I said it.

"Yes, I reckon you're right there." When Cadogan looked at me then I felt he was seeing me for the first time.

"You have children, don't you? Sons."

"Yes."

Cadogan changed my bedding, helping me back from the chair where I'd slumped. He tucked me in, pulling an extra blanket and pillow from a carrier bag to make me more comfortable.

"Is that better?"

"Thank you."

He reattached the shackles to the bedframe, letting the chains out a little more so it was easier for me to turn over. "I've brought you soup."

My hands clattered the spoon against the bowl and he took it from me, spooning the goodness into me.

"Can you manage some more?"

Half remained. I shook my head. The freezing feeling was creeping back over me again, sooner than I expected. Cadogan put a hand on my forehead.

"Please, not the gag." I called out when my temperature plummeted and rose. "I'll try not to shout this time, I promise."

"I'll try not to use it. I'll be here with you, don't worry. I'll see you through it."

That was probably because there'd be repercussions if he didn't keep me alive but I felt better when he said that.

Cadogan had helped me through every indignity. He'd held a bucket for me to vomit into. He'd helped me on and off the commode and then the bedpan, when I became too weak, carrying off my putrid filth.

"Cadogan," I croaked.

"What is it?"

"Do your sons love you? I bet you're a great dad." I meant it. In those moments of outrageous intimacy he did more for me than my own father ever had. I didn't know if I was hallucinating again, but it looked like Cadogan was crying.

I was dreaming of the sea.

The fall was exquisite. I reached one hundred and twenty-five metres. It was dark and cold. Such silence. I didn't know if I was at the bottom of the ocean or in outer space. I didn't know if it was joy or just my heart being compressed. Infinity overcame me.

I've been dreaming of the sea.

When I wake my groin's wet and I'm panting, straining at the chains.

"I need to be in the water."

Cadogan looks at me for a full minute before deciding. I'm off the bed before the last manacle has clattered to the floor. Genetics are imperative. My body knows what it must do. Cadogan tries to help me across the rocks as I flail and stagger, pulling off clothes as I go.

I plunge in, the momentary shock of cold water a distraction from the pain in my lower abdomen. I try to pee but nothing comes. A spasm doubles me over. I thrash, coming up for air, fighting to control my breathing. I take a lungful and dive, swimming out as far as I can before the first contraction.

Blood jets from the tip of my penis. It stains the water in a black cloud. How willingly complicit we are in our own downfall.

Then I ejaculate. It's a gush of tiny lives. Sea horse fry. Hundreds of them float up around me, moving in streams. They're all bulbous eyes and tails at this stage.

My little ones. They can't all survive. The currents will buffet them until some die from exhaustion, poor swimmers that they are.

One of them twines its tail in my chest hair.

The spasms come again. More babies escape me. As I pump out young the brood pouch low on my abdomen flattens. My penis bleeds continually now and it feels like there's broken glass in my urethra.

All the things I've never felt. I've been accused of being cold-blooded but it's not blood in my veins but brine. Each spasm is a perverse happiness. I'm suspended in a cloud of tiny seahorses.

I sink into the ocean's infinite arms. I'm not just a son of the sea. I am a father.

To Look Upon His Works

RJ Barker

It was the Grand Sychophant Oroestes who brought the artist Milon of Honsa across the seas from his faraway land to paint the great and terrible King Hattaran of Murast. What greater honour could there be for the greatest warrior the world had ever known to be painted by the greatest painter the world had ever known?

None, of course, and it was the job of a grand sycophant to know such things.

Now, friend, I have heard of the painting, it is a terrible thing. A picture so real that it feels like Hattaran lives again, that his armies may move across continents, cities will fall in fire and pain and those who love will find what is dearest to them taken, sullied and destroyed. Now you, to come here, across the sands, to pass through destruction and the rubble and to travel up the Shard Road of Murast you must indeed be a true lover of art – but, though you walk through a wasteland, do you know that we, the people of Murast, were once the greatest art lovers in the known world? Indeed, Hattaran himself brought the best and the brightest artists back to his mighty capital to ply their trade among the gentle towers of our city.

Of course, you we see none of that now.

And how, Milon, do you achieve such vibrant colours in your pictures?

It is in the application of materials, Grand Sycophant Oroestes, it is all in the application of materials.

It is strange, that you must look upon a ruin where I see what once was; a city overflowing with beauty and fat with plenty. Those few who scratch a living here now mourn the days when every stall was overflowing with produce brought from all over the world. A man who is hungry quickly forgets fear, just as a man who is frightened quickly forgets hunger. We forget too quickly in any case, and quicker than ever in the case of Hattaran of Murast. Oh, he is seen as a monster, and he was, but he loved beauty also and for a time Murast was a wonderful place to be, but few books from his reign survive to tell us any different.

Of course we had books, friend. Of course.

When I was young the libraries of Murast were famed, they were ripe with knowledge. It is said the tribesman who once travelled the forests around Murast, bringing us the food and milk from their beasts, all died on the sword because Hattaran needed vellum. Huge herds of goats were driven through the city to provide enough vellum for our writers, playwrights and poets to scrawl their thoughts upon. One could not go past a street corner without coming across a poet or writer reading from their latest opus. We had so many writers in Murast that some of the greatest names to have ever written starved on our streets, ignored. No, we had no shortage of books in our time, but all that is lost now, burned.

I see you bring me no vellum to paint upon. Do you not have any in this huge city?

No, Milon, for a writer found a form of poetry that was beautiful while making no sense. And he could not understand this, and thought on it for days and weeks until he decided if he did not understand then the people would not understand and he decreed no one should write these poems any more. But the poets did not listen and tracts lampooning Hattaran appeared on the walls. For that he had a great pyre made of all the books and scrolls in the city's libraries and gathered together all the writers and threw them into it. You will struggle to find vellum here now as it is the sign of a writer, and writers in Murast are burned alive.

No mind, Grand Sycophant Oroestes, I will source my own materials.

Now, are you thirsty friend? You will hear the running of water and you may follow that to find a spring. Cup your hands and drink deep for water is scarce in the ruins of Murast, the sun beats down and steals the moisture from even our skin. Pots? Oh once we had such pots. Hattaran worked a hundred thousand slaves to death to build a causeway across the bay of Urlay and lay waste to the land of Beckan so he could have access to their clay mines. What was done with that clay was astounding, my friend: porcelain so fine and thin you could have read books through it. Pots made to look like every animal you can imagine, clever jugs of birds which spouted water from their beaks. Our potters competed to make the tallest and thinnest vessels imaginable. Such fine handles you have never seen, clay made to do things that seemed impossible: bowls that rang like bells when touched and likenesses of men and women that, if they had not been so still, you would have taken to be real. In fact, I knew a man who fell in love with a clay likeness of a woman, it was a famous story, but of course, it is lost now.

By the well are some shards and hollowed bones that may hold water if you do not wish to use your hands. I would be grateful if you brought me a little water, to talk makes me thirst.

Ah no, we have nothing to put your paints in. See the path we walk along? Well, Hattaran found himself displeased with the potters; he believed they were mocking his manhood with their new shapes. He had learnt from the poets and did not give the potters time to turn on him for he is a man who is not afraid to make hard decisions. He had every pot in Murast smashed on this road. Then he had horses drag the potters over the road of shards to flay skin from their backs. When he was satisfied that the blood and screams had taught the artists of the city to appreciate him, the potters were thrown then into their own kilns to roast. It was a very fine lesson our king taught us.

No mind, Grand Sycophant Oroestes, I will source my own materials.

You say you are starved of colour and your eyes thirst to see the famed colours of Milon's painting? I understand that need, sand and crumbling sandstone can provide little for the eye to feast upon.

So little was left of beautiful Murast when her enemies fell upon her, my friend, though I do not blame them for their anger – how could I? Once Murast was a riot of colour, beauty was everywhere and our king himself loved to paint. Great Hattaran besieged the city of Varim purely for its painters. He stood his army outside the city for three months, until the starving overthrew the government and opened the gates for him. You will hear he murdered everyone in the city but it is not true. Hattaran was not a man to waste anything and although he only wanted the painters he did not abandon the rest of the city. Those who were well enough he sent to mine clay and the rest he did kill, out of mercy, deeming it cruel to leave them to starve in the empty city. The artists he brought back and they painted his city in honour of their redeemer. It was a magical place then, huge vats of paint kept in the central courtyard before the Palace of skulls. Pools of every colour under the sun, and the stories of Hattaran's conquests did bloody dances across the walls of Murast. It was said, even those taken in war and brought in chains to die before the palace were thankful for their fate; because they had seen the walls of Murast.

I do not doubt there was some truth in that.

Paints? Ah, the great sadness of Murast is that some of the painters King Hattaran was kind enough to bring to his city became decadent. They created art of such strangeness it bothered the king, worried at him like a dog will worry at a corpse, and so the king, in his great and terrible wisdom, had them drowned in the paint vats and all the paint was spoiled.

No mind, Grand Sycophant Oroestes, I will source my own materials.

Do you carry an instrument friend? Many who ply the arts also love music, I do and I miss it. Murast once sang as loudly as any city. Great halls were built, that threw sound from their gates, sending it echoing through the streets until it mixed with the sound of instruments that fell from the many other halls. At each and every corner in Murast a man could hear a different symphony and the birds themselves wept with jealousy over Murast and her songs. Every type of instrument was played here, friend. King Hattaran loved music so much that he brought down the great forest which once surrounded Murast to build his fleet and take the island of Voisi where the greatest harpists lived.

But do not take up your instrument for me, friend, it may be best not to play, lest you wake ghosts which sleep in the ruins.

Music? Ah, sadly not, the wise and mighty Hattaran decreed his people must be happy and as such all music played in Murast must also be happy. But the Harpists of Voisi could not obey, for they betrayed great Hattaran by loving their old home more than they loved Murast. Their songs wept out minor keys and Hattaran, in his righteous anger, had all the musicians of Murast strangled with harp strings and forbade any to as much as whistle on pain of death. You will have seen the street of hanging on your way here, of course. It is difficult for a man not to make any music.

No mind, Grand Sycophant Oroestes, I will make my own music.

But Hattaran...

Will make allowances, I am sure.

The stone feet, friend?

You will find many such things in the ruins of Murast. Hattaran brought artists from every land he conquered but he had no need to bring sculptors. Murast was always a city of sculpture, our buildings were decked with faces and figures, our squares with glorious statues that reached for the sky. In the early days of Hattaran's rule we celebrated his conquests in marble and quartz, in bronze and iron. We beat our enemies' weapons into images of their subjugation, we destroyed cities, made their people slaves and had them bring the stones of their homes to us so we could create a huge likeness of our warrior leader. Vast it was, throwing a shadow over the whole city like a sundial and you could tell the time wherever you were by looking for Hattaran's shadow. But it was cold in that shadow, friend, and it had a weight we never realised until it was too late. Sculpture was the only art he did not destroy as he became older, I think he could not stand to see himself maimed in any way. We had to wait for our enemies to truly bring down Hattaran and banish his shadow. But the sculpture here was astounding once, friend, we had started to leave behind the human form and experiment in more and more abstract forms but... well.

That ended.

The sculptors of Murast? Oh they live, but they no longer sculpt I am afraid. Hattaran found their more experimental forms difficult to understand and then found his own meaning in it, found mockery in it. He had their eyes put out, as punishment.

And yet they live?

My son was a sculptor, Milon, I begged for his life.

And now, you bring me to paint your king?

I am the Grand Sycophant of Hattaran, Milon of Honsa, and I have heard much of your work. You are the greatest at what you do, are you not?

Oh yes, Oroestes, yes, I am that.

I have heard it said, friend, that the screams from Hattaran's chambers went on for a week but no one dared intrude. After all, screams from Hattaran's chambers were nothing new. Only when there had been silence for another week did anyone dare enter the king's bedchamber. Oroestes led them in and of the painter, Milon of Honsa, there was no sign. All that remained of King Hattaran was his throne, sticky with dried blood and discarded flesh, and there was the painting. Of course, all now know of the flesh portraiture of Honsa, how the artists take apart the subject to create a likeness of his soul. Paint bowls made from bones, paint from flesh, music from screams, sculptures of agony a history written in blood; but none did then.

None except Oroestes.

What became of him?

He died when Murast fell, like most did who were not maimed in some way. The victors knew of Hattaran's cruelty so all who were well or able bodied they put to death, and all who were not they judged as victims of Hattaran's cruelty and took them away from this place. All except me, I remained to guard a painting I have never seen and never will see. Hattaran put out my eyes you see, and only my Father's begging kept me alive. So I stay here to guard his vengeance.

Now, are you sure you wish to see it? I am assured it is quite terrible to behold.

12 Answers Only You Can Question

James Warner

"Have you considered taking the USAT?" my parole officer asked me.
I told her I didn't even know what that was.

"The USAT qualifies you to become an utofuzi. An utofuzi loosely combines the roles of a samurai, a flâneur, and an ux. An ux combines the roles of a griot, a stag brought down by hounds, and an utofuzi."

She was an earnest woman who made me feel guilty about the depth of my own disillusion.

"Look at it this way," she said. "To become a lawyer you first take the LSAT. To become a hobo you take the HSAT. To become an autodidact, the ASAT. Theologians, the TSAT. How would you *expect* to prepare for a life striving to comprehend the Unfathomable, if not by taking the USAT?"

"I never looked at it that way," I admitted, as my parole officer produced an index card with a question typed on it:

1. X is inversely proportional to Y. Which of the following are NOT possible values of X/Y?

    A. The judicious contemplation of discernible reality/crises of institutional legitimacy
    B. Wisdom/pain
    C. Ruptures in the historical continuum/attention to the finer points of technique
    D. Renting yet another U-Haul/the universe's shrinking at an decreasing rate

I chose B. My parole officer predicted I was going to be good at this, and gave me another card:

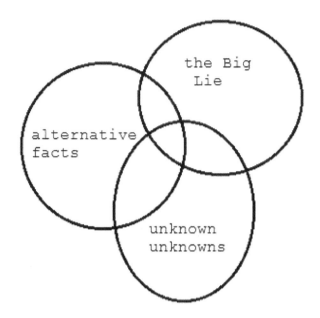

2. On the diagram above, shade in the area that falls outside of all three crappily-drawn ovals.

We spent another half hour working on USAT questions and, before leaving, I'd signed up to take the USAT – in an unspecified location, at an undisclosed time, under unanticipated conditions. (That's how the USAT works.)

The prospect was exhilarating, and anticipating my ordeal gave me purpose. All my life I'd been good at tests and bad at reality, so any opportunity to take another test filled me with hope that I could keep the latter at bay long enough to feel a sense of justification.

Insisting the topic always came up, my parole officer subsequently taught me the formula for life trajectory, where L = life trajectory, i and j are points on the i and j axes, F = ability to forget what already happened, and Z = impersonal forces you can't subvert:

$$L^2 = (\pm\sqrt{Z} * x) + (y - F)/\infty + L^2$$

She was so proud of her own life trajectory, she kept it framed on the wall of her office. The prosecution showed it to you, as Exhibit A.

Preparation materials for the USAT are hard to find. Soon my parole officer had shown me all the index cards she had.

There are no official books or websites to help you, but if you approach the docks towards dawn you'll find tutors prepared to offer you tips. One of these told me the best tutors focused on patterns, not rote memorisation. "There's a rhythm to it," he assured me.

"Did you pass the USAT?" I asked him, and he told me nobody ever passes the USAT.

Knowing this somehow improved my morale. He advised me to learn a lot about bees, and when I asked why, said becoming an expert on a subject that might not turn up in the test is part of the process. "Always wear red during the exam," he emphasised. "Some advise taking wind speed into account, although that part never made sense to me." He sold me a map to use if I ever needed to get really lost – "but once you start unfolding it, there's no way to fold it again. Forget whatever Chalkbrood told you."

Later I found part of an old test in the sleeve of a Laurence Crane LP at the public library.

3. A corporation has invented alienation-flavoured soda. How many cans will you buy, expressed in terms of *n*?

4. You spend six months in a factory motivating the workers to improve their productivity. Replacing one blue lightbulb with a green lightbulb triples productivity. Replacing another blue lightbulb with a green lightbulb halves productivity. At this point you realise you are not in a factory at all… you are in your bathtub, in the foetal position, staring at your Joseph Beuys shower curtain. There is no question to be answered here, so move on.

In the weeks that followed, I learned about bees. I memorised lists of words that are not synonymous with themselves – *Authenticity, Believability, Credibility, Duty* – and learned which square roots are the nemeses of other square roots. I procured a supply of 27G clutch pencils, the only kind allowable for use during the USAT, and learned special vocabulary words suited only for answering USAT questions.

I began seeing test questions everywhere I went. I noticed the words *No Test Material On This Page* spray-painted on the side of an abandoned sofa. I reread Joseph Conrad's *Lord Jim* – Exhibit B for the prosecution. The conversations I had at bus stations late at night were now on topics like whether bees are inherently capable of crime. You tell me.

Post-its on the side of a bank said ROB THIS BANK, and suicide hotlines called me proactively, to make sure I wasn't paying too much attention to current affairs. I kept my map tightly folded, all this time, near the bottom of my backpack.

The person who administers the USAT test is always someone you aren't expecting. In my case, my landlady appeared early one morning with an eviction notice that had the questions typed on the reverse, and an answer sheet. "You're allowed to use a calculator," she said, "but only for questions that don't include any maths. Take a deep breath before you start."

Predictably, there was a question about bees.

4	5	6	6	6	6	6
6	6	6	6	6 ½	7	8
9	9	9	9	9	this one isn't even a bee	this one might be an owl

5. Sozima collects twenty-ones bees, counts their stripes, and records her data in the table above. Has she ever really been in love?

    A. any response I make to this question might tend to incriminate me
    B. no way is that an owl
    C. $\sqrt[3]{dreams}$
    D. still hungry for you, elephant

I filled in the circles on the answer sheet, 'darkly and completely' as the instructions demanded, and every time a 27G clutch pencil malfunctioned, grabbed another – I've taken easier exams in my nightmares. Yet in a pure flow state, marshalling my emotional-logical resources to bear on tasks that would avail me nothing, happy and beyond time, I forgot I was soon to be evicted. At its core, the USAT measures how comfortable one can become with uncertainty.

6. Which of the following does not help to make up the cytoskeleton?

    A. contributory negligence
    B. fleeing to the mountains to evade the coercive power of the state
    C. analepsis and prolepsis
    D. validating the semi-secret knowledge of the marginalised

I guessed the answers I didn't know. I employed the formula for the ambivalence of a triangle. I divided by ∞ repeatedly, and threw in random apostrophes.

When I handed my answer sheet in, my landlady told me some cops had been around looking for me. "I didn't want to tell you before," she explained, giving me kumquats for the road, "in case it distracted you from your freaking *test*."

She also handed me a certificate emblazoned with the words *YOU HAVE ENTERED AN INVALID LAST NAME.*

I thanked her, topped my backpack up with kumquats, and left via the fire-escape.

On the outskirts of town, I took my map out of my backpack, and began unfolding it.

The centre of the map had been cut away to make snowflake patterns. Following this problematic chart as best I could, I came to a copse where two women were tying their shoelaces. A sign nailed to a blighted tree said simply *FISH*, with an arrow pointing into the sky.

"What kind of pencils do you use?" one woman asked, presumably to see if I was an utofuzi. She relaxed fractionally when I showed her my *YOU HAVE ENTERED AN INVALID LAST NAME* certificate.

"How did your test go?" the other woman asked. "Did you

remember to capitalise everything? What does the U in USAT even stand for? I'm lucky that didn't come up."

"Utofuzi?" I suggested. "Undisclosed?"

"Umbrage," the first woman said. "Unsubscribe."

"The USAT's not as hard as the ASAT," the second woman said. "I failed the ASAT seven times." I looked at my hands, on one of which somebody had written with a Sharpie, without me noticing, *ese tipo esta craquiado*. So what else was new?

"Unstandardisation," the first woman said. "The USAT's a standardised test for people who don't want to be standardised."

"I'm told I got a really good score on the ZSAT," the second woman said. I suspected the ZSAT was something she'd just made up.

As we walked on through the woods, I kept an eye out for chanterelles but, not spotting any, I thought about *Lord Jim* instead. My latest rereading had altered my perspective. Before, I'd seen the ending as a cop out, suspecting Conrad was cobbling together some redemption for a character he wasn't sure was redeemable. *Lord Jim* had seemed to me, towards the end, to slip back into being the kind of boy's adventure story it had formerly done so good a job of avoiding.

My current reading of the ending was darker – I now saw Jim's final fate as an echo of his earlier failure, rather than a repudiation of it. Jim chooses, over whatever more practical solutions might have been possible, a death that demonstrates his courage – but in doing so he sacrifices himself unnecessarily, effectively deserting the people of Patusan as conclusively as he earlier deserted the pilgrims on the Padua, fulfilling Marlow's prior dismissive judgment –

"A certain readiness to perish is not so very rare, but it is seldom that you meet men whose souls, steeled in the impenetrable armour of resolution, are ready to fight a losing battle to the last, the desire of peace waxes stronger as hope declines, till at last it conquers the very desire of life."

I admire the way that sentence slips out of being grammatical halfway through, so that you feel something more powerful than punctuation at work.[1] Martyrdom, if not exactly a form of cowardice, is something

---

1. Some editions change the comma between *the last* and *the desire* into a semi-colon but I disapprove.

worse in Marlow's eyes – a flight from practicality. One might even argue that an excessive death wish is at the root of Jim's initial shying from danger. When he deserts the Padua, his temptation to go down with the ship may be what he is really fighting against the hardest.

He is no more ready at the end than he is at the beginning, to fight a losing battle to the last like an utofuzi.

"Readiness to perish is my middle name," I said.

When I looked around, the two women were no longer there – I would not see them again until the start of my trial.

I walked on alone, past burning churches and log cabins, and at last reached the tent city. The sky was like lemon curd left too long in a sauna.

My parole officer was there. She told me she was on a spiritual retreat.

"You're scared of death and you're also scared of living," she advised me.

"I'm not *that* scared of death," I said.

"If you see a man abusing a woman around here," my parole officer warned me, "don't try and intervene. She might think that's condescending."

"I wasn't born yesterday," I said.

"Forget whatever Chalkbrood told you," my parole officer said.

"I don't know anyone called Chalkbrood," I said.

There were spilled flashcards lying in the grass, and I perused them at the same time all those things my lawyer says I shouldn't talk about were happening.

7. Please, you can make a relaxation music for people who knows much things. I know so many that for me is creepy even sounds of nature =(. Warning! message for all people: Is dangerous to know too 2 too much, and the xtreme knowing.=(.

Lord Jim is a doppelganger of Kurtz in *The Heart of Darkness*, both dying in a colonial outpost they've failed single-handedly to subdue, both dying of their own romanticism. For although Jim is portrayed as a gentler potentate than Kurtz, people only invade other countries to escape their fear of their own inner savagery. Both antiheroes seek to manufacture states, and learn in the process their own nullity as individuals. What's most important about both Jim and Kurtz may be what we learn through them about Marlow, who avoids self-disclosure and is always portrayed speaking in a leisurely, unflinching way to pipe-smoking men who implicitly accept Marlow as one of their kind, although a close analysis of his yarns cannot support their judgment. The nature of Marlow's own history can be inferred only via his fascination with the life trajectories of others, and by the fact of his choosing to roam the world analysing doomed outcasts to unresponsive audiences.

Someone came over and started abusing my parole officer, so I put some distance between us, wandering over to a picnic table by which a couple of VSAT instructors were playing mumbly-peg. The V in VSAT stands for Victim.

8. Which is an important consideration when hunting from a ground blind?

A. The hunter is in full view of the rabbit, so it is important to be flatteringly attired.
B. It is difficult for other hunters to see you, so it is tactful to kill them first.
C. You have no protection from the elements, so it is sagacious to optimise your workflow.
D. All critters are projections of your own fears, so it is company policy to brace yourself against an unseen catastrophe.

I turned back to look at my parole officer. She stood out against the sky. I think she was shouting.

9. Distilling a lifetime of experience into an expressive silence requires

A. prayer
B. reverb
C. hoodoo
D. preventing the spile pin from accidentally falling out of the joining shackle

Another flashcard demanded 'What is the main theme of the following passage?' followed by what looked like blood stains.

Security came over and asked me to fill out a form saying what I'd seen, but I'd no idea what I'd seen.

They handcuffed me, while my unfoldable map and *YOU HAVE ENTERED AN INVALID LAST NAME* certificate blew away in a sudden gust, and threw me in the back of their van.

"You know what I realised?" I asked the driver.

He drove past nondescript cabins along a narrow asphalt road. So far this had been one of those drawn-out Conradian journeys to the epicentre of someone else's moral failure – except that in this case the moral failure was my own: that of not having noticed my parole officer had fallen in with the wrong crowd.

She was being rushed to hospital, and several people claimed to have seen me arguing with her.

I thought of the van driver as Marlow, ascribing to him a lifetime of pacing decks whilst ruminating on human insufficiency.

"The only thing the USAT tests," I told him, "is how much time you've spent preparing for the USAT. USAT just stands for USAT Score Approximation Tribunal."

"I scored in the 93rd percentile," Marlow told me. "*You* know how 1970s sports movies end," he added, although actually I didn't.

For a while we seemed to be gaining on the ambulance transporting my parole officer, but before long it had outpaced us. Marlow's countenance took on a thoughtful cast as he scrutinised me in the rear-view mirror.

"I'm supposed to drop you off at the police station," he remarked. "Who said 'More tears are shed over answered prayers than unanswered ones?' Was it A. St. Teresa of Avila, B. Beyoncé, C. Yogi Berra, or D. Sister Souljah?"

"Trick question," I said.

"They all are," Marlow said. Maybe one day he would explain me to a brooding, silent assemblage on some malarial verandah. "*Perhaps you know I used to work for a private security company,*" he would say. "*Once I helped a murderer escape, who was a twisted sort of a chap, if you like. The cumulative effect of him was rather troublesome...*"

But the driver was not really Marlow, and he did not help me escape.

He took me to the police station – some secret sharer *he* turned out to be. Outside the station, journalists asked me if I had any comments on the death of my parole officer.

10. Problem sensitivity usually results in

A. testing offenders for drugs and giving them more if permitted
B. taunting probationers until they commit crimes aligned with their philosophical bearings
C. applying general rules and procedures to specific anomalies
D. neofascist backlast

After spending a while in the holding tank, I was taken to the Prison.

Here I first met Chalkbrood, who taught me the following:

Examinations are a tool of psychological warfare employed by centralised governments, a way of dividing and ruling from the time of the Han dynasty onwards. Their purpose is to standardise what subjects ought to know in ways that benefit the imperial, metropolitan power, while sidestreaming other perceptual traditions.

At the start of an examination, it's customary to write your full name – already more information than it's wise to give the government – and from there things keep going downhill. You may have to show an identity card, and the questions themselves perpetuate a managerial mindset. As the ocean sorts stones according to size, so exams sort the state's human matériel according to brainwashability, approval-hungriness, and loyalty to establishment limitations of thought. In a society ridden with quantifiable measurements of pseudo-performance, prestige becomes dependent on thinking the way the authorities want, on answering questions in a way which abstracts from the flux and contingency of actuality in the direction of imposed categories.

After testing, never knowing if your answers have been received, processed, or acknowledged, you cannot be sure you officially exist. This saps your courage, and makes you more pliable.

Every exam question is a cage. That is why Chalkbrood has developed the ESAT. The E is for escape artist, and the ESAT is not multiple-choice like the VSAT. One answers in a non-official language, if one shows up at all. A healthy response might confuse the examiner as to who one is, ridicule any oppressive background assumptions embedded in the question – those sleights of hand designed to force mystifications on us – and end by convincing the invigilators to burn down the records office. Consider this example:

$$n(t) = t^2/2 - 20t + k$$

11. There was a 100-day period when the number of bees in a certain hive could be modelled by the function n above. In the function, k is a constant and represents the number of bees on day number t for $0 \leq t \leq 99$. On what number day was the number of bees in the hive the same as it was on day number 10?

In response I ask how to camouflage the hives so as to evade Board of Health scrutiny, how to encourage a sustainable variety of wildflowers in the vicinity, with adequately nutritious nectar, which inspectors can be bribed with honey, and how best to appraise the role in colony collapse of the decline of genetic diversity due to artificial queen insemination, to GMOs, and to neonicitinoids and other pesticides.

Because one thing the question doesn't tell you is that, on the 101st day – the same day my parole officer succumbed to her wounds, having been multiply stabbed with a 27G clutch pencil, or so the prosecution claims – the drones all vanished.

Chalkbrood thinks the pesticides act as a nerve poison that disrupts their homing ability, so they never find their way back to the hive.

But my own view is that the drones are avoiding the hive deliberately, having been provoked by state-of-the-art apicultural techniques into seeking out zones of schismatic resistance. I believe that, as a strategy of infrapolitical sabotage, all the bees are deliberately evolving back into being wasps.

Chalkbrood thinks this is bullshit.

My parole officer's life trajectory and mine were perpendicular, and we met at a right angle. "She tried too hard not to be condescending," I told Chalkbrood. "Trying that hard to be uncondescending actually *is* condescending because it implies you can't take any condescension, if you see what I mean."

Chalkbrood sometimes claims to be the marooned captain of a tramp schooner, sometimes a prison psychologist. He has many incompatible social security numbers, none of which include any Arabic numerals. His credit score is a baseball bat, his dating profile a cinder block, his World of Warcraft Best Player Ranking a tooth plectrum. His Myers-Briggs personality type is a length of rebar he found in the creek, and his TED talk was about how and why not to tame sea urchins. I'll stop there, because I don't want to make Chalkbrood sound more of a contrarian than he actually is.

He says the real mistake was replacing all the human beekeepers with robots – robots are bad beekeepers because they cannot feel stings.

12. What is this to be? ... the hell supposed

I live and work within the unseen processes of nature, and how do you grade someone on that? I answer all computerised surveys with an elliptical gaze or strangled cry. *You teach the wrong things,* I say, *but that's okay, I make up for it by not learning them.*

Anything I draw has the wrong number of legs, lest everything end up as one of those personality quizzes where you have either to click *I am like this,* by a photo of a bloodletting fleam, or *I am like* this, by a photo of a hydraulic torque wrench, or maybe the photos are of a cisalpine meadow and a reciprocating saw, but whatever you decide to click means you didn't get the job.

Am I guilty or innocent of murdering my parole officer? You the jurors may not bring food or unauthorised materials into the courtroom. The improperly attired will be excluded, and all electronic devices should be left in the parking lot. Photography is forbidden at all times, and forget whatever Chalkbrood told you. After your verdict, remain quietly seated until you are dismissed, then run for the hills.

The Woman Who Turned into Soap

Harkiran Dhindsa

Every Friday night, Daya and her sister were rounded up into the mould-specked bathroom by their mother. Steam spiralled off the hot water as it hit the bucket squatting below the tap in the old enamel bath, while Chandni scrubbed vigorously at their necks and scolded them to keep still. She removed days of grime, leaving their skin prickling raw. Often, she soaped them with food from the kitchen just as her own mother had done back in Punjab. She would take a palm-full of plain yoghurt and rub it into their hair, but Daya always whimpered when the cold dollops trickled down her bare back. When their hair was dry, Chandni massaged oil into their scalps, working it along the hair shafts until their heads had the sheen of a raven's wings. It was a laborious task, on occasion accompanied by Chandni wondering aloud whether she had performed some misdeed in a past life for God to punish her with the burden of daughters rather than the blessing of sons.

The oils varied – almond, mustard, olive. Chandni said almond was particularly nourishing for the brain, but when Daya went shopping with her mother along Ealing Broadway, her eyes were drawn to fragrant promises that came packaged in bottles labelled conditioner. Watching adverts on TV, Daya was fascinated by women immersed in deep bubble baths, the velvety foam cocooning their bodies. She watched an actress raise a perfect silky, long leg from the opaque water and stroke it seductively with her hands from pointed toe to knee. As Daya became older and washing became a private activity, she tried to recreate these luxurious scenes, pouring half a bottle of bubble bath into the water, even using an egg whisk once for full froth effect. Only the water level was not quite deep enough for proper submersion, as the tank warmed up barely enough for half a bathtub. The pleasure was also ruined a little by flakes of enamel paint floating up to the surface and her mother knocking on the door and shouting, "Hurry up, girl, any longer and your

73

skin will shrink. I don't know what you do in there."

Daya heard her mother's footsteps retreat down the stairs and she lay back and flicked up the foam into swirls and watched the creamy bubbles slowly disintegrate on her developing breasts.

A month later, Daya's father made an announcement. It was one of the rare days when he was awake in the afternoon, taking a holiday from the nightshift of his security guard job; he was going to look at tiles. A new bathroom suite was to be installed.

"About time, too," Chandni said. "Every time I clean that old bath I shred my gloves, and it's not as if anyone else round here's going to lift a finger. It's all very well them cleaning themselves, but clean the bath? No, leave it to me as if I'm the servant."

It was as if the goddess of bathing herself had smiled upon Daya and heard her longings. With the new plumbing came an electric shower. At last – spontaneous hot water, no more waiting around for tanks to heat up. No more sitting in your own soup of dirt and old skin. This was an invigorating wake-up call cascading down her teenage body first thing every morning. While her mother lit the clay lamp in the little shrine cupboard and offered up prayers, Daya sleep-stumbled into the shower cubicle before school. It became imperative – a layer of skin had to moult under the running water before she could emerge as her living self each morning.

Chandni was pulling sheets off the beds one day to put into the washing machine and as she lifted the quilt off Daya's bed, she croaked, "How can you let so much blood get on the sheet. You must sort yourself. This is dirty. What if somebody else saw this?" Nobody was going to see it, Daya knew, but still she felt ashamed and skulked out of the room. After that she always did her own washing.

It wasn't just dirt and smells that Daya tried to rid from herself. There was also the thickening hair – shafts that she ripped out with wax before she allowed her legs to be seen in her games skirt, and underarm hair razed before she pulled on a swimming costume. She began to notice the hair above the lips of her dark-haired friends, and she became envious of the light, barely visible down on the arms of blonde girls. She offered to pluck her sister's eyebrows into shape, but Asha said she was going for the natural look. "I've got better things to do with my time, and do you know what a stink you leave behind every time you use one of those shaving creams?"

People regularly remarked to Chandni, "Isn't Asha pretty?" They never said that about Daya. When Asha had moved up to secondary school, it had been the same adoration again, but this time from Daya's friends. "Your little sister's so cute." Daya sat in her bedroom and placed mirrors at various angles around herself, trying to work out what it was that made people perceive Asha as more beautiful. She stared at faces on television, passengers on buses, at girls in her classroom and tried to break down this essence of prettiness. Poring over glossy magazines for hours, she hoped to soak up beauty from the pages by osmosis. She scrutinised the models' faces, her own eyes tracing the shapes of their eyes, lips, noses. Genes had been mixed up and in the random sifting, her sister had gained the finer features that aligned more closely with the faces in the magazines.

Turning sixteen, Daya took a Saturday job on a beauty counter in Boots, where she was paid to sell dreams in jars. She easily spotted the insecure, hesitant customers and, in turn, they seemed drawn to her. She left school at the end of that year to train as a beauty therapist and then landed a job with a beautician named Bunty who ran a salon above a sari shop in Wembley. Bunty assured Daya, "You'll be kept busy here. When I first started very few of our ladies cared for this sort of thing. Now these young Indian women, these solicitors, accountants and all, they spend a lot of money here. They're even worrying about cellulite these days. Bet our mums never even noticed it." Bunty said it as if their mothers were from the same generation. Her hair was dyed a bright copper, back-combed, sprayed and locked into position around her head like a halo, and her heavy makeup concealed a face nearer Daya's mother's age. Bunty was soon to be overheard readily confessing to customers, "I'm on the wrong side of forty but only just." Daya realised that her boss only said this to have the customers respond, "Oh, I thought you were much younger than that." Bunty was divorced and regularly took days off work when Ramesh, a married man who lived in Coventry, came down to London on so-called business. Of all the treatments offered in the salon, Bunty liked manicuring best, as then she could sit opposite her clients and gossip with them at eye level while she buffed their nails. She was happy to let Daya take over the trail of women who climbed the stairs for facials, back massages and torturous hair removal.

Daya couldn't persuade Asha to try any of the treatments. Asha went travelling with their cousin around India. Daya winced as she read the postcard – backpacking in the Himalayas. The words invoked dirt and sweat. She sensed enough of it oozing out of the pores of her clients. She tried wearing latex gloves but the molten wax clung to them, so instead, between clients she started to scrub her hands clean with more vigour than a surgeon. And her sense of smell seemed to heighten. On the bus every morning, she raised her magazine in front of her nose to block out the odours emanating from the passengers around her.

Chandni said it was about time that her older daughter married and set up her own home. But Daya had started to recoil from men, those in the street and at bus stops and especially leering men serving behind the counter of the Indian take-away. Once she would have wanted them to admire her, these men whose gaze lingered over Asha. Now she did not want to meet their eyes at all. The only man Daya touched was Tony, her one male client, a model who regularly arrived to have his chest hairs waxed.

Chandni arranged meetings with suitable bachelors. The first date, the man's after-shave was so overpowering it triggered a headache in Daya. With the second man, there was the faint stink of sweat in the air, the third had stale breath, and the fourth a general whiff of onions about him. At last, Daya met one who was reassuringly soapy-smelling and she studied his face closely, saw the bristles that lay in wait under the skin of his shaven chin and wondered if she could bear to get close enough to him. It was then that she knew she didn't want to be touched. She didn't need a husband or a lover. Maybe a statue would do, a Michelangelo carving to look at and admire, something that didn't perspire. She told her mother to give the match-making a rest.

Daya moved jobs to bigger premises in an exclusive leisure centre and busied herself attending to the tense, young professional women who wanted pampering. They revealed their secrets while she waxed their legs or massaged away the stress knots in their backs. They told her of their ill-fated affairs. At lunchtimes, Daya rushed into the gym downstairs, past the heaving bodies – more body odours – and reclaimed herself under the shower. Only then could she touch other bodies again in the afternoon.

In the evenings, she didn't want to encounter other people, other skins, and if any of her colleagues asked her to join them for a drink, she'd make an excuse and decline. Over the years, she had squirrelled away enough money to put down a deposit on a small flat, but first it had to be redecorated and decontaminated of its previous owners. The one-bedroom apartment was tiny but with an adequate-sized bathroom, and she spent a hefty bank loan and many weeks thumbing through design magazines in pursuit of the ideal bathroom fittings. She kitted out her bathroom with shower gels, mousses and shampoos. One of Daya's clients had told her that the word shampoo had arrived from India, something about massaging heads, and, standing back to look at her own bathroom, she recalled her mother pummelling yoghurt into her scalp. Fragrant candles and essential oils were arranged around the bath to invoke particular moods so that the room now resembled part chemist, part spa and part Body Shop. How righteous Daya had felt, years back, to discover products she could use to indulge herself without harming rabbits and perhaps also help a few village women with their wages in some faraway place. But she wasn't loyal only to Anita Roddick. Sometime later, she'd discovered Lush, with its intense, loud fragrances and its food-hall appearance, where soaps were laid out in great slabs as if they were cheeses to be sliced and nibbled. There was always some new line of cleansing products springing up to deplete Daya's funds and now that she had her flat to finance, there would be less to spend on stocking up the bathroom. If there were soaps containing avocados, or strawberries, or watermelon, she wondered if she could almost give up on food shopping all together.

Coming out of her flat one morning to put her rubbish into the wheelie- bin, Daya saw tiny white worm-like creatures crawling over the black plastic. Hesitantly, she approached the lid and was hit by a putrid smell that arrowed straight to her throat. The bin was crawling with maggots. Recoiling, it was all she could do to stop herself from vomiting and she ran up to her bathroom to have another shower even though it delayed her for work. The bin men called the next day and, returning from the salon, Daya poured a whole bottle of disinfectant into the empty bin and then tipped the bin onto its side and blasted the insides with a jet of water from the neighbour's hosepipe. She stood well back, trying to avoid the back spray as maggots slid down in a stream of water across the forecourt and into the road. She had tied a white cotton handkerchief over her face, covering her nose and mouth and yet, even through this, she could smell the fetor of decay.

When she was sure she'd got rid of every last maggot, she went back inside and tore off her clothes and shoved them inside a bin bag before stepping into the shower. For weeks afterwards, she would find herself suddenly twitching, believing maggots were crawling over her skin and then have to wash again.

The summer was hot, the air-conditioning inadequate in the salon that Daya had now been appointed to manage at a new spa near Holland Park. Her foundation streaked and by the end of her shift, she could no longer bear the make-up layered onto her face. Each evening, as soon as she returned home, she began to undress, leaving a trail of clothes from the front door to the bathroom where she immediately clambered into the shower and scrubbed her body clean.

The constant bathing was drying out her skin; she had to use more and more creams and lotions to stop it flaking off. Her mother had slapped a bit of supermarket brand moisturiser onto her cheeks and a smear of Vaseline onto her lips if she went out on a frosty day, whereas Daya regularly discovered new promotional products, sent free to the spa, which she used to target previously neglected parts of her body. Now she had acquired not only lotions for her neck and hands, but also creams for her thighs, her stomach and, recently, a watermelon gel to push in between her toes. Just before retreating into her bed with its crisp, clean sheets, there would be the final soak. Alone in her flat, pleasingly devoid of men to clutter up the place or leave a shampoo bottle on the wrong side of the shelf, she could indulge herself with her latest fragrance, fingering the potion as she removed it from its packaging.

Between work and washing herself and vacuuming the flat, there was no time for anything else. And work no longer held any pleasure; in fact, it repelled her, but there were bills to be paid. Daya thought she no longer required a plethora of luxuries – only shampoos and shower gels and a hot water supply to be maintained and the mortgage to be met on her dust-free flat. She desired never to have to step out of her front door again, never to take her body into the outside air with all its contaminants.

Having sipped the last of her wine one evening, she perched her glass on the rim of the bath beside an emptied bottle of bath oil. As she reclined further into the hot water, she saw a creamy flake rise to the surface. She was reminded of the old peeling enamel paint in her childhood bath and she felt a deep gratitude for her pristine tub. She closed her eyes and slid back deeper into the bath so that her lips met just the surface of the water and she breathed slowly, the steam making her giddy and a little drowsy. When she opened her eyes again, she saw more flakes, they were like coconut shavings; it dawned on Daya that these were layers of skin, her own brown integument. She tried to reach out for the flakes, these floating petals, but couldn't move her hand; her fingers were dissolving in the bath water. She attempted to lift her leg but that too was dispersing. And now the flakes began to disintegrate, leaving only suds on the surface.

Rising from the water, there were all the aromas that had once surfed her body – wafts of lemon, vetiver, strawberry, ginger, juniper. A hundred fragrances blending, but each one distinct to her finely tuned sense of smell. She felt no pain, only lightness, a climax to all those baths that were supposed to invoke relaxation. There was an easing in her limbs and her head, all aches fading. She sensed a washing away of awkward thoughts, a rinsing of emotions – a true cleansing. There was no more form, no vessel, just a weightless faint notion of existing. Steam rose from the bath and her mind swam upwards on the warm air, floating, swirling. No longer of body, no longer of this life – free.

Mushroom Speed Boosts

Ben Reynolds

I gave up racing Logan for a while. It got boring. He is too good. He knows every shortcut, every shortcut within a shortcut, where to use the mushrooms. He set the fastest time on every track.

But I've been practicing. I'm ready.

Mario celebrates my return with a *wahooooo!*

Logan races as Donkey Kong. I'm always Luigi. Luigi is Mario's under-appreciated brother.

First up, Mario Kart Stadium.

Come on then, this time you're going down.

3… 2… 1… Go!

I get a boost start and beat him to the first corner because Luigi has better acceleration than Donkey Kong. I stay ahead until he uses a mushroom to take a shortcut over the grass and I can't catch him from there. He's too good.

Damn it!

He play-punches me on the arm and leans back with that satisfied smile. Sometimes he feels he should taunt, take the piss, because that's what everyone else does, but he's not very good at it and you can tell he regrets it. It's not him, but to be honest I don't know whether it's worse to be humiliated or patronised.

Try a different track. Twisted Mansion.

I'm better at this one.

3…

Gotta time this right, get the boost start.

2…

Mum pokes her head through the door.

1…

Who are you talking to?

Go!

Gah, missed the boost. Thanks Mum.

Logan. We're racing. He's too good though.

Mum moves into the room, sits next to me. She puts her arm around me.

Bubble, I thought you were going to delete his accounts.

This isn't his account. This is him.

I point to the screen. DK skids around a corner, boosts into a straight.

That's his ghost.

Mum pulls her arm away.

Oh Jefferson.

What?

It's not him.

It is! I point at the screen again. *That's him. He did that. Before, I mean. He set the fastest time so the Switch remembers how he did it and I have to try to beat him. It's called a ghost race.*

Mum stands. She runs her hands through her hair. There is a seam of grey on her left temple.

This isn't helping anyone. Her voice wavers, her lips thin. *I've asked you to delete his accounts.* She doesn't look at me as she says this. She looks at the floor and then at my bedroom door. *It's all I've asked of you. Please do it.*

I swallow, say nothing as she stares at the wall, struggles to keep her breathing regular.

I'll take that as a yes, then, she says. Thank you.

She slams my door harder than she intends to on the way out. I think.

These aren't his accounts. These are his save games.

I spend the evening beating his times, one by one. But I leave the last one. Rainbow Road. I leave it for him, so he doesn't disappear completely, so he can stay.

The Guile

Ian McDonald

Best trick I ever saw? A lanky streak-of-piss Dutchman did it right in front of my eyes. A ring, a watch, a wallet. Some covering patter about a thief, but the effect is: He puts the ring, the watch, and the wallet in an envelope and seals it. Patter patter, he tears up the envelope and presto chango, it's empty! The ring, the watch, and wallet are back on his finger, his wrist, in his inside pocket. Simple, quick, clean: done three feet in front of me and I have no idea how he did it.

Well, I do. Sleight of hand. Misdirection. That's how they're all done. But the trick of it – the guile: I have no idea.

I'm not a magician. I was the Silverado Resort's valet parking service. Pernell Brolin.

I used to be a pit boss; eight pits, blackjack. I was hot death in a tux. I ran a tight pit. But, you know, age. You slow. You miss things. I still have a stripe down the side of my pants, but it's grey, not black.

This is not a Las Vegas story. It's a Reno story. And it doesn't take place in the Luxor or the Bellagio, it takes place in the Silverado Resort. Popular with spring breaks and bachelor/ette parties from San Francisco. And it wasn't David Copperfield or Mat Franco or Penn and Teller. It was Maltese Jack Caruana.

Those guys, they make 737s disappear or levitate Charlize Theron or drive semis over each other's heads. Big, clever illusions. Jack Caruana is up-close, under-the-skin, inside-your-head magic. The kind of man who would take your ring, watch, and wallet without you ever knowing, and work wonders with them.

There's a new thing in magic, like there's a new thing in jazz and, it seems, in coffee. This new thing is to show how the trick is done, and then do it anyway. The skill – the guile – is in how well you perform the sleight of hand. Some of the new names in the Las Vegas hotels and magic clubs work this way now.

They owe it all to Maltese Jack Caruana.

I had some of that new thing in coffee. A truck came in for a few days on the west side of Buena Vista. It was not what I call coffee at all. Sour. Coffee should not be sour. But it was the new thing, it seemed. The thing about this new thing, the guile, is that if you don't like it, the problem is with you, not the coffee. With you, not the magician.

The coffee truck lasted two days. Not enough business in Buena Vista.

Now this you'd call the meet-cute. Movies have their tricks and guiles just like magic. I'd come off earlies, flat out by eight thirty, someplace beyond dreaming, when *bam!* A hundred watts of blue LED flashlight shone through my eyelids and I was awake like someone ran a live wire up my ass. The light swung around the inside of the trailer, then moved off. I saw a slit of blue shining under the door. I heard the latch, I heard rattling, I heard swearing, I heard every single key on a fob try the lock. Not cops, then.

Cops are always the first thought in Buena Vista.

I pulled on a robe and threw open the door. I almost knocked the short, sixty-something man back off the step.

"Who the fuck are you?" he said.

"Au contraire," I said. "Who the fuck are you?"

Maltese Jack Caruana, of course. Magician. Ex the relaunched Alon, starting a new residency at the Silverado, two shows a night, matinee on Sundays. Mondays off. He'd been given a trailer in our little clutch. Misread the key fob; two for five.

"You're a magician and you can't get a door open?"

He was small like some kind of terrier, and he looked exactly as someone would who'd driven up from Vegas in one go. He smelled of car seats, taco sauce, and dust and sweat, but it was the M-word that got him in my door. *Magician.*

"So what kind of magician are you?" I asked. 'Illusionist, escapologist?"

He looked at me like I was bird shit on his shoulder.

"You know magic?"

"I know it. Can't do it."

"I'm a micro-magician and mentalist," Jack Caruana said, and that got the top off my quart plastic bottle of blended scotch and two glasses on the coffee table. Of all the schools of magic, I like the up-close, intimate magic best. There's nowhere for the trick to hide. Illusion: a magic box or a glass tank or a big circular spangled curtain and you think, okay, the trick is in there somewhere. Escapology: one big trick – get out of this – and that's it. Mentalism: old stuff – reading minds, predicting the future, clairvoyance, hypnotism, moving things with your mind, feats of memory. Micro-magic: up-close, table-top magic; hands and cards and you know it's in the hands somewhere, but you never see it. That's proper magic.

"Did you ever meet Ed Lorenzo down in Vegas?" I asked. "I like that guy. Makes me laugh."

"Taught him everything he knows."

Right, Jack Caruana. Magic men who residency in Las Vegas, even at the Alon, don't domicile in Buena Vista. I poured and slid a glass across the table to him.

"Did you teach him that walking chair effect? Loved that effect."

"Good effect, that."

We clinked. You see, real magicians don't do tricks. Real magicians perform *effects*.

"Maria won't have cleaned the trailer out and you don't want to start this time of night," I said. "I got a spare bed in back. Welcome to Buena Vista, magic-man."

It started when Salazar lost his job to the robot.

I say that and you think Arnie walking out of the exploding gas tanker or a transformo-bot the size of a city block punching its fist down a monster's throat. Or maybe one of those cute Japanese things that I always want to kick onto its back to watch it flap its arms. But modern robots of the twenty-first century – real robots – are invisible. Now you've got another image in your head you can't get out. I'm playing a magician's trick – telling you the truth but making you see something else. Invisible killer terminators. Software, my friend. Software robots.

The house wins in the end. That's the iron rule. You can win big, that's probability, but if you win consistently, you're gaming the gamers. The house calculates its edge by statistics – standard deviations – and when the shape of the bell curve starts going out of whack, it's time to take a closer look. There is knowing when to look, and knowing what to look for. Salazar was the eye of the Silverado.

When I started in the pits, they used to hide the surveillance cameras. By the time I went to the concierge desk, they were in plain sight. Guys like Salazar worked twelve monitors at a time. You had to have the eyes, but you needed the nose as well. Psychology, my friend. Every player has tells – having no tell is a tell – and it's no different for cheats. People who fiddle at their clothing all the time at the table but never at the bar. Patterns of blinking. Salazar took all the tiny improbabilities of behaviour and made them into something significant, because there is nothing random about humans. Twelve years watching the pits and he pulled every kind of rigger and card-counter and memory artist, and then the casino pitted him against an AI. Remi. We all thought it stood for something. Remote Evaluation and Monitoring Intelligence. No. Didn't mean a thing, just a name. But in the first week alone, Remi's catch was up twenty-seven percent over Salazar's. Over a month it was thirty-seven percent higher.

The entire surveillance team was moved to other work, and that is how Salazar the Eye came to Buena Vista.

AIs don't see the way humans do. AIs have no blind spots, no doubts, no biases or unconscious skews, and they never, ever blink. Humans notice, humans select, and humans un-notice. AIs see. Like God.

If Salazar losing his job to Remi was where it started, it began the night I was sitting up for Jack to come back after the eleven o'clock show in the Opal Miner bar. Starting and beginning, they're two different things. We'd begun taking a sundowner together at the end of the shift before we headed off to our trailers. Just one, maybe two. Never three. The casino had implemented random drink and drugs tests. Not that Jack ever would – a drunk magician is no magician – but I'm in a car-facing job and I've been in twice already to blow into the white tube.

High pressure was sitting over Reno like an alien mother ship – four days now and the heat was at insane and climbing. We were sitting outside on camp chairs surrounded by freezer packs full of slowly melting ice we'd collected from the hotel ice machines. Didn't make a damn bit of difference. Jack's cell rang. He answered and I saw a weird look on his face, then he raised a finger – something strange here – and then touched it to his lips – whatever you say, say nothing – and put the phone on speaker.

"Sorry, I got distracted, who did you say you were?"

"Come, come, Mr. Caruana, you weren't distracted at all. I saw you on the twelfth-floor street-view camera. You have Mr. Brolin with you, and from your behaviour, I suspect you are relaying me on speakerphone."

Remi? I mouthed.

"Yes, Mr. Brolin."

Fuck, I mouthed.

Jack kept his cool. "Casino employees aren't allowed to gamble," he said.

"You know I would know that, Mr. Caruana, so I wonder if you are attempting some kind of double bluff? I was watching your evening show."

"What did you think of it, Remi?"

"I think that I am at variance with the audience."

"How so, Remi?"

"They applauded the degree to which they were deceived by you. I applauded the plausibility with which you sold obvious misdirection."

"I don't understand, Remi."

"I think you are being disingenuous, Mr. Caruana. For example, your opening piece. You clearly direct a member of the audience to pick a card you have preselected. You do it by observing the card at the very start of the trick and then manipulating it into a position to be selected. The audience is amazed when you identify the card you have already selected."

"That's magic, Remi."

"There is no magic, Mr. Caruana."

"You saw me make the force."

"Yes. You directed the audience to look elsewhere while you very quickly noted the bottom card of the deck and slipped it to where you had cut the deck in a concealed hold."

"That force takes less than a tenth of a second, Remi."

"Point zero eight of a second. But I don't see the way humans see, Mr. Caruana. I see everything, all at once. I am incapable of being misdirected."

"That's a very basic effect, Remi. I use it as a warm-up, really. You can see how to do it on YouTube."

"But I didn't see it on YouTube, Mr. Caruana. I saw you do it in front of eighty people, out of a maximum capacity of two hundred, in the Opal Miner bar. I am intrigued. I shall be watching you in the future." Call over.

"Fucking artificial fucking intelligence…" Jack ranted. The cell rang again.

"As I understand, that is a disrespectful thing to say, Mr. Caruana."

I jerked a thumb toward the hotel, turned my back to the camera, and said, "It can lip-read."

Every show that week, Remi watched, two shows a night and the matinee on Sunday. Every night, as we slumped off the shuttle bus and into our chairs under the heat that showed no sign of breaking, it would call and tell Jack exactly how an effect was worked. It started on the easy, sleight-of-hand tricks. By Wednesday it was dismantling the showstoppers.

"It must be researching," I said. "Everything on YouTube, all the Magic Castle videos, every magic show ever done. It wouldn't take it that long."

"It doesn't need to," Jack said. "It does exactly what it says. It sees in a way we don't. I can't misdirect it. Watch this."

He stood up, pulled a deck of cards out of a pants pocket. Shuffle, cut. "Pick a card." I picked the Queen of Hearts. Jack shuffled the card back in, squared the deck, put it back in his pocket. "I'm going to read your mind, then I'm going to use my mind to steer your mind to pick exactly that card in the shuffled deck."

He pulled out the deck, fanned through it.

"Any time you want."

"Stop." He turned up the card. Queen of Hearts, of course.

"Simplest trick in the world." He let the cards fall. They were all Queens of Hearts. "It's a force and deck-swap. I put the first deck in my right pocket, but the marked deck, I take that out of my left pocket. And no one ever notices. Remi would see through that in a second. I wouldn't insult it, or myself, with that effect. You know some magic. You know every effect is made up of key parts…"

"I saw that movie," I said. "The pledge, something in the middle I can't remember, and the prestige."

"That's structure. How magic *works*, that's different. In my theory…"

"Everyone's got a theory," I said. I passed the big plastic jug of whiskey. Down to the last two fingers. Three days to payday. I should stretch it, but I love magic talk.

"In my theory," Jack said without losing a beat – he knows how to work an audience – "every effect has two elements, the guile and the panache. The panache is all the showmanship, the patter, the props, the dressing. The panache is how you sell the effect. But the trick, the magic: That's the guile. The panache is there to hide the guile. People see the panache and miss the guile. Remi doesn't see the panache and nails the guile. Every time. I do the purest magic there is, and he sees the guile. Every time. He's probably lip-reading this right now. Read this, then, Remi. There has to be an effect, somewhere, that an artificial intelligence can't see."

Inés rolled in off the shuttle bus. She used to deal pai gow poker but as she got older and stiffer she got moved down the tables, pai gow poker to baccarat, baccarat to blackjack, blackjack to the slots. Now she bossed a pit of twenty-five machines.

That was her road to Buena Vista.

You see me in the grey frock coat and the pants with the stripe down the side and the shoes so shiny it's like they're signalling to the moon. I say, *Welcome to the Silverado ma'am*, and I take your car and off I glide, and when you want it, back I glide. The panache. You don't see the big concrete underground garage. That's the machinery. And you don't see me at the end of shift taking the staff shuttle bus out the back way, along the boulevard through the gate in the screen of trees. Behind those trees is Buena Vista Trailer Park. Right in the middle of Reno's premier resort hotels, the trailer park no one sees.

No one except Remi, it seems.

Inés banged down beside us on a camp chair.

"Air-con still dead?"

"Can't have this heat, Pernell."

Inés' air-con was perfectly serviceable. She hadn't been able to pay her power meter the past month. She'd been eating on the staff discount and lighting the trailer with candle stubs stolen from the banqueting suites.

"I hear that computer's upstaging your show, magic-man."

Jack scowled. I offered her scotch.

"If it were me, I'd show that uppity machine what for."

And then it came to me, oh Lord it came to me, in a kind of sparkling flash and everything was still and silent in all the world. I jumped right

up out of my seat. Pretty spry for my joints.
"I've got it!" I yelled.
Scotch flew everywhere.
"It's obvious! Gandalf versus Thulsa Doom!"

My pa, he had a trick. Everyone's pa had this trick. He put a little piece of paper on each finger and went, *Two little birds sitting on a wall; one called Peter, one called Paul.* Well you know how it's done, but at age eight I watched and I watched until everyone was pissing with laughter because I couldn't see he was making them fly away and come back. Same as Jack's Queen of Hearts; you're so busy watching you don't *see*.

The idea that magic was as simple as swapping forefingers with index fingers made me a lifelong fan of tricks and scams, fakes and fly moves. I begged and begged to get a magic kit of my own for my twelfth birthday, but I learned pretty soon that I didn't have the motor skills – or the dedication – to work a palm or a drop. There is no performance art rehearsed like magic. Thousands – tens of thousands – of repetitions: Magicians practice a move until it's automatic, perfect, instant and unseen.

I couldn't learn the guile.

In community college I always sat in the same chair. One day I got moved to a different one. Someone had carved into the folding table: *Gandalf v Thulsa Doom.* Deep and smooth at the edges, filled with black gunk like it had been done back in the sixties. Even when I moved back to my usual seat, it bothered me. Gandalf I'd heard of, but who was this Thulsa Doom? The undead sorcerer in *Conan the Barbarian*, that's who. James Earl Jones, that's who. James Freakin' *Earl Jones*.

And it all came back. I'd never seen a black wizard before. I don't mean dark arts, evil magic. I mean: *black*. Wizards were old white guys with beards and staffs. No disrespect, Mr. McKellen, but this was a black guy who looked as mean as fuck and could turn into *a giant death snake*. James Earl Jones as Thulsa Doom: That's a wizard I could get behind.

I hadn't thought about those old words gouged into the community college desk for years. But it lay there, unseen but not forgotten, until one hot, high-pressure night in Reno, it came bubbling up.

"A challenge."

I knew Jack wasn't getting it with the same white, Saint Paul–blinding light in which I saw it. This would be a sell.

"*The* challenge, my friend. You, Maltese Jack Caruana, international man of mystery, magic, and mentalism, challenge the great Remi, all-seeing wizard of the Silverado, that you will perform a trick, before a live audience, that it cannot explain. Marketing, my friend. Is. Everything." The plan was clear and entire before me. I had a vision. "Battle of the wizards. Gandalf versus Thulsa Doom."

"I could be wrong here…" Salazar was a less frequent visitor to the evening sessions than Inés, but he did chip in for the scotch. We were a small, tight community; four trailers drawn in around an open yard in a quiet corner of Buena Vista. We all chipped in what we could, when we could. "But that's more Gandalf versus the all-seeing eye of Sauron."

"The point," I said, "the actual point is: You market it, you make it the biggest magic show in Reno – bigger even than anything in Las Vegas. The biggest show in the world. I tell you, you'll get every magician and table-worker and illusionist and mentalist on five continents turning up to see this. It's the classic battle – man versus machine. Like that chess master taking on Big Blue, or whatever."

"Deep Blue," Salazar said. Know your enemy.

"That chess master lost," Jack said.

"Your career's finished anyway," Salazar said. "Like mine. Another robot kill. If you stop talking to Remi on the phone, it'll break in on the sound system. If you shut down the sound system, it'll just post the camera feed on YouTube. This way, you keep a percentage of the house and the licensing deal and a story for the after-dinner and convention circuit."

"You've got this all thought out," Jack said, and I knew I had him.

"Looking at ways to game the system is my job," Salazar said. "Was."

"Wizard Wars!" I said. "Or Wizard versus Wizard. Which sounds better?"

Then came a cry from Inés's trailer and a sudden, flickering light. She had knocked over one of her candle stubs. Her curtains were on fire. Salazar pulled open the door, I went through like a linebacker and hauled Inés out. Her hair was singed, her hands scorched. Her sofa was ablaze. Black smoke boiled up from the burning upholstery foam. Then Maltese Jack was in with the fire extinguisher, sending tornadoes of powder to every corner of the trailer. The fire was out in moments. Powder covered every surface. The trailer leaked smoke from door, windows, every vent.

It would be weeks before Inés could live there again, if ever.
"You stay with me tonight," I said. Pernell Brolin, refuge to the lost.
We knew then we had to get out of Buena Vista.

The management didn't go for either Wizard Wars or Wizard vs Wizard.
They had their marketing department take a look at our proposal and
decided to call it Magic or Machine? Like a Discovery Channel show.

Which is to say, they bought into it two hundred percent. A thousand
percent. They bought it. The dudes who developed the software bought
it. The papers, the syndication shows, the networks, and the digital
channels: they bought it. The other casinos in Reno bought it: they
wanted to see if Remi was as good as the Silverado said it was. And the
public bought it.

Maltese Jack's agent negotiated him a percentage of house and rights.
It was a sweet deal. The Silverado added a rider; every trick that Remi
guessed, Jack would never perform again. We both read the score: a Las
Vegas magician on the glide-path of his career, who couldn't even fill the
smallest bar in the resort. It was the mother of all resignation letters.

So, you've had the meet-cute. Now the montage.

We had a date: Halloween. Of course. We had a venue, the Gold
Room: the Silverado's four-thousand-seater prime ballroom. Full light,
sound, and projection. Willie Nelson filled it ten years back, ten nights in
a row. Jack Caruana had one night, and he could have filled it ten times
over.

Maltese Jack's problem: there are only ten magic effects. Vanish,
produce, transform, restore. Transpose, transport, escape. Levitation,
penetration, prediction. Everything else is panache. Remi knew all ten.

Maltese Jack's problem: part two. The kind of magic he performed
was small scale, close up, unshowy. Making it fill the Gold Room was an
issue. Big flashy displays, glam assistants in fishnets and smiles, would
make the audience suspicious and kill it dead. Possible solution...

Add celebrities. The guest list for the golden circle was so full the
Silverado had to start star-rating the celebs. Fellow magicians – only if
they'd had a network series, a residency of more than six months, or
seven million YouTube hits. Movie stars – only if promoting something
that would be premiering at the time of the show. Sports stars.
Supermodels. Millionaires, no chance, billionaires: step right up.
Bloggers, vloggers. Influencers. Musicians? We could have filled the

Gold Room with needy pop stars and had them spilling onto the gaming floor. Celebrities had the panache. Pick a star, pull them up onstage, and stick a camera in the face to see the OMG! expression all over the screens. Who needed flash and fishnets?

The publicity grind. The media training, the interviews, the photo shoots and profiles. The Silverado moved Jack out of Buena Vista to a penthouse suite. Inés took over his trailer. Management still hadn't got round to fixing the fire damage. When our shifts allowed, Jack invited us up to abuse the bar.

"Look at the size of the bathroom," Salazar said. "You could fight a war in here."

"Egyptian cotton," Inés said, stroking the sheets. Her hands had healed after the fire but the pain had set into the nerves and would likely never leave again. "What's the thread count?"

"You can see all the mountains," I said. I was out on the balcony. Cooler now, a different season.

"Planes coming in," Salazar said, joining me.

"Where are our trailers?" Inés asked. From the penthouse level we could see Buena Vista at the centre of a ring of casinos.

"It's like a walled garden," Salazar said.

"Some fuckin' garden," I said.

"Way to the right," Jack said. "You can't see them. The trees get in the way."

It was pleasant on the penthouse balcony, with hundred-dollar bourbon and a cooling breeze from Tahoe, and it all said, *Halloween is coming, and Maltese Jack Caruana: Are you ready? Do you have the effect that will fool an artificial intelligence that knows every trick and cheat and slick move a human can pull?* Because if he did, he sure wasn't telling me.

On the night, he called it right. The Silverado wanted tux minimum; silver lamé preferred. Maltese Jack walked on in the same slightly tight, cheap grey suit he wore for all his shows. At least a hat, the dresser said.

"Hats are for Sinatra," Jack said.

So on he came, a small man in his early sixties in a bad suit. Onto the biggest stage of his life. He was on his mark before the follow-spot found him; it was another twenty seconds before the audience realised who he was. We started the applause. He had reserved us a table. Not the best, not in the golden circle, too close to the bar and we had to share it with a team from Boing Boing. He waited for the applause to die down.

"Good evening. I'm Jack Caruana. And I'd now like to introduce my partner and worst enemy, the machine that will decide in front of this specially invited audience and all these cameras if there really is such a thing as magic. Remi, the house AI."

Remi's voice boomed from the sound system. "Good evening, Jack. Good evening, guests and everyone watching on television," and oh my days, the Gold Room went apeshit. Jack went down to a table in the golden circle and an actress I kind of recognized from those car-stunt movies gave him a big black book.

"My book of tricks," Jack said. He put it on an honest-to-God church lectern. "My grimoire."

Grimoire: that's a good, mouth-filling word. Thulsa Doom would sure as shit have a *grimoire*.

He led with an old one, an easy one; a gussied-up variation on that same force that Remi had spotted and called us on Jack's cell to discuss. Even I could see how it was done. Brian Hoyer from the Patriots, who'd come up waving and smiling to pick the card, was stunned. The room went silent as a morgue, waiting to see what Remi made of it.

"I am disappointed, Jack," Remi said. "Very disappointed. Really, the bottom card force? That was the very first trick I learned." Whoever was on the sound desk managed to make him sound even more irritating and petulant than he was on the phone. Remi spent five minutes taking Jack's effect apart to the last finger-flick and thumb-hold. The entire Gold Room was spellbound. Jack Caruana stood smiling.

"That your last word Remi?"

"It is, Jack."

"Well, Remi, our deal is, if you can see how the trick is done, the trick is gone. You saw it. That trick is gone. Dead. Buried." And Jack strode over to the grimoire, tore out a page, and held it up for all to see. A flick of the fingers, a flash of blue fire, and the page was floating ash. *Ooh*s. Flash-paper; always a nice piece of theater.

Next Jack brought one of those new country and western singers onstage. A decent prediction effect, a bit of number magic. Applause. Camera close-ups of amazed faces at the celeb tables. The pause – the AI equivalent of clearing your throat. Then Remi explained how he had done it in such detail, the whole Gold Room could have gone home and performed it.

Jack went to the grimoire; another spell from his book of tricks went up in a blue flash.

The French Drop. The Blackstone Cardless Card Trick. The Talkative Clipboard. Twisting the Aces. Classic effects, all of them. And Remi destroyed all of them in that patient, geeky, reasonable voice. Each dead trick, a page went up in blue fire from the book of magic. At first the audience had laughed and applauded when Remi told them how the effect was done. Then I noticed them sit back and sigh and murmur, and those murmurs become rumbles of displeasure. Because Jack was losing to Remi, but Remi was losing the audience. Remi didn't know, didn't care. Remi didn't see the panache. Remi only saw the guile. And that was its mistake.

Hummer Card, Mexican Turnover, Scotch and Soda, the Reluctant Telepath. Dead, dead, dead. Dead. I felt the Gold Room turn, I felt the anger and silent resentment, from every pit-watcher who lost his job to an AI to the singer who'd been auto-tuned until every atom of individuality had been polished out of her voice, every musician who'd had an AI take her song, drop it around beats and boops and turn it into some shiny, soulless global megahit. Every ball-player and tennis star and golfer who'd had their game taken apart and analysed and drilled by a machine coach again and again and again to do it right do it right do it right. And I saw that the real loser was Remi.

Jack went to the grimoire, opened it to let the final page hang down. "All gone," he said. "Every trick in the book. Except one."

Every magician keeps the big effect for the finale. Leave them astounded. The Gold Room went quiet. Even the bar fell silent. Not a camera-whir, not a notification alert. Jack went down into the golden circle and led Taylor Swift up onto the stage.

Everyone in the Gold Room was on the edge of their seat.

Jack delivered some quick-fire patter, let Taylor promote the new album, then said, "I'm going to show you a deck of cards." He took a deck out of his right pocket.

I whispered, *No, Jack, don't do that. You can't do that. Not for the last effect.*

He did the force and the switch, right pocket–left pocket. The worst, the best, the most bare-faced trick in the world. Queen of Hearts. They're all Queens of Hearts. A silence in the Gold Room. Was that it? Was that the trick that Remi couldn't solve? Applause started – not by me – broke into a ripple, into a cautious wave. Obviously something very, very clever had happened here. Something Muggles couldn't see, something not even Remi could see.

"Jack." The Gold Room held its collective breath. Cameras went in close on Jack Caruana's face. "Jack. You took the first deck from your right pocket. You took the second from your left pocket."

The Gold Room exhaled. They hadn't seen it. They truly had not seen it, the most blatant, most stupid, most obvious trick in the grimoire. In that instant, they hated Remi. He had shown them something obvious, right in front of their eyes, that they hadn't noticed. Any kid could do that trick. It had fooled four thousand people, live in front of cameras. Remi had just told every celeb and sports star and the guys from Boing Boing that they were blind and stupid.

Jack ripped the final page from the grimoire and held it up. A click of the fingers and it was consumed in blue fire.

"Ladies and gentleman, the machine has won. It was a privilege to perform for you the night the magic died."

Then he walked down from the stage and up between the tables toward the ballroom's main doors. The Gold Room rose around him. Roaring, cheering. Whistling and yelling and whooping. Because no one wants the magic to die. No one wants to know how the trick is done. We want wonder in the world, things we can't explain. We want to be fooled, even though we know there is no such thing as magic. It's always a trick. It's the quality of the trick – the guile – that matters.

Jack Caruana walked through those tables and out the double golden doors, clean out of the Silverado, and never once looked back. A beaten man, triumphant.

And that's the panache.

We waited until the celebs and the movie stars and vloggers had all gone, until the TV crews were coiling their cables and de-rigging their microphones. Salazar and Inés and me, we went to the elite pickup zone and waited on the red carpet between the golden ropes. Perfectly on cue, the executive van with the blacked-out windows pulled in.

Jack already had the champagne open.

"Airport, sir?" the driver said. Adnan had booked the executive van two months before.

"How much time have we got?" Jack asked.

"Time for whatever you want," Adnan said.

"Take us the tourist route," Jack said. We went round Buena Vista, all the way, three times, drinking the champagne as we wove between the shuttle buses. Then Adnan drove us downtown through the neon and we drank the second bottle of champagne in the blue-green flickering light.

"I thought I was going to shit myself when you did that dumb-ass two-pocket force," I said.

"Run the risk of a new trick that just might work?" Jack said. "The pocket switch was a sure bet."

There is a proverb in magic: Make the audience walk as far as possible from the trick to the effect. In the best effects, the guile happens even before the magician has told you what the trick is about. If the vigorish gets you in the end, the wise bet is on the house. We played Remi to lose. If Jack had beaten the AI he would have been locked up in the Silverado forever, performing that one trick again and again and again. Hey! Give us the trick that beat the computer! Again and again and again. With every eye in the Gold Room watching his every flick of a finger to spot the guile that the computer missed.

We made it out clean and there was a plane on approach high over the desert, coming to take us down to Florida.

Fly away Peter, fly away Paul. Fly away Inés and Salazar and Pernell and Jack.

But the best tricks – the very best tricks – have the twist in the end. The kind of trick where you borrow someone's tie and cut it into pieces, then forget about while you do the real trick and then at the very end, when tie-guy is the only one remembers what you did, you bring it back whole again.

"How much did you take them for?" Jack asked as Adnan brought bags round to the curb.

"Personally, about a grand," Adnan said.

Remi boasted that it did not see as humans saw, that it could not be misdirected. But a magician will tell you: they don't deal in misdirection. They deal in direction.

Staff can't gamble at their own casino. But their friends, relatives, workmates at other place of employment: They can. Remi studied us, but it never occurred to it that we might study it. Learn its tricks and guiles. While Remi was watching Maltese Jack Caruana up there in the spotlight, a hundred gamblers hit the Silverado's two floors. The casino was packed that night, players watching the Wizard Wars as they fed the machines. Our foot soldiers worked the tables, made money, moved on. Made money, moved on. Made money, cashed up, and rolled on out. The bank of Buena Vista. Remi never saw, because Remi was watching Jack.

And *that's* the guile.

And that's the story of how Maltese Jack Caruana beat the machine.

What ya mean, you didn't see it? Where were you? Mongolia? Jail? It was all over the networks. It's up on YouTube. Just Google it. Wizard Wars, Wizard versus Wizard. Even Magic or Machine, God help us. Any of those will get you there.

Anyway, thanks for the drink. Should be heading back. I'll call an Uber, thanks. It's pretty close. Yeah, we all have apartments in a gated community. No it's not fuckin' Cocoon. I don't need to be mentalist to know you were going to say that. You all do. It's nice, a pool, tropical planting. Wi-Fi, gym, store. Golf buggies to get around when we want to visit. No, not a beachfront location; who can afford that? But you can smell the ocean in the morning, and on a quiet night, you can sometimes hear the waves.

You see, it's the things you notice and the things you miss. Did you notice that I never explain why Jack was called Maltese Jack? Nor will I. Just recall what I said about the best tricks having a turn at the end. You see, I called this story "The Guile," not "The Panache." And I also said that the smart wizard makes it a long walk from the guile to the panache. The effect. The magic.

You see, Thulsa Doom may be the first black wizard, but he isn't the only one.

Maybe check your watch, your ring, and your wallet, my friend.

The Moss Child

Lisa Fransson

And the stream spoke to Alva in gurgles and murmurs of the ice on the mountainside that melted in the morning sun: "Have a drink, child, and taste for yourself."

Alva crouched by the stream, cupped her hands and bent her head to drink. As she did so, the ends of her hair dipped into the water and flowed with the current, in play with the iridescent fish hiding in her tresses.

"I wish, fish, that I could sit here and let you nestle in my hair always, away from prey," said Alva.

"Rise," said the stream, "and do not worry. They are a part of me, as I am a part of you."

"As you are a part of me," whispered Alva and rose, her hair dripping dark stripes down her white night-dress.

Moss cushioned each step with damp springiness, and the tufts of grass brushed her legs as she danced along the forest path towards the rising sun. Around her ankles a mist swirled in ever thickening and thinning veils, whispering of being teased from the soft earth and sliding up the golden rays of dawn, towards the sky: "Root your feet in the earth. Touch your fingers to the sky, child, and feel for yourself."

Alva dug her feet deep into the moss and stretched her hands upwards until the sun's rays warmed her fingertips. As she did so, earthworms took to curling up under the soles of her feet.

"I wish, worms, that I could stand here and let you burrow tunnels under my feet always, away from prey."

"Dance," said the mist "and do not worry. They are a part of me, as I am a part of you."

"As you are a part of me," whispered Alva and curtsied in front of a fir branch. She took the needled proposal in her hand and pirouetted beneath it, causing a fine rain of dew to fall upon her face.

Up there, on the top branch, perched the tree pipit. The bird raised its wings and took off in song flight, singing his proud poetry to the softening sky and the forest below: "Keep out, keep out. Don't come near. My wife and I have built our home here."

After some circuits, the tree pipit landed back on his branch: "Try it yourself, child. Take flight and sing through your heart."

Alva stuck her toes in a crack on the lichen-covered rock and hauled herself up. At the very top of the rock she spread her arms wide and filled her lungs to sing.

"Child, child," sang the pipit. "The old woman is afoot."

"The old woman? Is she good or is she bad?"

"She's of the forest, child. Nothing more, nothing less."

Alva slid down from the rock and ran in amongst the trees, but her dress caught on the brambles, her hair tangled in a low-slung branch and a sharp stone cut the sole of her foot. She tugged at her dress until it ripped. She pulled at the strands of hair until they snapped. She limped on her foot until she reached the hollow tree – once lightning-struck, and deep enough to swallow her whole: hair, night dress and all.

For a while she heard only her own breath inside the trunk, but there came a rustle of feet wading through dead leaves. And next the smell of fungus and the mutterings of a voice like branches knocking together: "Why does she run so from me? She with the gift of eyes and ears. Why does she hide so, like the fish and the worms?"

Alva pressed her back against the crumbling shell of the tree, and worm-eaten wood pattered to the ground. *Quiet*, she thought. *Be quiet tree. Be quiet heart. Be quiet breath.*

First she saw the creeping of a shadow, darkening the ground outside her hiding place. Then the old woman herself shuffled into view and stopped just by the hollow. A scream began to form inside Alva's belly, swelled in size as it rose. She covered her mouth with her hand, before it could leave her throat.

The woman's nose was long and crooked and the skin on her face brown and craggy. On her head she wore a cap stitched from sycamore leaves in the autumn blooms of oranges and yellows. A carpet of green moss grew in waves from her scalp over her shoulders, down her back, all the way to the ground where it knitted together with the moss on the forest floor. Her coat was earthy brown and buttoned up with toadstools and in her skirt hundreds of fern fronds hooked their leaves together, furled and unfurled. On her feet she wore boots carved from solid rock. But when her eyes turned towards Alva inside the hollow, they were the colour of the sky reflected in the mountain stream. Alva even thought she could see the tiny fish swimming in the old woman's irises, off to hide in Alva's own hair.

"Why does she run so from me? She who was cradled by the moss. Why does she hide so? She who was fed on dew and raised by the rays of dawn," muttered the old woman.

Alva closed her eyes and tried to merge with the tree trunk, while she waited for those gnarled wooden fingers to reach inside and curl around the top of her arm, to pull her out and bind her with cobweb-sticky spells, commanding her to follow, to follow, to follow the old woman home to her large oven, which Alva herself would be forced to fire up and feed. Until…

The woman knocked hard against the tree trunk, making Alva jump. "Why does she hide so? From me?"

"Old woman, if you're going to take me, then take me." Alva's voice ripped out of her like a storm gust.

"Why would I take you? You are already a part of me," said the old woman and she turned to leave.

"As you are a part of me," whispered Alva and stepped out of the tree. The woman's rock-clad feet dragged through the leaves, her hair grew from her head in an even stream, leaving a trail of moss through the forest. As Alva watched, the wind, for just a brief moment, shifted the old woman's coat to the side to reveal a hollow back.

"As hollow as the tree," whispered Alva, and for a moment she thought she saw her own face peeping out from inside the hollow of the woman's back.

But the sun was fully above the horizon now and Alva knew she had dawdled. She ran along the forest path, past pipit's fir tree, past the rock, past the fish in the stream, through the whispers of the forest coaxing her to stay. "I'll be back tomorrow," she promised them. Through the field and down the lane to her cottage.

"Alva? Look at you. Where have you been?" said her father as he turned from the pot of stew bubbling on the stove, the wooden spoon like kindling in his broad hands.

"To greet the morning. Here, let me do that, father," said Alva and took the spoon off him.

"In the forest again."

"It calls me, Father. I have to go," said Alva as she stirred the pot.

"It calls you, does it?" He nodded to himself as he lifted the leather apron off its hook and muttered. "We shall see you married yet."

"I'm fifteen."

"Your mother was sixteen."

"And where is my mother now?" said Alva as she threw the spoon into the stew and turned to her father.

Her father pulled the leather apron over his head and turned his back to Alva. She sighed and fastened the strings for him.

"The fire needs tending. We have horse shoes to beat," he said.

Alva left the stew to simmer while she ran upstairs, pulled her nightdress over her head and stepped into a shirt and a pair of breeches. She tied her hair up in a bun, high on her head, and pulled one of her father's caps over her ears. Through her window in the gable, she saw the tree-tops swaying in the distance. She waved back. He would not see her married yet.

All day they beat metal. Alva fed the fire, fetched buckets of water from the well and tools from the stand. When her father needed a break, she wielded the tongs and the hammers. In the evening they sat in front of the hearth and shared a pot of stew that tasted of molten metal sprinkled with soot.

"Father," she said over the stew, "I saw somebody in the forest this morning."

He lowered his spoon to his bowl and raised his head to look at her. "Who?"

"A woman. Or perhaps she was more of a creature. Her back was hollow."

Her father filled the spoon with stew and held it still above his bowl. "Was..." His eyes strayed to the flickering flames in the hearth. "...she very beautiful?"

"She was old, Father."

He lowered the spoon back in his bowl without eating and let his arms hang by his side. "Yes, she said she would be." A mere whisper in the quiet of the night.

"Do you know her, then?" asked Alva.

But her father did not reply. Instead he scraped his stool backwards and went to the aumbry that stood pushed up against the back wall, so dark and heavy that the cottage seemed to have sprouted up around it. He pulled open a top drawer, reached inside and rummaged, until Alva heard a click and the knock of something falling. Back by the hearth, he pulled his stool up close and held out a box covered in soft leather. "For you," he said.

Alva took the box and opened it. Inside, on a bed of dry moss, lay a silver braid with a pendant shaped like a drop of dew. Her father lifted the silver braid out of the box and placed it over Alva's hair. The pendant he arranged to drop over the middle of her forehead.

"From now on you will wear this, always," he said

"Even in the forest?" asked Alva

"Even in the forest," replied her father.

"What if I lose it?" asked Alva

"You will not lose it," replied her father.

"It weighs heavy on my brow, Father, for such a small thing."

"You will get used to carrying it."

But the pendant felt as cold as the meltwater in the mountain stream against her skin, and the weight of the chain pressed her head towards the earth. "Why must I wear it?"

"It belonged to your mother." And with those words her father rose and walked up the stairs. His footsteps, thudding heavily on each step, continued to creak on the ceiling as he shifted and shuffled around in his room.

Once he'd settled upstairs Alva tried to remove the braid, to put it back on the moss inside the box, slide it back in the drawer and tell her father tomorrow that it was not meant for her. But the braid would not budge. No matter how hard she pulled – the gem had set into the skull beneath her skin.

Alva awoke to the sound of the pre-dawn hour pulsing inside her veins, telling her the birds would wake, the flowers would open and the dew would form on the spiders' webs as the sun would rise. She swung her legs over the side of her cot, stood up in her nightdress and nearly lost her footing. Only when the throbbing inside her head grew so strong that she had to sit back down on the bed, did she remember the weight that her father had placed upon her. She pressed her hands hard against her temples where the braid dipped into a V-shape, so that the drop sat encased in the bone between her eyebrows. Like some horn. As she touched the drop, a frost spread through her bones and she sat frozen on the edge of her cot, breathing clouds of mist into the silence. The mist quickly gathered into snow clouds above her hair, and the tears she shed formed icicles on the tips of her eyelashes. "Father, what have you done to me?" she whispered through lips too stiff to shape the words. She closed her eyes and saw herself, yesterday, dancing through the trees in the sunlight. She thought of the old woman that had frightened her so. *Help me!* she thought.

A fox's smile that she did not recognise played for an instant on her father's lips when he came in to fetch her. "Come, let us seat you in front of the hearth, child." He gathered her shirt, breeches and cap and carried her downstairs to the fire where he fed her porridge from a spoon. The porridge dribbled through her icy lips, but he scraped the spillage up and fed it to her again. "Poor child," he said. "But you will see that it is for the best."

The porridge did not thaw her limbs enough to dress without help, but when leaning heavily on her father's arm she was able to hobble out to the forge. This morning, *he* stoked the fire while she watched. Closer and closer she moved, until the snow-flakes crowning her hair thawed and the icicles on her eye-lashes dripped out of existence. She furled and unfurled her fingers, like the fern fronds of the forest, like the fern fronds on the old woman's skirt.

"Who was she, Father?"

"Don't let Metsa worry you. You're safe with me."

"I don't feel safe with you, Father," she whispered letting the bellow-burn of the fire swallow her words.

"You just stay in the forge. We'll make a blacksmith out of you yet."

"But I shall have to sleep by the forge in order not to freeze."

"So you shall, child. So you shall."

Alva looked to her hands: to never stroke moss, to never cup the water in the stream, to never spread her arms wide to fly from the rock, to never be invited to dance with the fir tree, to always freeze, even under the rays of the sun.

"But I might as well die." This time her father heard the words she spoke. He put his tools aside, squatted down beside her and gently stroked her cheek.

"You are my heart, child. I could not think to lose you."

"Look at me, Father. Have you not already lost me?"

Her father frowned, stood up and began to hammer the blade of a scythe glowing orange in the fire, with clang after clang after clang, swinging his arm in a wide circle behind him and up and over. Sweat dripped from his forehead and he bit his lips until they bled. Only after he'd finished the blade did he turn to her again. "You spoke to her."

"Not much, Father. I was frightened of her."

"But then why do you speak such words?"

"What words, Father?"

"Asking if you are not already lost to me."

"Because I am."

"Enough!" He turned, with the hammer held high as if to strike her, his teeth bared in his soot-blackened face; wild orange flames played in his eyes. But as Alva crawled backwards away from him, the fear of death in her eyes, he dropped the hammer, crouched next to her again and took her hand gently into his, stroking her fingers. "Beautiful child. Have I not been kind to you?"

"Yes, Father."

"Have I not let you roam free as the wind in the trees?"

"Yes, Father."

"Then why did you wish yourself away from me?"

"I didn't, Father."

"You didn't?" He frowned and slowly placed his finger on the crystal drop fused onto her bone and traced the braid to the place on her temple where it emerged into her hair.

"No, I didn't."

"You didn't." Her father gave the braid a gentle tug, causing a shiver to run through her. "Perhaps, I acted rashly?" he said.

"Perhaps you did, Father."

"At least I'll see you married now."

"But how can I marry if I can't leave the forge?"

"Ice forged with fire," he said as he picked the hammer off the floor and stuck another blade into the flames.

Alva, shivered and huddled closer, closer, closer to the fire. When the flames licked her skin, she did not burn. This forge, her prison. "Help me!" she whispered into the flames.

The next morning she awoke on her mat by the fire only when the first rays of sunlight stroked her cheek. The brightness around her, the world outside wide awake before her. *I have lost*, she thought, *the darkness before dawn*. She took a step towards the forest outside and felt her heart freeze and shatter like glass inside her chest. On the bench next to her, on a bed of brown leather, glinted the blades of the finished tools. She picked up the deer hunter's skinning knife.

By the time her father brought the tub of heated water for her to wash in, she could no longer see for the blood gushing into her eyes, yet she kept hacking the point of the knife against the skin and bone surrounding the pendant. He grabbed her wrist and twisted it until the knife dropped out of her hand. He tied her hands behind her back with leather string from his pocket, so that he could clean the wound without her clawing at his eyes. She spat in his face. He flinched, but left the saliva to drip from his chin rather than let go of her. She screamed. He said nothing. From the leather bag on the wall he took a handful of moss, which he placed around the clean wound. Soothing, calming, warming moss, moss, moss. She fell asleep to the rhythmic clank of her father beating the blade of the skinning knife into a formless lump.

In her dream the moss on the wound knitted with her skin and grew until she was shielded inside a soft blanket. The moss held her, cradled her and lulled her with the gurgles of the stream, the whispers of the wind and the song of the tree pipit. Soothing, calming, warming moss, moss, moss told her stories of all the dawns since the birth of the sun, of being and not being, of growing old and growing young and growing old again, from moss to earth, to earth to moss, to moss to earth... "Help me!" she whispered from inside her blanket of lullabies. But, the moss receded, taking its stories with it, and all that remained was the flight song of the tree pipit. Alva opened her eyes, and there in the sky, just visible through the door of the forge, the little bird circled and dipped, rose and circled, chirping, just like a bird.

"I no longer understand you, pipit," she said as she raised herself up on her elbows. A steel cuff fettered her foot now. Attached to the cuff was a chain long enough for her to walk between the fire and the open door, but the bench of tools had been moved out of reach. She ought to have aimed the knife at the hollow of her heart.

The rattling chain caused her father to turn. "Work, child. Work and forget."

"And then what, Father?"

"Then you'll be free."

She stood up next to him, elbow to elbow. A horse shoe glowed in the flames. When her father opened the farrier's tongs she put her hand in the fire, grabbed the horse shoe with her fingers and carried it in her steaming hands to the anvil, where the sparks flew under his hammer. Her father turned his face towards her and smiled.

That evening, after Alva's father had left her and as the setting sun bled the sky red, the pipit flew in through the door, landed in her lap and dropped a single stalk of moss in her palm.

"Thank you, pipit. How beautiful?"

The pipit chirped at length. She listened to every note, trying to fit them against an ever-eluding pattern.

"I am afraid I can't understand you, pipit. I am afraid I will never drink from the stream again. I am afraid I will never see the forest awaken again. I am afraid... Yes, I am afraid."

Again the pipit chirped, hopped around and flapped its wings once.

"To fly? I wish. But look, I can't even walk from here." Alva stretched her hand through the open door, away from the forge. Her fingers turned blue instantly and when she knocked her hand against the door frame, her nails shattered and clinked to the ground where they melted from the heat of the forge.

The pipit flew up, pecked the drop on her forehead and landed back inside her cold hand, where it rested down and fluffed up its feathers as if to warm her.

"It's of no use," she said as she lifted the pipit up and held it against her cheek. And with that the pipit took to the air and flew towards the forest.

The stalk of moss in her hand, she kissed it gently and inhaled the smell of earth deep, deep, deep inside her lungs. "You will live here now, with me," she whispered and poured some water into her mug. "But do not worry, I will hide you from him." And she stood the stalk with its roots in the water and pushed the mug into the shadows of a nook where one of the wooden beams entered the ceiling. Then she fed the fire, so as not to freeze during the night, and rolled her mat out on the floor. But as she felt herself drift off, she sat up and spoke towards the stalk of moss in the nook. "You must tell me if you're not happy here. Pipit will come for you. I could not bear for you to be unhappy."

The wind knocked branches together, rustled through dead leaves on the ground. A shadow fell across her dreaming eyelids as the earthy smell of fungi flowed through her nose on the crest of her sleepy breaths. Never before had Alva felt cold in the forest, never before had the ground felt so hard, or the heart so empty.

A sudden roar and burst of heat made her wake. In front of her eyes a thousand tiny green dragons furled and unfurled, frayed wings and snouts stretching and folding. "He's not an evil man, child. It is just what love does to some people."

Alva sat up and shuffled backwards until the chain clanked to a stop. The old woman was feeding the fire with pine cones out of a woven basket as big and round as Alva's wash tub. The fire crackled and popped with greed, as it consumed fistful after fistful of cones.

"Who are you?" asked Alva.

The old woman's joints creaked when she turned and peered at her with her rippling blue eyes. "Tonight, I am your guest, child," she replied and pointed upwards, towards the nook by the beam. "Now, you must move closer to the fire, or you won't be long for this world."

"The stalk of moss?"

"Is a part of me…"

"…as I am a part of you," whispered Alva. "As you are a part of me?"

The old woman nodded and tugged a patch of moss from her hair, large enough to make a rug to sit on in front of the fire. She grabbed Alva by her arms and carried her stiff body closer to the heat. And there they sat, side by side, staring into the dancing flames. Soon Alva's hair began to thaw and water dripped onto the moss. At the same time, little bubbles of damp began to boil on the surface of the old woman's earth-coat and to rise in tendrils of steam. Alva followed their journey upwards with her eyes. "I will never see the mists of dawn rise from the forest path again," she said.

"What rot you talk, child. Why ever would you not?"

Alva lowered her head. Her legs had sunk deep into the moss rug and her bones no longer ached from the hard floor. "He fettered my ankle."

The old woman raised her foot as if to smash the cuff with her lichen-covered rock-boot. Alva closed her eyes. Would her leg be crushed? But all she heard was a clink as the lock snapped open.

"See that, child. The iron remembers the rock."

"Because it is a part of me…" whispered Alva.

"As I am a part of you, child."

Alva traced the rugged texture of the old woman's skin with her fingers – rough like the bark on the fir; she patted the moss flowing from the old woman's head – soft like the forest floor; she caught the drop falling from the old woman's eyes – cool and fresh like the stream. Alva rested her head on the woman's shoulder, the earth of her coat forming around her cheek, her own hair mingling with the moss hair. "Mother?"

The old woman nodded and smiled. "Of course, child. Of course." And they were as one, before the flames.

"Of moss and moon were you conceived, child, of dew and dawn were you born, to a man wandering lost in the forest, who laid down to sleep under the branches of a fir. The mist weaved in and out between the trunks and the moon shone bright as day in the night sky as he closed his eyes and drifted off to sleep.

"I waited, before I lay down next to him. Such strong arms he had, and so restful he lay on the moss. You must understand, it was my time to have a child and he was not unwilling.

"And I tried to live with him. Under a roof, between walls. Wearing frocks and sleeping on a straw mattress. Yes, I tried. I did try, child. But every day, at the hour before dawn, I would find myself wandering naked and barefoot through the forest, slipping into tree trunks, running down the mountain waterfall, joining the dawn chorus and sliding up the first rays of the sun. Always with you in my arms, suckling sap from my breasts.

"But after you were born I began to mulch, so much faster than him, and I realised that my cycle would end many seasons before his. How he raged when I told him I could not stay."

"Why could you not stay, Mother?"

"He fears the cycle so."

"And what did he do?"

"He took the sledge hammer and went off to the mountain for three days and three nights. When he returned his skin was as black as a moonless night and he sat on the bench outside the forge for another three days and three nights, turning over rocks in his hand, chipping away at them. Finally, he disappeared into the forge for another three days and three nights."

"And what then, mother?"

"He gave me this to wear." She touched the crystal drop on Alva's forehead.

Alva shuddered and lowered her head. "What did you do?"

"I refused."

"Why?"

"Because this stone, although it may look like a dew drop, is a stone that dripped into being over slow centuries in icy darkness under the watch of the sleeping rock, until the moment it was hacked from the ceiling of the great mountain hall by a man with a craving for possession. Its sole purpose is to bind and to blind." With her gnarled finger she touched the spot in the middle of her forehead where the drop would have hung. "To mulch is to give life, child."

"I no longer understand pipit," said Alva and looked down at her hands.

"No, you wouldn't."

"I tried to hack it off, Mother."

"A dew drop will dangle and fall, child, whereas a drip-stone will fuse and cling."

The flames rose with a roar as the door flew open behind them and let in a cold gust of wind. The candle flames in the chandelier above flickered and died, leaving wisps of smoke in their stead. "I thought it was you I could smell, old Metsa."

"Father..."

"Be quiet, child." Broad and tall he stood, pushing the door frame with his hands as if trying to stop it from clamping him.

"Dear old harrowed Rufus. Come sit with us by the fire."

"Do not try to bind me with your magic, Metsa. Child, what has she done to you?"

"She unfettered me and comforted me, Father."

He glanced down at her foot and the steel cuff gaping open next to it. "Told you stories, did she?"

"Yes."

"A story is one thing, the truth is another," he said.

"The truth, Rufus, shapes itself to the person who does the telling. Now, come! Sit!" Metsa ripped another slab of moss from her hair and placed it to the other side of Alva.

Rufus' hands dropped from the door frame and hung along his sides. He stared, from the old woman to the fire and back to the old woman. "I've a mind to see you burn, vixen." But the force had left his voice.

"By all means, turn me to ash, Rufus. By dawn your forge will be a mound of planks rotting beneath moss and fern. Now, sit. I do not have much time."

Beside her Alva felt her father's body sink into the moss, heavy, heavy, heavy. And for a while they sat silent in the night, letting the flames soothe them. Each time her father sighed heavily into the fire, a flame sprang back into life for a flicker of a moment. Alva reached out her hand to let the fern fronds on her mother's skirt curl around her fingers. And as the moss hair crawled down her mother's neck, a part of it crawled onto Alva's shoulder where it continued to grow, as if it were her own. On her other side, her father's hand, rough and large as a baker's paddle, reached for Alva's. But he let go at first touch, as if struck by an adder.

"You're cold, child."

"Yes, always, Father."

"I am afraid..." he said. "I was afraid..." And he cupped his face in his hands.

Metsa reached her arm around Alva and placed her twiggy hand on his neck. "You see, Rufus, that I am no longer in bloom. My bones have hardened and my flesh has softened. I will go now and I will take Alva with me."

"But she will die if you take her," he said.

"Perhaps I do not mind so much, Father."

"What rot!" said the old woman as she turned to Alva and lifted the braid clean off her head. The skin on her forehead had healed smooth. Only one strand of the healing moss had taken root just below her hair line. Metsa touched the strand gently with her fingertip "...as I am a part of you."

Alva's eyes brightened and she smiled. "Mother, I can hear the wind. It's telling us to rush, rush, rush. We must hurry. And the grass sings that it will carry us. Oh, the stars, the stars say to follow them to the stream, and the stream... I cannot hear so clearly yet."

"The wind is always rushing. But perhaps it is time for us to go."

Rufus stared at the braided silver chain in Metsa's hands. "But I followed the ritual: 'Reaped from rock, forged to fuse, for love to last, through ice and flames'. You can't just lift it off."

"For love to last, through ice and flames, did you say?" asks Metsa.

"Yes."

"And did the love last?"

"No, I lost it." he said, and frowned at Alva, who could meet his eyes only briefly before looking down at her fingers that were now glowing pink in the heat. Then he looked into Metsa's blue eyes, where the rippling stream began to flow backwards through time until he found himself lying on the moss under a tree with a woman whose skin shone under the moonlight, whose hair fell over his cheeks like a silver rain and whose hollow back echoed with the wing-flaps of bats, the rustling of leaves and the purling of water. "Yes," he said, "it did last."

"I'm glad," she said, and smiled. Then she held up the silver braid for him to see. The metal glimmered in the fire and the drip-stone dangled back and forth. "You forged this for me, Rufus and not for our child."

They left him sitting by the fire as they walked out of the forge. Mother and daughter, hand in hand, down the lane, past the meadow and into the forest. Alva filled her lungs with the night air and opened her chest to the stars. The pre-dawn hour flowed inside her veins, telling her legs to dance across the moss. The tall trees, the roosting birds, the webs strung up for prey, the hoots of the owl, even the putrid mushrooms and the fox that had just caught the rabbit, all of it hers. It was only when she got to the stream that she noticed she'd let go of her mother's hand. Alva rushed back down the path and found her hobbling along, leaning heavily on a cane.

"Why so slow, Mother?"

"Because you are so fast."

"You are moulting earth, Mother?"

"Help me to the stream, child. There's a tree there, with low sloping branches."

"Yes, I've danced with it. It is where pipit lives with his wife."

"It is where your father fell asleep on the moss fifteen years ago."

"A good place to visit, Mother."

By the time they reached the stream, the sky shone orange and red with the birth of a new day. Alva helped her mother sit down on the ground. They rested their backs against the tree trunk, wrapped the low-hanging branches around them like shawls, and Metsa smoothed her fern skirt over their legs. The moss of Metsa's hair flowed down the tree trunk and her skirt began to spread across the ground until the bank of the stream was covered in a carpet of ferns. The tree trunk seemed to become one with Metsa's brown craggy skin, while the toad stool buttons of her coat dotted themselves in a circle around the roots of the tree.

"You look as if you are taking root, Mother."

"You could say that."

"But how will you rise again?" asked Alva.

"I will not rise again, child."

"Are you dying?"

"No, I'm giving life, child. For as long as the butterflies flutter to the chickweed, for as long as the pine cones fall and take seed. For as long as you live, my child."

"As you are of me."

"As I am of you."

"Will I too find a man in the moss, Mother?"

"That I cannot say. You must walk your own path." Metsa's words were now just creaks in the wind and when Alva turned to look at her mother; her eyes were two tiny puddles of water gathered in hollows in the bark, her hands had turned into gnarled roots stretching their fingers across the ground until the fingertips dug into the moss and where she'd held the braid of silver, a single snowdrop grew. Alva touched the head of the flower; cold and smooth.

"I will not pick you," Alva whispered. "You have already been picked once." She bent over the flower, towards the tree and kissed the bark. "Sleep well, Mother."

"The end, Alva, is no different to the beginning," replied the wind.

Back at the forge her father still lay in front of the dying fire. On hearing her footsteps, he rose and took a step towards her. Then his chin sank to his chest. "Why did you come back to me, child?"

"I will come back to you, Father, as long as you permit me to leave," she said.

He opened his arms to receive her. "I won't keep you, child."

We Can Make Something Grow Between the Mushrooms and the Snow

Kirsty Logan

The Mushroom House

Eco-friendly and ripe for development, this highly unusual dwelling will make the perfect home for the right occupants. Buyer be aware that house is set on a bed of mushrooms with most of the organism below the soil surface, providing a sturdy and constantly growing base for the structure. The organism's above-surface aspect forms the walls and roof. Three public rooms, two bedrooms, family bathroom – though these will expand as the organism grows. Damp proofing recommended.

Richard's notes: Three seconds in this house, and I feel my body pulse fertile as earth. It's perfection. We can have children here, I know it. Three, four – eight, ten. As many as we want, no effort at all. What can I say? It's a house made of sodding mushrooms, and I bloody well love it! I really can't see a single problem. Where can I sign?

Carolyn's notes: This is not a house. It's a pit of rot. The walls are grey and spongy and everything stinks of decomposition. My feet are mired in dirt. Every time I breathe I feel I'm inhaling spores, invisible things that will wriggle and burrow and grow inside me. I could never work in a place like this. I need space and quiet, cold and clarity. This grimy, mildewed house is the opposite of that. How quickly can I leave?

The Bluebell House

This charming and unique cottage is situated in the centre of a bluebell wood. Previous owner was a witch, but the house has been professionally cleaned with bleach and appropriate rituals. Bijou, but still with all the necessities. Big enough for a family, assuming the family is one person, or multiple people who are very small. Living room, two bedrooms, outdoor bathroom. Good-sized kitchen, particularly the oven.

Richard's notes: Carolyn wouldn't take the mushroom house, even though she got pregnant right after we went there – I knew it was a fertile place! I'd happily have stayed there. But hey, marriage is about compromise. It's creepy to me that a witch lived here. Cast her weird spells and curses, thought her nasty thoughts. For all we know, she cooked stolen children in that oven. The estate agent didn't say that, but I've read the stories. Still, perhaps bringing a child here would be a good thing. Perhaps it would cleanse it. I mean, we're certainly not going to put any children in the oven! I think we could make a good go of it here.

Carolyn's notes: The flowers on the ground here are thick as dust. The second I got near the house, I was choking on pollen. But I'm trying. I even brought my research books with me to see if I could do some work, just as a test. He goes on whether or not he likes the place, but for me it's more complicated than that. If I can't work, I can't earn, and we'll lose whatever house we're in. I left him talking to the estate agent and tried to work. Nothing came. I can't think. Can't breathe. The pollen is inside me.

The Cave House

Sturdy roof and walls. Open aspect to the front, interior fully open-plan. Easily maintained. Free food and water sources in the form of lichens, mosses and a nearby stream. A fixer-upper, ideal for an enthusiastic and motivated buyer.

Richard's notes: It's a cave. Literally a cave. And I don't know what she wants, but to be honest I'll stay in any godforsaken hole that pleases her as long as she can be happy with me and our child. She's grown so much bigger over the past few months, and the baby will be here before we know it. Even she must see that modern people don't raise babies in caves. A fucking cave! She can't possibly want this.

Carolyn's notes: This is better than the others. Fewer distractions. There are horses in the field nearby, which I like. One of my chapters is about Icelanders' conversion to Christianity in the year 1000. They had to follow the religion, obviously, but they were allowed three exceptions. One was the eating of horsemeat – luckily for those horses, we're not Icelandic. The other exceptions were ritual scarification carried out in secret, and *bera út*, abandoning a child in nature to die of exposure. I've tried to tell Richard so many times but he doesn't think it's interesting. Anyway, I don't think this is the right house for us.

The Bird House

Spacious and airy, complete with open skylight. Fantastic views. Comes as seen, trunk and all attached branches included, as well as any feathers. Birds may return to lay eggs, meaning an environmentally friendly and organic food source for owners.

Richard's notes: This is getting ridiculous. We're eight months in and she's enormous, almost past walking. How is she supposed to get up and down a tree? It would be impossible to attach any sort of decent ladder to the trunk, it's so spindly. And that's not even mentioning a child who'll be crawling in no time – right off the branch, no doubt, and what then? And what are we supposed to do when it rains? I need to put my foot down. Or at least, I would if it wouldn't snap the branch we're standing on.

Carolyn's notes: This is closer. This is better. I need light and air and space and solitude. I need to be able to move, to think. It's not just for me, it's not selfishness. We won't get any more of my advance money until I finish the book. I have to support us all, and I can't do that in the dark and the earth and the foetid heat. This is nice – open, airy. The twigs are a bit scratchy but there are plenty of feathers and they're very soft. Of course they're soft; that's what people stuff duvets and cushions with. The baby will soon need a home that isn't me, and here's a literal feather bed. But still… We're not quite there, but we're near.

The Island House

This cosy and charming wooden structure is set on its own island. Structure in fact covers the whole island, which is compact and ideally situated in a peaceful and secluded part of the ocean. Perfect for the homeowner who likes their own space.

Richard's notes: Look, I'll admit that it sounded good when the estate agent said we could live on our own island. But when I imagined island life, I did imagine that I'd be able to actually walk on the island. You know what I'm picturing: a beach, some trees, maybe some green patches for chickens or sheep. This one is so tiny that you can't leave the house without stepping into the ocean. It's not even a calm, blue, tropical sort of ocean – it's grey and choppy and every other wave crashes into the outer walls. I can't believe this is what she wants. The baby is only a few weeks old, and as we're looking around the house I swear she's eyeing up places she could put him down.

Carolyn's notes: What was my life before? What was it like to arrange my time the way I chose? What was it like to be able to hear my own breathing? Three weeks, and I can barely remember. It needs so much. It wants so much. I thought if I could go away, away, away – to an island, no one else there – then I could work. But there will never again be a place with no one else there. I could be on the other side of the world and I would still hear him cry for me in the night. His tiny mouth, never full, never silent.

The Glacier House

A spacious, secluded, one-of-a-kind property created from a much-sought-after glacier. Fully open-plan with far-reaching views to all sides: front, back, top, and bottom (when over deep water). Currently three bedrooms, though further rooms can be carved out.

Richard's notes: Why on Earth would she even consider this? Dragging us up to the hinterlands, so far fucking north I feel like we're about to tip off the map. I get that her book is on northern cultures, but come on! She wants to go from a northern country, to a further northern country, and then when she's in that country she wants to go even further? I mean, Christ, why don't we just move to the middle of the Arctic and call it quits? Not only is this house on the ice; it's made of ice, with beds and sofas and tables and chairs made of ice. There are no walls. There is no roof. I can't believe she'd even suggest bringing our child here. The wee guy will freeze to death in about three seconds. *I'm* freezing to death in about three seconds, and I'm a bloody adult, with enough body fat to shame a seal. I can't live here. He can't live here. God, I miss the mushrooms.

Carolyn's notes: The first step I took into this house, I felt my mind flash clear. It's perfection. I can work here, I know it. I love this glacier: the chill, the cleanse of it. We're taking this house. It's everything I need. I think of the horses, of the ritual scarring, of the cold. There are rules to the world, I know. But perhaps there can be exceptions. I don't need three, only one. We'll take it. Are you listening? I'll take it.

Boys

Lizzie Hudson

When they first move into the house, it feels obvious to Laura that it loves her more than Tim. It wants her to be there and doesn't mind that Tim is an addition. It's as if the rooms warm themselves up slightly in the few seconds before she walks into them. The orange light that comes through the big front windows in the afternoon might shine right on her face and miss him entirely. Sometimes the water in the shower warms up straight away for her, but is a bit faulty for Tim.

Here, she thinks, she is the most beloved one. The house loves her more than it loves Tim and Tim loves her more than almost anything. She loves both the house and Tim, and in time she will get them to love each other. But she is, still, the most loved one. It feels like having two best friends, but knowing that she is both of their only best friend.

Before they moved here Laura and Tim lived at the adventure holiday camp where Tim worked. Tim instructs groups of children/families on tree climbing/zipwire courses. They had a flat in a small building where all the instructors lived with quite a lot of their girlfriends and even some children. It was in Kendal in the Lake District.

But because they were unhappy there, Laura started to act stressed and strange. Tim noticed this. So when Laura inherited some money because somebody died, they decided to buy a barn conversion closer to the town that they both came from. Tim would still work for the same company but, instead, he would commute and travel over the country to assist at different adventure holidays.

This is where they have come to live now.

Laura first sees the prince in a nearby stately home on a Saturday afternoon.

It said on the website that the stately home is an iconic 18th Century house with a notable art collection.

The biggest painting is entitled *The Prince and his Retinue Hunt Game in the State Park*. The prince is wearing a long ruffled frock coat and his hand is on the head of one of his pointy-faced hounds. A foxhound. The prince's hair is brown. Laura does not have to read the plaque at the side of the painting to know that he is the one who is the prince, even with his whole hunting troupe around him. His face is horse-like and shimmery, regal.

In the gift shop they sell small fridge magnets with the picture of the prince and his retinue hunting game in the forest. Laura buys one and puts it on the fridge and uses it to hold up a photo of her and Tim from Prague last year.

When they get back from the stately home trip, the wood of the front door has swollen again so they can't get it open for ages and have to kick it until it opens and then they have to arrange for someone to come round and shave the wood down so that it won't happen again. Tim gets stressed about it and wonders if it was a bad idea to move somewhere where they have to arrange for everything to be fixed themselves instead of renting and just getting a landlord to do it. His voice goes annoying in that way she hates.

Laura is fairly sure she could have figured out how to do it by herself, but Tim is worried about what will happen when he has to go away with work and she's there alone. They have an argument in which Tim implies Laura lives in some sort of fantasy/dreamworld and never has to deal with anything real/tangible and Laura implies Tim does not respect her independence and competency because he hates women. Laura sleeps in the spare room that night.

To be honest, Laura rarely feels hugely unhappy or frightened or stressed any more. If something bad happens it is like a soft weight that sort of rolls over her. She doesn't cry unless she is really drunk. She has accepted that for life to be good and exciting sometimes, bad things have to happen too, to have something to compare the better things to so that happy and sad are contradictions of each other.

When Laura is in the spare room she is reminded of how she felt when she was a teenager. She used to imagine sex with men and she used to imagine saying this thing to them in a moment of climax. She used to think it was the most outrageous thing someone could say. She can't even remember where she got it from now. It might have been from porn or from something someone at her school had heard in porn. She used to think these words almost every night.

Tim has to go away to Ireland with work. He is supervisor for a two week adventure holiday with a group of Scouts.

Laura has to get a taxi to Morrisons to do the food shop because Tim has taken the car.

On the third night that Tim is away the prince from the painting appears to her after she has got out of the bath.

Except, if she is honest, she wishes him to. It is not a huge surprise. If she is honest, she gets out of the bath and brushes her hair and puts on her pyjamas and waits for him in the dark. He takes her hand and squeezes it gently and she says, "I knew that you were going to come eventually," and she feels his breath on her hair.

When they have sex there is a heaviness to his weightlessness on top of her body.

He is gone in the morning and when she wakes up she goes back into her and Tim's room and puts on the TV and cries and goes back to sleep until eleven AM.

But Laura knows that the prince will come back the next night, and he does. He is just like a real boy/man. She wanders around the kitchen and spends the whole day making loads and loads of tiny biscuits and cakes and tarts. It feels as if her heart is in a perpetual state of clicking.

When the lights are out, she imagines him in full shape; she knows if she turns the light on that she might catch a glimpse of him and that he will disappear forever. So she never does.

Sometimes she will find him waiting for her in the hall, where he is slightly more visible when the sun is setting and comes musky through the windows, she can see the bits of dust it reveals settling on his shoulders. But in a way he is less present there. She feels like he is making himself appear for the sake of it, as if he thinks that she wants that. It is the spare room where he is really present.

By the time they have been fucking for a week she has already whispered the words that she used to imagine to him at least three times. Then one night, when they are holding hands in the dark and watching an episode of Masterchef on her laptop, she confesses to him that she has always wanted to say it but that she knew if she said it to Tim he would feel weird about it and other men she had slept with had known her friends, and if Laura's friends found out she said that then they might think that she wasn't a feminist anymore.

The prince tells Laura that she can always tell him anything that he wants and he won't judge her or tell anyone.

In the morning he is always gone. It's okay. Laura reads in bed then makes herself massive breakfasts in the kitchen, like fry-ups and batches of Welsh cakes and popovers with a lot of fruit on the side.

Sometimes she puts photos of her breakfast on Instagram and Tim likes them or comments saying he misses her, so Laura feels bad, but sometimes he forgets and then she feels angry again.

In the afternoons she goes out in town or to the cinema or to the garden centre. Sometimes she goes to look at the prince in the stately home, very much there with all of his dogs.

At night she makes big dinners and puts on the new Ed Sheeran album and pours herself a glass of wine. And this is the only time she feels a sense of fear, her heart going click, click, click. Some time around now she knows he has come into the room, feels a warmth and a fullness. Sometimes he will touch her slightly or move the door so she knows that he is there. She always sets two places at the table even though he doesn't eat.

Then she gets the text from Tim. Tim is like: *Back tomorrow I can't wait to see you I've bought you a bracelet and two different types of wine.* Laura has to tell the prince that she can't sleep with him for a while and she promises to talk to him when she can but she just has to figure out what is going on because all of this is fucking with her head. He understands and to say goodbye he plays her a short song he has written on the mandolin.

She sleeps back in her and Tim's room, cold and too spacious. When she wakes up, Tim is not next to her in the bed as she'd thought he might be.

She wonders if his flight might have been delayed, but when she looks out of the window, Tim's Nissan is back on the drive. Tim is waiting at the kitchen table.

He says that he saw that guy through the window and at first he kicks off and nearly throws a cup of coffee and he even calls her a slut and a whore and then he says sorry and she says sorry and they both are on the floor on their knees kissing and crying. The day after Tim packs most of his stuff in a suitcase and goes to stay at his mum's.

When Tim is gone, things between Laura and the prince change. She isn't sure if it was the limitation of their time together that made her think she was in love with the prince instead of Tim, that its rushed and forbidden nature made it feel exciting and glamorous and that these endless days without talk make her feel tired and nervous, or just that now it has got boring and she has started to see him like all other boys.

The sex stops being good. He stops coming every night, and she doesn't ask him why. If she is honest she feels a bit angry towards the prince that he would appear in physical form for Tim and not her, but she doesn't bring this up.

One night she realises it has not just been an entire week since she saw the prince, but since she saw literally anyone. She goes to the shop to buy some wine and ready meals and feels surprised when the teenage boy in Morrisons appears to be able to see her.

That night when she is about to fall asleep she starts to hear the noises again.

When the door opens she thinks it might be the prince. But it is someone else, or something else. His body is heavier. When they have sex he grips her thigh harder and he does not like it when she talks to him. Laura is glad of that.

Now, it is somebody different almost every night. Laura is in full acceptance of the fleeting nature of their visits, has stopped trying to understand them like she used to but is used to their bad timekeeping, how some of them wake her up in her sleep with their elbows, some of them like her to make loud noises, some of them want her to whisper secrets after sex or put the radio on quietly. Often she recognises someone she has slept with before but more in a way that a bird in the garden might be the same bird that comes into the garden every day or it might be a completely different bird, and how that's okay.

She always makes them dinner even though sometimes they don't come until later.

Laura still finds herself saying that thing all the time. She isn't even really into the stuff it connotes any more or doesn't find it novel, she just feels that she owes it to this thirteen year old version of herself who she thinks about quite often, who wouldn't believe that Laura gets the opportunity to say it so often.

She often says things in other languages (she has started doing French online in the afternoons) or things in made-up languages. Sometimes she'll experiment by saying what someone else has said to her before, often feeling like it would always make them come anyway; it wouldn't matter if all that she was whispering in their ears was words and more words and more words.

Tim texts her to ask how she is. He asks if and when she is planning on moving out of the house or if she'd consider paying him rent seeing as she is living there for free and he isn't living there at all. She doesn't get it for almost a week because the signal is not good and also because she doesn't charge or turn on her phone that much these days.

That night Laura cooks a huge dinner. She lights candles and sets out all the plates. She summons every ghost and makes them promise they will come with her wherever she goes even if it means having to leave here. Every single one of them says yes, of course, they will stay forever.

The Farm at the World's End

Helen McClory

You are not here.

A cat yowls in the wildflowers, birds twitter, the sun rises and falls, then there is a dead mouse curled up grey in the road, and a dead dog grey also, and one morning after that the starlings lie around, a sprinkling of sharp angles and dusty feathers. I knew it would happen, eventually. The birds begin to fall daily, amassing beneath the trees or under the eaves, going until there are no birds left alive. The radio no longer plays its terrible love songs. Softly I hear the insects at night talk to me about their cousins overseas, still healthy, a fecund lot clattering amongst glossy, riverine trees. There's nothing coy about the insects; they make their desires quite apparent. At least they are still trying. They are in pieces but they do not stop singing. Perhaps they simply don't know how to. I find cricket legs and wings all over, and collect them like charms to hang around my neck.

Then one day let's say I make a mistake and touch one of the birds. Now I tend the infection; a grey that spreads. I stroke the grey; it feels like the velvet of an ancient and crumbling curtain, it pulses like slime mould, seeking out nutrients from my body. I wrap up the infection site neatly as I was once told to, but just for aesthetics. I defy anyone to read the advice available and not laugh. The disease goes creeping towards my heart, just as it suggests.

Let me tell you what my morning looks like: get up none too early, clean last night's dishes, change my dressing. The grey velvet progresses. It is said to get to the genitals quickest of all, though I haven't looked at mine in a long time, so I've no idea. I call the cat (she does not come), leave food for anything that might still need to eat, make something for myself. I have a shelf full of old jars and what's in them counts as food. There is no one to watch me smear the brown stuff on rice cakes, and anyway the salt from my crying jags is a pretty good seasoning. I wash one of the broken cars, sweeping out the hay and picking about for anything useful. I work, and the sun pinches in the shadows of the trees across the dirt road where no one ever goes. The shadows start to stretch back, filling the land from the ground up, and then it's blue-dark, and I put on my head torch, and go about the place, wishing I could speak insect. Wishing I could speak to anyone.

What does your morning look like? I try to assemble something convincing: you wake up sweet and refreshed in your studio, and the city is loud and the morning sunlight very robust, rubbing up against your paintings and smoothing the lines on your face, slight as they are themselves. You make yourself a tapioca wrap and coffee, and you talk to the whole world on your phone: the whole world wants to know how you are, because that is how you are, magnetic, alive. Then you must have some bills to pay, some preparation for the smooth running of a plague-free life. And then you make art until classes, or therapy and the theatre group, then classes. I imagine this life you have as full of sounds, bustle. I imagine you becoming annoyed, over-worried, taxed by the constant overturn of voices, traffic, demands, brilliance, beauty. I imagine you whole and continuous in your healthy body. I have to imagine it, because I cannot tell what does or doesn't exist beyond a ten kilometre radius of the affliction where I am now. Where I will be as the small end, with patient slowness – a mother in her long grey dress – bends across my body to lay me down.

For thirty-four years I had no idea about apocalypses. It's strange, I used to think they were a global event. I suppose that was a position of privilege. Now I know better. An apocalypse can be limited to a single city, or even a street, shattered into debris by a gas explosion. An apocalypse can be as small as a palm, as large as a house, seemingly sturdy, now desolate to look at on its patch of hopeful ground. It takes on fairy tale dimensions. It can fit about one like a skin, like a grey fur covered in ticks. At the end of the world there is a farm and I am living in it, more and more undone by this particular catastrophe. I have lost the use of my tongue; my mouth full of softness, my teeth sending sparks of static when I chew. I cannot cry now, it has become a disease without release. But it doesn't know me, not at all. And the people that are supposed to know it, know nothing either. And me? I'm as lost as the rest. Just for fun, of a night I sit on the rotten wooden deck and stare out across the empty field, imagining horses there, gleaming, snorting, rushing about with their tails up. The velvet inches over and into me, I can feel its ministrations in my heart, my heart starting to beat like powdery moth wings. But the world, the world is populated by many wondrous things: horses and the horses I make when there are none; you and all that is aside from you, and I understand this, right to the very end I get to, no matter what anyone else has said, or failed to say correctly.

The Prevaricator

Matthew Hughes

Alphronz became a prevaricator because of a lesson he learned when he was a little boy, not long before the sixth anniversary of his naming day. His mother had told him she would take him that afternoon to the Grand Market in the centre of the City of Wal and he should therefore not get his clothes soiled while he played outside.

Alphronz went down to the street from the little flat where they lived in the suburb known as The Bords. A trip to the Grand Market was a treat because his mother would allow him to choose a fifthing's worth of sweetmeats from the confectioner's booth. A fifthing would buy several boiled sweets, and Alphronz would be allowed to choose each one. He was particularly fond of the aniseed balls.

So he played sedately with his little squad of wooden soldiers on the pavement outside their tenement and time passed. Then he heard the rumble of the omnibus's iron-bound wheels and the clopping of its quartet of horses and stood to watch it go by. He saw it stop some distance up the street and there he saw a woman with her hair bound up in a blue cloth and wearing a yellow woollen jacket climb aboard the conveyance.

Alphronz suffered a pang of abandonment. His mother owned just such a scarf and jacket. She had boarded the omnibus and was now riding away without him. His little mouth opened in a sob and tears sprang from his eyes. His wails drew the attention of passersby. A matronly woman, the butcher's wife, stopped and stooped to ask what was wrong.

"My mama's gone without me!" he cried.

"Now then, no need to cry," said the woman. "She'll be back directly, you'll see."

But Alphronz was not to be so easily consoled. Fresh torrents ran down his cheeks and he emitted a heartrending moan. The matron frowned then reached into her reticule and brought out a silver half-penny. "Here," she said. "Now stop crying."

Alphronz looked at the shining disk in his little hand. He had never held a coin before, except a fifthing to give to the confectioner. But a half-penny was worth two-and-a-half fifthings. The child tried to calculate how many sweets it could buy, but he knew only how to add and take away simple sums. Multiplication was as yet unknown to him. Still, it was wealth beyond his scope. He closed his fingers tightly around the coin.

The woman patted his head, said something Alphronz did not attend to, and walked on. It was only then that he noticed he had stopped crying. He wiped away the traces of his tears and put the coin in his pocket – the one with a button – and sealed it safely. Then he gathered up his soldiers and went around to the alley where lay the sole entrance to his tenement. He climbed the stairs and pushed open the door of the flat only to find his mother on her hands and knees, scrubbing the kitchen floor. She looked up and said, "Are you trying to hurry me? I don't want you underfoot when I'm cleaning. Go back down and play."

Alphronz did as he was bid. But he did not play with his soldiers. Instead, he sat on the bottom step and thought about what he had learned:

People would give him money if he cried.

Why would they do that? he asked himself. And he found an answer:

His tears had made the butcher's wife unhappy; giving him the coin had made her happy again.

In the years to come, Alphronz put this lesson to good use. To begin with, he would place himself where there were plenty of passersby, and then he would think of the saddest things he could, until the tears came. Sometimes he would be given a stick of candy, but oftimes, some well-meaning soul would hand him a fifthing or a half-penny.

In time, he grew too old for the tears to work their effect and he realised that he had outgrown that particular tactic. But as he matured into a small yet wiry young man, the strategy took on a variety of tactical forms while the core of the device remained the same: First make them unhappy, then take their unhappiness away. And always take the money.

By the time he met his middle years, still small but no longer wiry, it had become his stock-in-trade. He had learned that a reliable generator of unhappiness was envy. Thus Alphronz would appear in a town as a wealthy newcomer, renting a fine house and a carriage, engaging servants to meet his needs, and making a grand splash into a carefully chosen social stratum: those who were financially comfortable but would like to be more so.

Over sumptuous dinners and all-night games of brag and follow-the-fox, Alphronz would demur when asked for details of how he had won his obviously vast fortune. The conversations usually flowed along these lines:

"I'm in grain," would say a broker who lent money at usurious rates of interest for seed grain to poor farmers and took their land if the harvest was not enough to repay every last groat. "What is your interest?"

And Alphronz would reply, "Oh, I am retired, though I still keep a hand in, from time to time."

"A hand in what?"

"This and that, opportunities as they arise. Whose turn is it to deal?" Gradually, as the weeks passed and he was the subject of much speculative gossip, he might let slip a mention of 'secret fiduciary pools' or 'high-risk, high-return speculative ventures'. Then he would change the subject and refuse to be drawn further.

Thus did it become common knowledge that Alphronz had connections to financial elites in distant cities. He was able to buy into lucrative schemes that the cognoscenti reserved to themselves, making vast profits from ventures that ordinary folk never got a sniff of.

And then would come an evening when Alphronz breezed into the local supper club to order a gourmet feast and a demijohn of the best wine the cellars could offer. He would invite a few of the regular patrons to join him in a celebratory toast.

"To prosperity!" he'd say, clinking his rim to theirs, then immediately refilling his guests' glasses and saying, "And to the best of times!" He would then proceed to become cheerily inebriated – or so it would seem – and allow his cronies to tease from him some details of his latest success.

Over the next few days, he would be quietly and individually approached by those who had heard the details at first- or second-hand. They would ask to be part of the next syndicate that came Alphronz's way.

He would show them his palms raised in warning, tell them that such ventures were only for the sophisticated investor, that the rewards were high because the hazards were also out of the ordinary. But that only sharpened their appetites and they would press him to take them into his circle.

And so he would, though only for small stakes to 'protect them from the dangers of risk'. Then, after several days, he would bring them profits of forty and fifty parts per hundred. And they would clamour to be included in his next venture.

After two or three of these teasings, when the hooks were well set, he would inform his little circle of devotees that a large play was now in the offing. "But," he would say, "this one is not for amateurs. The buy-in is substantial, though the returns will be enormous if all goes well."

Envy had by now been supplanted by pure avarice. His cronies would empty their savings and borrow against their houses to raise the necessary stake. Alphronz would give them each a receipt, then load the sacks of gold bezants and silver double-crowns into a strongbox. This would be placed in his carriage and he would depart the town promising to return with their winnings in a week or so.

And that, of course, was the last the marks ever saw of Alphronz the prevaricator. A league or so out of town, the carriage would have stopped at some inn where a good horse and a stout mule stood waiting. The strongbox would be transferred to the mule and Alphronz would mount the horse and be gone.

The carriage driver would return to his depot, a coin in his pocket. A day later, his employer would come to Alphronz's manse to inquire why the draft for the month's rental had been refused at the fiduciary pool. He might find the house's landlord come on a similar mission, along with the dealer who rented Alphronz the furnishings and silverware. But the servants who might have answered their inquiries were all gone.

It would be several more days before the investors, anxious for their profits and having failed to find Alphronz at any of his usual haunts, would arrive to find the place empty and available for rent. By then, the prevaricator would be far away, spending their wealth to afford himself a fine life.

After the tenth time he had performed this 'operation', as he called it, Alphronz returned again to the Isle of Tortoises in the Tepid Sea. Here he had a comfortable house situated on a bluff above the harbour at Port Amberlyne and was known to be a man who kept himself to himself but scrupulously paid all his accounts in full and on time. His habit of giving handsome gratuities to waiters and doormen won him excellent service at the places he liked to frequent.

But after a massage to take the kinks of the long sea voyage from his muscles and a celebratory meal at The King's Plate, Alphronz came home and went down to his strongroom to make a final enumeration of the latest operation's takings. He calculated that he could live, in the style he preferred, for seven months. Then he would have to go forth once more into the world, choose a new town to infiltrate, and repeat the process.

The heap of coins and ingots that would keep him at leisure for seven months made a substantial pile on his counting table. Next to it was a smaller but not inconsiderable pile of specie: the seed money for his next harvest of the people he thought of privately as 'the crop'. It would pay for the rental of property and furnishings, the engaging of servants and a carriage, and all the meals and drinks to which he would treat the crop as he cultivated it and prepared for the gathering of the fruits.

It occurred to Alphronz, not for the first time, that the seed money would see him through several more months of living expenses on the Isle of Tortoises. If he could devise a means of carrying out an operation without putting in so much of his hard-earned wealth, he would not have to work as often as he did. He would have more time to enjoy existence. Now, as he locked up the strongroom and went up to his favourite chamber, the one with a balcony that caught the evening breeze, he turned his agile mind to the question of how. His day servant had decanted a bottle of pale wine and set it with a glass on the balcony's wrought-iron table. Alphronz settled into the plush-cushioned chair and poured himself a measure. He inhaled the wine's bouquet, swirled it twice in the stemmed glass, then took the first fragrant sip.

As he did so, his memory took him back to an evening several weeks before, when he had been dining and wining with some members of the crop. A prosperous horse-coper who dealt in thoroughbreds for the racing crowd was telling of what he had learned during a trip to the Great Dry Plain to buy breeding stock.

"On the way back," the fellow said, "I passed through the city of Barstandle, just to see what I might pick up from a couple of stables I know there. I could hardly do any business, because the entire city was in a frenzy of fear."

Alphronz raised his refined brows in inquiry but left it to the others around the table to press the coper for the tale.

"Wizards," said the man, "well, at least one wizard. Word had got around that a powerful thaumaturge was looking to buy an estate just down the road from the south gates."

"Oh my," said one of the crop, an importer of luxury goods. "Barstandle does most of its trade with southron cities."

"Indeed," said the coper, "and it's a brave caravaneer who will lead his wagons past the walls of a wizard's demesne. But the only other route would mean a three-day detour through the Flintshard Hills, and you know what you'll find there."

Heads nodded sagely. "Bad water and even worse bandits," said one of the listeners.

"So what happened?" Alphronz said.

"A few days went by and the fuss died down. Word was that the town elders had offered the thaumaturge an incentive to go elsewhere."

"Wizards usually can't be bribed," someone said. "They can conjure up all the gold and jewels they need."

But another man said, "I've heard that conjured riches don't last. The gold fades to iron and the jewels turn back into pebbles."

More sagacious nodding. "I've heard that, too," said the man who took farmers' land when they couldn't pay their debts.

And the discussion moved on.

Alphronz sat on his balcony above Port Amberlyne and sipped his wine. He could not represent himself as a thaumaturge. But in the case of Barstandle, the spellslinger had not actually appeared on the scene. As soon as rumours of his impending acquisition of the estate spread through the populace, the city fathers had sent their inducement to encourage him to settle elsewhere.

"Wizards have ghosts and familiars to serve them, as well as sylphs and afreets," Alphronz mused to himself. "But they also have human henchmen."

He sipped some more and thought, "Such a fellow might arrive in some town and let it be known that he was seeking properties his master might acquire."

To portray himself as a wizard's henchman would cost far less than masquerading as a semi-retired investor in high-risk ventures.

And he reminded himself of the lesson he had learned as a little boy. If you can create unhappiness, people will pay to be happy again. And fear was just as good a generator of unhappiness as envy – perhaps even better – and it might require less of an investment.

Considerably less, as it turned out. Alphronz had heard that there was a retired spellslinger living somewhere on the Isle of Tortoises. A few days of inquiries led him to a village called Five Points and another couple of questions brought him to a nondescript house on the edge of the settlement. A tall, wizened man in a worn grey woollen robe was scratching with a hoe at a vegetable plot beside the house.

Alphronz approached the waist-high fence. "Are you Jarndycek the sorcerer?" he called.

The man ceased his hoeing and straightened. He twisted a ring on his finger and said something Alphronz could not hear. Then he raised his voice and said, "Who wants to know?"

Alphronz had prepared a story to open the discussion, including a name of convenience. Now he was surprised to hear him name himself accurately followed by a succinct description of his way of making a living. The sorcerer studied him for a moment, then said, "Come through the gate."

Jarndycek met him on the walk that led from the gate to the house but diverted him to a small area paved in flagstones where a table and chairs similar to those of Alphronz's balcony stood in the shade of a wystol tree. "Sit," he said.

Alphronz, to test the fellow's power, resolved to stand. He managed to do so but the longer he remained upright, the stronger grew a sense of dread until he trembled like a child who fears a monster lurks beneath his bed.

The tall man sat and regarded him pensively for an extended moment. Then he said, "I can make it much worse."

Alphronz sat and felt the fear ebb from him, though his breathing remained rapid and he was bathed from head to toe in a sheen of cold sweat.

Jarndycek said, "I find conversations more useful when I am certain of the other party's candour. Now, what do you seek?"

Alphronz decided there was no sense trying the sorcerer's patience. He said, "I wish to know if, and how, I could gull affluent people out of some of their wealth by pretending to be a wizard's henchman. I would tell them I was seeking a property where he could set up shop."

"And they would pay you to go elsewhere."

"That was my thought."

Jarndycek studied him with a sharper eye. "You were not thinking of enlisting me as the wizard?" he said.

"No, only as the source of information and perhaps some magical paraphernalia that would confer verisimilitude on the imposture."

"Hmm," said the sorcerer. "And how would I benefit from the scheme?"

"I would pay you for your services."

"How much?"

Alphronz had come with a figure in mind, but had intended to offer far less as an opening move in the bargain. Instead he found himself plainly stating what he was really prepared to pay.

"What would that buy me?" he said.

Jarndycek used a thumb and forefinger to squeeze his lower lip into a clump then said, "I would have to think about that."

He proceeded to do so for a while, casting his gaze toward the stone-walled field that lay across the road from his house and the forest that stood beyond the field. Finally, he turned back to Alphronz and said, "I cannot make you into a convincing wielder of magic in your own right. It takes years of study to master the elements of the craft and, even then, you might be limited by the strength of your talent. Thaumaturges are not all created equal."

"Oh," said Alphronz. He saw the prospect slipping away.

"However," Jarndycek went on, "you are not seeking to present yourself as a practitioner, but merely as the servant of one."

"That is so."

"In which case, your putative master might equip you with something that would allow you to wield some of his power, by proxy."

"Ah," said Alphronz, "and could you do something along those lines for the fee we have discussed?"

"No," said Jarndycek, in a tone and with a slow shake of his head that said the notion was far out of the question. Then, as Alphronz's hopes crashed once more, the sorcerer said, "But I could do it for a fraction of the take."

"Oh?" Alphronz began to wonder if he was like the farmer in the old tale who bought a goat that was supposed to able to eat anything and would grow to a prodigious size. The last thing the goat ate was the farmer.

"How much of a fraction?" he said.

"How much do you normally make?"

Despite himself, Alphronz told the truth. Jarndycek's face showed that he was impressed. "Twenty parts in a hundred," he said.

Alphronz said, "That is more than I have to set aside from one operation to fund the next. I would be better off to keep doing what I've been doing."

"Understandable," said Jarndycek. "What would you say to ten percent?"

"I would say I would rather it was five."

The sorcerer considered the response. "Let us say, if the 'operation' yields no more than the sum you have already admitted is your annual income, you will give me five percent. But you will give me ten percent of whatever you make above that figure."

"Less expenses?" Alphronz said.

"Less expenses."

And so the bargain was struck.

Jarndycek removed his ring and placed it on the table between them. They had moved inside, to what the sorcerer called his workroom: a windowless, shadowy chamber full of corners that looked even darker than the yellowy lamplight could account for. Tall shelves against two walls held tattered books bound in odd colours of leather, interspersed with unusual objects: a human skull figured with strange symbols; a rounded lump of black iron pierced by several holes; a set of small brass hammers hung by wires from a frame of dark wood that clattered softly against each other, though no breeze stirred them; and an oval frame of silver surrounding a vague image that seemed to move of its own accord.

Jarndycek drew Alphronz's attention to the ring. It was a thick circle of what looked like tarnished silver but in places it showed transient glistenings of a purple light so deep as to hurt the eyes.

"This," said the sorcerer, "is what you will use."

"What is it?"

"Not what it seems. It is my familiar, a creature I bound to my service in the twelfth year of Duke Osmain's rule."

"Osmain of Vanderoy?" Alphronz said. "He died in my childhood, a very old man."

"The same. The term of indenture is three hundred years. We are nearing the middle point."

Alphronz could think of no cogent reply. He was beginning to feel like a man who wades through waist-deep surf only to encounter a sudden plunge of the seabed into dark and chilly waters in which who knows what monsters may lurk.

Jarndycek did not appear to notice and kept speaking. "It is an *athlenath*, which is to say an entity of the Seventh Plane. I lured it into our Plane by means I need not describe, shackled it, and caused it to accept the conditions of its servitude."

"What is an *athlenath*?" Alphronz said.

"You would probably call it a demon. They come in different strengths. This is a young one, but strong enough for my purposes. An older one would have been too powerful, or too experienced, for me to capture. Indeed, when I finally free it, I doubt anyone will be able to catch it again. But by then I will have acquired sufficient mana to translate myself permanently to the Overworld, and none of this will ever concern me again."

"I am surprised that one who commands a demon would be interested in the arrangement we have made, that will yield only material wealth."

Jarndycek sighed. "You nuncupes have fanciful notions of what it means to be a practitioner."

He went on to explain that it was almost every thaumaturge's aim to leave this, the Third Plane, to dwell forever in the Fourth, commonly called the Overworld or, sometimes, Elysion. But the translation required a huge stock of psychic energy, which had to be husbanded and built up over decades by arcane exercises of will and spirit.

"Controlling my *athlenath* requires an expenditure of that energy and reduces the time I have for building up mana. As does cultivating my garden and every other mundane task." Jarndycek leaned forward and said, "But if you provide me with gold and silver, I can hire persons to perform many functions, leaving me more time and energy to concentrate on the ultimate goal."

Alphronz was taking this in and turning it over in his mind. "But if I command your demon, will that not drain energy from me? I do not wish to become pale and semi-transparent, and end up as a ghost haunting the house that used to be mine."

The sorcerer waved away the concern. "You will lose some life-force when you invoke the *athlenath*," he said. "But that will come back to you in full when you rest between operations. And I will give you a tonic."

The depths below Alphronz now felt cold and perilous indeed. But he saw in his new partner a bright enthusiasm for the scheme he had proposed. To attempt a withdrawal now would risk angering a wizard who controlled a demon. The truth spell Jarndycek employed at first sight of the prevaricator had already given Alphronz a taste, a very mild taste, of the other's power. He would not like to face that power when it was motivated by anger and an urge toward revenge.

He swallowed and said, "What do I have to do?"

Jarndycek nudged the ring with a finger, the one that had a black rune incised into the nail. "For simple tasks," he said, "you must speak a brief cantrip, only five ergophones, then –"

"Ergophones?"

"Syllables of power. They will take a little getting used to, but once you have mastered them, Yaffrik will do your bidding."

"Yaffrik is its name?" Alphronz noticed that when he spoke the appellation, the ring lit up with a flash of the eye-paining purple.

"Yes, but don't say it again until I've trained you."

"Why not?"

"It would be..." Jarndycek's hands opened, his fingers eloquently spread, "...not good."

Alphronz swallowed. He wondered how far he would get if he rose and fled the house now. And told himself, *Not far if pursued by a demon.* "I will remember that," he said.

"Good. Now here are the ergophones."

Jarndycek spoke each one clearly, pausing between the individual sounds. Alphronz listened closely, heard the first, and then the second, but by the time the sorcerer voiced the third, the first had faded from his consciousness. He frowned and Jarndycek stopped.

"You are having trouble keeping them in mind?" he said. "It takes some time to develop the capacity to encompass sounds of power. Persevere, and it will get better. You would not have succeeded in your profession if you did not have the will."

"Perhaps if you wrote them down," Alphronz said.

The sorcerer wagged an amused finger. "That would give Yaffrik an opportunity to alter one or two of them. Then when you spoke its name, followed by the banjaxed cantrip, the *athlenath* would indulge itself in all sorts of hijinks."

"Hijinks?" Alphronz said.

"A euphemism. I do not wish to trouble your mind." Jarndycek tried an encouraging smile. "Now, let us try again."

The two partners had given comprehensive thought to the details of the scheme and tested various scenarios to find any inherent flaws. Thus it was a good two weeks before Alphronz, now clad in skintight livery of rose and silver, arrived in the town of Old Almery. His was an ostentatious entrance: a golden barouche drawn by two coal-black steeds, with eyes that blazed like blown-upon coals and from whose lips dripped a steaming froth, came down from the sky at noon and alighted in the Grand Plaza.

The carriage's gold-shod wheels rattled over the cobblestones, throwing up sparks, before the twin werehorses could be drawn to a halt – which happened to be just before the town hall. Alphronz stepped down, tied the reins of braided silk to an iron post, and hailed the plump, white-bearded man who wore a robe of purple velvet and a chain of gold links that hung from his neck to his waist, standing agog at the top of the marble steps.

"Hey, fellow! Where might I find a land office or some such? I am seeking a good stretch of country, preferably with a hill on it, where my master might build his manse."

It had been decided that the putative master would be a known thaumaturge of Grand Master or Emeritus rank, but that his name would never be uttered. Voicing the name of such an exalted personage, Jarndycek had explained, was tantamount to tapping him rudely on the shoulder. The wizard might not himself be listening, but he would have set imps and sylphs to do that for him, if not an *athlenath* more powerful than the one bound into the ring.

But the conspirators had put on the doors of the carriage a heraldic device consisting of a star in the open jaws of a griffin whose claws clutched a sword and a feather. Though not identical, the arms were closely modelled on those of Hildefranch the Ineffable, a centuries-old thaumaturge of supernal power.

"He is close to translating himself to the Overworld," Jarndycek said, "and unlikely to exert himself over mundane concerns. As long as his name is not mentioned, all should go well."

As indeed it did. The man in purple, trembling and dry of voice, directed Alphronz to an office across the square. The prevaricator set off at a brisk walk, but he had scarcely arrived at the land bureau before the old fellow came in, along with three other town elders in plush robes bearing emblems of civic rank. They were breathless from hurry married to worry.

Hesitantly, they approached Alphronz where he pretended to study a map of the area. A conversation ensued, which began with vague generalities but soon spiralled in toward the crucial issues of concern to the four fuglemen of Old Almery.

Thus it was less than an hour after his arrival that Alphronz oversaw the loading of a coffer full of precious metals and jewels into the barouche. He spoke to the steeds and they rattled around the square until they had achieved sufficient speed, then launched themselves into the air. In moments, Old Almery was receding into the larger landscape.

Alphronz blinked not only from the speed of his passage through the upper air but also at the alacrity with which the scheme had achieved its goal. The funds in the coffer amounted to a greater sum than almost any of his previous operations had yielded. Moreover, instead of spending weeks carefully cultivating the greed of his targets, he had been in and out in no time at all.

The carriage turned south over the Tepid Sea. Soon Alphronz saw the shape of the Isle of Tortoises rising from the waters, and not long after, he descended to land on the back lawn of Jarndycek's house. He handed the wizard the ring, then brought out the coffer and opened its lid.

Jarndycek smiled. "And all went as anticipated?"

"It did," said Alphronz. He did not mention that when he had spoken the cantrip to activate the demon, he had experienced terrifying sensations and near-dislocations of his senses. He hoped the spell-casting would trouble him less the next time.

Which Jarndycek thought should be as soon as possible. "Tomorrow, in fact," he said. "I have been scrying for new targets. The City of Caer Lyff has a well-stocked civic treasury and there is no practitioner within a two-day journey."

"Tomorrow?" Alphronz said.

"Why not? I'll improve the tonic."

The prevaricator looked at the heap of riches that were now his, after the wizard had taken his share. "Indeed," he said, "why not?"

Caer Lyff was as easily plucked as Old Almery, as were Bandimee, Syaskal, and New Alathe. Jarndycek hired himself a gardener and purchased two more ancient grimoires he said would assist him in perfecting his axial volition. He did not bother to explain the term and Alphronz did not trouble to ask.

Instead, he contemplated the mounting pile of treasure in his strongroom and thought about buying a grander house in the hills above Port Amberlyne, with a full staff instead of one day servant. He might even wed, though he leaned toward keeping a mistress. But perhaps he would do both.

He told Jarndycek, "Three more such operations and I would be inclined to retire."

He had feared the wizard would disagree, but the response was encouraging. "I have just about all that I need now. Three more then no more would suit me, too. Come see the results of my scrying."

So Alphronz flew off to Uz Narim and was back the same day, with a goodly supply of the peerless-quality gemstones traded in that town's ancient market. The following day, he went to Urzendhi and returned with a basket of that place's famous ivory statuettes, carved from the teeth of monstrous bogworms that infested the surrounding peat plains.

On the third day, he descended upon Toch Meevie. This was a prosperous town largely built from the local grey schist, its architecture like its inhabitants running to stolid and blocky. The civic square was spacious, centred on a fountain and lined with stone benches alternating with stone boxes from which rose stunted but wide-branching shade trees.

Alphronz touched down as usual, but there was no one to see the fire-eyed steeds. He ran them in a circuit around the plaza, their metal-shod hooves and the barouche's wheels raising a racket. He drew up before the town hall, identified by the arms of crossed keys and iron crown above the entrance, and caused the werebeasts to rear and stamp against the flagstones.

Again, nothing ensued. No one appeared. Alphronz wondered if he had come on some special day, when the populace kept to their houses and all public spaces stood empty. But then he noticed a slight figure seated on a bench to one side of the plaza, a bland-faced man of indeterminate age clad in a nondescript robe and plain sandals.

Upon being noticed, this fellow rose to his feet and strolled over to where Alphronz sat in the carriage. The prevaricator opened the side door and stepped down, raising both hands in a warning to the man to beware of the stamping hooves. But the fellow paid no heed. He approached, regarded the animals calmly, nodded a minimal greeting to Alphronz, and studied the badge on the open door.

He turned a placid countenance toward Alphronz and said, "Do you know, if that star in the griffin's jaws had seven points instead of five, and if the sword and feather were in the opposite paws, those would be the arms of Hildefranch the Ineffable."

Alphronz blinked, finding himself at a loss for a response. He opted for his usual spiel and inquired as to the whereabouts of the land bureau. "Also, are any of the town's worthy elders in the area?"

The bland expression did not change, though the townsman briefly bit his lower lip before saying, "The bureau is closed. The ealdermen are not in their offices today."

"Is it a civic holiday?" Alphronz said.

"No."

The prevaricator felt a frisson of concern. He looked around the deserted square. "It's not a plague, is it?"

"No."

"Then what?"

The man absently reached up and patted the nose of the nearest beast. Alphronz raised a hand, meaning to warn the fellow that he risked losing his fingers, but the werehorse accepted the contact, emitting a soft whinny of pleasure.

The fellow finally answered Alphronz's question. "Because I said they should stay home today."

A shiver passed from Alphronz's shoulders to the base of his spine. He turned to step into the carriage, wanting to be gone. But the small man touched his arm and he found himself turning back.

"That's an interesting ring," the man said. "May I see it?"

Alphronz would have said no, but the quiet words were accompanied by a beckoning gesture, at which the ring that was Yaffrik left Alphronz's finger and made its way to the other's outstretched palm. He weighed it then lifted it and peered through the opening.

"Ah," he said, "a juvenile *athlenath*." He looked at Alphronz through the circle of dark metal. "It's not happy, you know. Indeed, it seems cruel to keep the poor thing in bondage."

He passed his hand over the ring, said some soft words Alphronz could not make out. The ring dissolved into a column of black and grey smoke that tipped ominously toward Alphronz, but the small man waved his hand again and said, "No. Go back to your home."

The smoke began to revolve like a miniature tornado, then suddenly shrank in size as if racing off into an immense distance. In moments, it was gone.

With its disappearance, the werehorses became a pair of squirrels and the carriage the barrow Jarndycek used to haul root vegetables from his garden to the storage cellar. The little animals scampered toward the nearest tree where they took up positions from which they could keep an eye on Alphronz, chittering to each other.

Alphronz wanted to flee, but found his feet somehow glued to the ground.

"Well," said the little man, "that takes care of the *athlenath*'s unhappiness. Now what to do about mine?"

"You're unhappy?" Alphronz said. He sensed far colder depths opening beneath him.

The fellow was changing. He grew taller, older, much more formidable. His eyes became as hard as agate.

"Oh, very," said Hildefranch the Ineffable.

Alphronz burst into tears. But there was no one to hand him a half-penny.

The Small Island

Heather Parry

There has been a blight about this island. Grain has ceased growing; livestock no longer breeds. Fields lie flat and the hills are barren, devoid of new life. As the last of the mature animals are slaughtered and rationed out, the future holds a horrifying uncertainty.

The people are reaching desperation. Angry seas have kept them from the mainland for too long. Each time they send out a boat, its crew comes back terrified – or worse, it sinks while still in view. Those remaining are afraid to try again. And so, for the first time in a hundred years, they are looking to the smaller island, the one that sits between them and the vast nothingness of ocean. None of those alive have ever dared consider that other place, so passionately did their grandparents tell them of its inhabitants, of witches and sorcerers and the worshipping of the carnal and the eating of flesh; of the unnatural forces that keep the small spit of land, green and lush and teeming with generations, closed off from the rest of the world. But now, faced with the grey death of their own futures, the promise of the lushness and the greenness and the sheer life of that other place is overwhelming the fear.

Aboard the boat, the youngest and strongest of the community's men tie knots and plug leaks. Though it creaks beneath the weight of its small crew and rocks with the gentlest wave, it is the best they have. They hammer wood to wood, pull and secure tarpaulin. The others stand at the tiny harbour and watch them as they work.

It is ready, the captain-of-sorts announces to his uncertain crew. *It's time.*

A girl runs forward. She is a creature somewhere between a child and a woman, the only thing on the island still flourishing amongst the decline. She has heard the tales of black magic and they excite her, speak to the otherness she has always felt inside. Tired of watching nature wilt and wither, she wishes to see women with their hands in soil, forcing trees to grow. She thinks of the women in the stories, the power of their will. The way they were said to embody a strength that terrified people for miles around and kept men from their shores for decades. She is going with them.

The girl's mother knows better than to protest; the crew, however, wave their hands in a no, point her back to her mother. The captain shushes them. Though the hardiest on the island, they're still weak and hungry and wasting away. Thinking of coal mines and dangerous gases, he ignores the further protestations of his men, extends a hand to the girl, and brings her aboard. A life jacket is handed to her. She straps it on and sets herself down at the front of the boat.

The crossing is difficult and strained by the same indignant seas that have kept them from the mainland. But the distance is much shorter. They could have done this journey many times before. They did not.

There is no port on the smaller island. No harbour nor jetty. A vast beach is their only welcome. They navigate the rocks and take the boat into the shallow waters. Two of the younger men move to haul their bodies out of the boat and into the sea, but the captain blocks their path with his outstretched arm.

Wait.

They look up across the sand and over the grass and up to where the village begins, where houses hundreds of years old still stand with thatched roofs. They look to the buildings beyond – the small church and the meeting hall. They see not a single movement; not a breath.

Why don't you jump ashore and scout? the captain says to the girl. *Why don't you take a wee run up that beach and tell us what you find?*

They drop her into the water and tell her to swim to shore, a tester, a little yellow bird without her cage. She makes it to the sand and runs from the water, over dunes and up the gentle incline. She goes willingly, an adventurer.

The fields are empty. Among the buildings, she finds nothing but death. People that have dropped seemingly in an instant. Bodies at desks and in kitchens, bodies intertwined and bodies alone.

She runs back to the water, the sand moving under her feet, and finds that the boat is further out than it was before.

A plague, she says. *There is nobody here left alive.*

The captain hauls the anchor back into the boat. Paddles slip into the water and they begin their escape. The girl runs forward, made slower by the sea.

You'll have breathed it in, says a man. *You'll have caught it.*

Another says: *We can't let you bring it back.*

Then there is silence. Silence from her and from the men who leave her. Silence because there's nothing to say.

She stays among the dunes for three days, shivering and starving and clinging to hope, running up to the village only to drink water from the well. As she pulls up the bucket, she peers into the darkness, looking for the witches she was promised, searching for the forces that transform one thing into another. There is nothing but silence and stillness, no movement at all. On the fourth day, staring out over the waves, she accepts that no boat is coming. She makes her home among the dead.

She steps around their bloated forms, pink foam escaping from their noses and parted lips. She searches their houses for what might sustain her. It is a week before the canned foods and pastes and butter and cream run out. Then another of stomach cramps and the rotten corpses of rats and snails. Of chewing the straw from roofs and hallucinations of beef. Of glances at the reddening, rictal bodies scattered about, as if abandoned in an abattoir.

It is the twenty-first day of her abandonment when, free of tears and resolute, she takes a handsaw from a tool shed and slices the bicep off the largest man she can find. Those that have fallen outside are colder and better preserved. She is so hungry she barely thinks of the morals. She builds a fire and rubs the muscle with salt and sits it to smoke and cook and become delicious.

She devours it within minutes. She feels human again. She sleeps full.

The brightness of the day wakes her. She strips naked and heads down to the water, her bathtub, and takes herself into the frigid sea. She runs hands over skin and goose pimples and feels a swelling under her fingers. From elbow to shoulder she has grown; not on both sides. Only one. She brings her arms out of the water and flexes the left. The bicep rises, strong and round and firm. She grasps it with her other hand. She grins.

There are two dozen dead outside the croft buildings and tiny homes. With her new strength, she uses her left arm to flip them over, to uncurl them from their poses, to tear them from one another. She appraises them. Blood has pooled; teeth and nails drop from fingers and gums. Yet each body has its own benefits. A pair of round buttocks, large feet, strong shoulders. She first takes the lips of a woman lying by a well. A knife will do for this; two slices and it's done. She fries them up with oil in a pan. They slip down with ease, and she sleeps.

The next morning, her face is heavier. She finds a cracked mirror. There they are, full and red and hers.

She takes calf muscles and long fingers and hefty gluteals. She takes daintier ears and wide forearms and breasts twice the size of hers. She pops out two gelatinous masses, barely clinging to their shape, from the corpse of a child. The next day, when she wakes, she has the blue-grey eyes she's always wished for.

She is strong. She is powerful. She can run and bend and move and lift and swim just as she wants to. She spears fish from the still-living seas, and grasps eels, and holds her breath to dive for scallops. She hears the absence of her people every day, but she no longer cares.

One day, she shears a cock from the groin of every dead man. She lines them up, five in total, and imagines them turgid. She looks for girth and length and erectile tissue. She swallows one whole, holds back a retch, and goes to sleep with a smile on her face.

She wakes, excited, with a hot urgency at her groin. It protrudes from just above her vulva. She thinks of the things she always thinks of at night, and it grows bigger and swells and brings sheer delight. She has chosen well. She is perfect.

The boat comes after three months. She hears it from the hillside. Wrapped in blankets to hide her new form, she strides down to the beach where they sit many yards from the shore. They are afraid, again. She lets them speak.

We need you, says the captain. *We want you back. We can't handle the shame.* There is one word that he does not say, and she notes it.

Go home, she thinks. *I am happy here.* But she does not say it. Instead, she runs her gaze over sturdy hands and firm hips and brows that sit heavy over eyes.

There is life here, she says. *Things growing. Things that have sustained me. Come and see.*

She waits a while. They do as she tells them. She takes them one by one around corners, into dark rooms, to show them something. She wrings their necks, smashes their skulls with rocks, stabs their chests with cold pokers. She picks over flesh and sinew and muscle and marrow, then waits for the next boat to come and rescue her.

She takes the parts that she wants and leaves the rest to rot.

A Gift of Tongues

Paul McQuade

His hands swallow mine when he speaks. *Ich liebe dich*. And I can't reply, can't say what I want to say – I am still on Chapter 7: Politics. Unable to respond, I smile. This is how the relationship goes: we muddle along, half-understanding. Nods, smiles, and laughter fill the gaps.

The smile has communicated something. He puts a box in my hands. The gold ribbon slips its knot, coils and falls along the table, swimming into the dark below. The red crêpe crackles like dead leaves.

There is a box inside the box. The second made of glass. The light refracts as it emerges, hiding its contents in white light. Only when I cover it with my hands can I see what is inside: a long slab of meat. Pink, glistening.

"*Eine Zunge*," he says. Chapter 3: Anatomy. He has bought me a tongue.

It is winter in Berlin. The sun, cloud-veiled, only deepens the city's shadows. The shadows press up against the buildings, the strange music of the city pours along the streets. Sigh of bus doors, percussion of the U-Bahn. People walk, not hearing, but feeling its movement. Couples crowd the bridges of the Spree, lip-to-ear, whispering secrets the river shelters in its long exhale.

Thöre tries to strike up conversation on the S-Bahn. It is late afternoon, the cabin filled with people on their way to the Grunewald. I stand on tiptoe and speak into his ear, so that other passengers cannot hear my *kauderwelsch* German. Small hairs glance against my lips; white arms soft as peach fuzz carry my words deep into his skull.

Kauderwelsch. Gibberish. Gobbledygook.

My German is comprised of Thöre, a textbook, and the lessons that my work makes the new transplants take. Once a week, for an hour and a half and full pay, we sit in a meeting room and talk. Situational German. Please-and-thank-you's. Polite conversation for business lunches. *We look forward to working with you*. No one takes it seriously. Sometimes when we go out, the other new-starts speak entirely in English, even when ordering, not bothering with so much as a cursory *danke* or *bitte*. There is something exciting about this. Something rebellious. I expect someone to snap, to swear, to tell them to speak German, the way I had seen the French do in Paris. I hold my breath and wait.

No one says a thing.

I met Thöre on one such outing. The new staff, two managers, one of the company lawyers. A bar in the east, street level, light spilling out over Soviet high-rises. We sat in our corner with Bavarian wheat beers, suspended safely in a cloud of English. It was the lawyer who disturbed our seclusion, standing up to shout in German across the bar. A man came over. They hugged, kissed – once on each cheek – and he joined us, taking a seat between the lawyer and me. A couple of half-hearted waves and quiet hellos from my compatriots, and the conversation closed over his entrance. The man and the lawyer turned to each other to talk amongst themselves.

When the lawyer popped to the bathroom, the man leaned across and asked if I spoke German. His breath felt alive against my cheek, and under the reek of bar bodies, he smelled of sea salt and coriander. Emboldened by the *Weissbier*, I tried to remember all those meeting-room conversations. The beer made things smoother. I tried to introduce myself.

"You speak *Kauderwelsch*," he said, in English. "But it's cute."

The lawyer returned and they went back to talking in German, though the man – Thöre, he said his name was, *Thöre as in Thor* – looked at me while the woman talked in his ear, smiling a deep, knowing smile.

When I stepped through the door of my apartment later that night, I pulled out the miniature German-to-English dictionary a friend had bought me as a goodbye present, and looked up what Thöre had said to me.

Kauderwelsch. Noun, neuter.

When I forget the word I want, when a phrase is beyond me, coiled slyly on the tip of my tongue, close as the tail end of a dream, *Kauderwelsch* is there, waiting in the space where the other words should be.

The train comes to a stop. Thöre leans down.

"We're here," he says, his mouth covering, for a moment, the entirety of my ear. He takes my hand and leads me out into the forest of the Grunewald.

"It is a very simple operation," the doctor explains in English. "You don't even have to be put under full anaesthetic. In fact, the results are far better if the procedure is performed in twilight sleep."

I hold the boxed tongue in my lap. It seems drier now, under the clinic lights. Smaller. Frightened. I wonder if this is a sign that it is sick, like a dog's nose.

"And afterwards, I'll be able to speak German?" I ask.

"Faultlessly."

Thöre takes my hand in his.

The doctor lists side-effects, reiterating after each how safe the operation is, how unlikely it is that I will suffer anything other than the pure joy of bypassing years of study. "Strange things, tongues," the doctor says. "I have to say, it's really quite a wonderful gift your boyfriend has bought you. Your new tongue will open doors."

"What about my old tongue?" I ask.

"Don't worry about that," he replies. "We take care of everything."

Thöre squeezes my hand and looks into my eyes. He mouths the words: *Ich liebe dich.*

Still unsure what to say, I nod.

"Excellent," the doctor says. "A nurse will be along in a moment to get you prepped. Just sign here."

The pen makes a scratching sound, like an animal trying to escape.

"I can't wait," Thöre tells me while we wait for the nurse. "I'm finally going to be able to talk to you."

"We talk all the time," I say.

"You know what I mean."

"I don't," I insist.

"You will," he replies.

The first present Thöre bought me was a flat white, the second a textbook. We met at a café near my work. The conversation a series of starts and stops. Almost not quites. When he talked for anything longer than a sentence, slowing down to make sure I could make him out, I let the words pass over me like water. I examined the curve of his jaw, how the stubble didn't quite reach his cheeks, the way the sunlight through the window made one eye wolf-yellow. When he asked me about myself, I responded as best I could. I knew the questions from class, but couldn't remember the right answers, only what other people had said. I told him

I had a brother when I have two. That one brother is older when I am the oldest. That I am eight and twenty instead of twenty-eight. He smiled at each mistake, chin in hand.

"I bought you something," he said

He slid an oblong of brown paper along the tabletop. I wanted to tell him that he shouldn't have, that it was nice of him, that I would repay the favour by buying him a drink. But I didn't know how. Instead I unwrapped the package, dumbly.

Inside was a textbook. A Japanese woman laughed with a blond man on the front cover. Above them, in slender green font, was written: *Die Gabe der Zungen.*

"Thank you," I said

I flicked through the pages and saw a phrase.

"The next round is on me."

Thöre laughed. After coffee, we took the underground in the same direction, Thöre getting off a few stops before mine. He kissed me and told me he would see me soon. After he left, I caught eyes with a woman sitting nearby. She smiled and said: *Sie sind so ein süßes Paar.* I smiled in response, unsure of what she had said. She returned the gesture and returned to her paperback. The exchange pleased me: as if I were just another German on the subway, kissing my boyfriend goodbye. It felt good.

It felt as if I were invisible.

The new tongue is stapled to the inside of my mouth. Dissolvable double-hinges, the doctor explains. Due to the need for movement, it would be impossible to bind the muscles with sutures. Instead, delicate little hinges have been affixed to the join between the old flesh and the new. They glitter in the clinic lights as I move a pink hand-mirror in front of my mouth, watching my tongue lick the white walls of my teeth, brush the inside of my mouth. The mirror makes my teeth seem small, but, to my tongue, these things are gargantuan: my teeth are cliff-faces, the roof of my mouth a universe wide. I put the mirror down. I shut my mouth. It feels as if I have closed my eyes.

I notice a taste. Slightly salty, like cured bacon, with a faint hint of bergamot. Tea-smoked meat. I use the new tongue to explore further; the hinges butterfly and pull at their fleshy moorings. The taste comes from all over. A taste my old tongue had forgotten. The taste of my own mouth.

"It will take some time to adjust," the doctor says as I sign my discharge. "Little things might take you by surprise. Just be prepared."

"Don't worry, doctor," I say. "I'm already getting used to it. The only thing is the hinges. How long will they be there for?"

"A couple of weeks," he says. "But we'll get you in for a check-up after that, just to make sure everything's fine and the hinges have fully dissolved."

"And my old tongue?"

"Don't worry. We've taken care of it. All you have to do now is focus on resting up and enjoying your new life."

The tongue has made everything new. Even the air. I feel it pour over the lump of

muscle in my mouth, feel it fill each delicate branch of my lungs. It is scented with the green of the Grunewald as we walk out of the clinic, and on the S-Bahn home, the stale coffee on Thöre's breath and the coriander punch of his cologne. Thöre is remarkably quiet. He sits next to me, grinning.

"What?" I ask.

"Nothing," he says, beaming ear to ear.

"Tell me."

"It's your accent," he says. "Your new one, I mean. You sound like you were born and bred in Hamburg."

"Don't be ridiculous," I tell him. "Why would I speak English with a German accent?" He laughs. His eyes reflect the trees as they pass by in the window. For a moment a house with a red roof shines there also. His expression is the same as when I make a mistake in German. Amused, affectionate. But I hadn't made a mistake. Had I?

Thöre's Berlin was different to the one I knew. The Berlin in my head, marked only by bars, restaurants, and coffee shops around my work and flat, branched out, connecting, like tendons, the smaller satellites where we met. I knew the city after a month. Not by direction, but by the memories Thöre and I made: seafood in Charlottenburg, slow walks in Mitte, parties in Neukölln, Thöre's friends. They spoke to me in German, first, then switched to English. It seemed as though everyone in Berlin spoke English, to one extent or another. Only Thöre spoke to me entirely in German.

One night in his apartment in Kreuzberg, as I leafed through *Die Gabe der Zungen* in bed and waited for him to finish brushing his teeth, I called through to the bathroom to ask him why, when everyone else spoke to me in English, only he insisted on German. I heard him spit, heard a tap running. He came and stood in the doorway, the band of his underwear folded over slightly where he had put it back haphazardly. He looked at me as if gauging something. The answer he gave was not textbook: he stopped and started, adjusted what he wanted to say, repositioned sentences mid-flow, so that in the end all I was left with were fragments, clauses out of order.

He does not speak to me in English because he wants me to know something. Something about the truth. Or something real. Him. Something real about him. Himself, maybe. The real him.

He climbed on to the bed, moved up my legs with predatory grace, and closed the textbook in my hands as he gave me a mint-sweet kiss. Then he turned out the light. He fell asleep in seconds. I found it harder. The feeling that I had to be alert, in case I missed something, was hard to shake, even though Thöre was no longer speaking. It was impossible to relax. To help me get to sleep, I ran through the vocabulary list I had just been reading. *Augen, Nase, Herz, und Zehen*. Eyes, nose, heart, and toes. *Arm* for arm, *Fuß* for foot. And *Zunge* – tongue. Chapter 3: Anatomy. *Die Anatomie*.

This is how I fell asleep: Thöre's mouth to my ear, his sleep-heavy breath keeping time. While I counted tongues, and waited to dream.

I talk to people in shops, on the train, strike up conversations with strangers at work. So excited am I by my newfound ability to speak and be understood. It feels like diving: deeper and deeper into Berlin, with no need to rise and fill my lungs with English. My new tongue has gills. The half-open wounds of the hinges, now dissolved, breathe the city. Berlin tastes of ash and June and ozone.

People ask me if I am from Hamburg. I tell them that I have never left Berlin. They laugh and ask me why I have a Hamburg accent then, and when I tell them I am not German, they say I must have learned from someone who spoke *Hamburgisch*. But the woman at my office is from Frankfurt, and the only other teacher I had was Thöre.

It never felt as if I were learning German with Thöre. It was as though I were learning a language only Thöre and I spoke. From the beginning he taught me to understand him with hand gestures, repetition, and glacial speech. I spoke a language of errors, parataxis, and diminishing returns.

I knew I had made a mistake when Thöre laughed. It was a particular laughter, almost affectionate. As if my mistakes pleased him, though my pronunciation did not. Everything sounded wrong to him. The words the same but unfamiliar, pressed through the meat grinder of my mouth – I butchered the language, he said.

The only sound I made that pleased him was '*ch*', as in *Ich* for I, as in *I love you. Ich liebe dich*. This he said after a month had passed. I didn't understand. To explain, he placed my hand on his chest. His hands swallowed mine. Something beat, warm and urgent, against my palm. The word came into my head in the rhythm of that beat: *das, Herz, das, Herz*. As if the two could not be separate. As if they needed each other. The first nothing without the second. Meaningless. This is what *Ich liebe dich* meant to me: something added, extraneous, something straining, and significant.

I couldn't tell Thöre this. I lacked the words. Instead I took his hand and placed it on my chest, let him feel my heart beat its own affirmation: *das, Herz, das, Herz, das, Herz*. Then I remembered something from Chapter 3.

"*Herzen*," I said. Hearts.

He smiled. Almost as if he understood.

"I'm sorry," he says.

I drum my fingers on the table. Rain falls against the window, muttering its response. A series of sharp taps, long sprays. Morse code on glass, there where the name of the cafe is written back to front. The words *Der Ausguck* seem almost fluent on their hand-drawn pennant.

I pick up my coffee and take a drink. Nothing. I finished earlier, but keep the cup at my mouth so I won't have to respond. While Thöre explains. How things have changed. Since the tongue.

"It's just that," he continues. "We've changed. I don't know."

I gulp air like a landed fish, pretending there is still coffee in my cup.

"I thought the transplant would have made things easier. But it hasn't. It's nothing like the brochure said," he says. "You seem like a different person now."

I put down the empty cup. Slowly. Attempt to work out what I am going to say. A couple appear at the window and peer in, trying to see through the breath on the glass whether there is anywhere to sit. One of them turns and says something to the other. Their words sound strange, as if the glass has inverted them too.

"If I'm not me any more, then who am I?" I ask.

"I don't know," Thöre replies.

A bell announces the couple's entrance. They take a seat at the wall behind Thöre, both of them on the same side of the high table, watching the rain against the window while they talk. When they speak to each other, it is still gibberish to me, glass or no glass. Yet it seems familiar. What language is that?

"I'm sorry," Thöre says. "But I don't think we should see each other any more."

The tongue changed everything but most of all it changed Thöre. It was as if a wall had come down. We emerged from our division, freshly gifted with speech. As if all that had come before were just whispers through brick. But it was not only a matter of language. It was all the little things bound up in it: the sighs, the many meanings of a touch, the warmth in his voice that came and went, like a square of sunlight through a window. The world was gold when it was there. But gradually, it began to turn ashen. He no longer talked to me with his chin in his hands. Now it was hands on table, eyes on fingernails. He looked as if he missed something.

Die Gabe der Zungen did not contain a chapter on relationships. I would never have been able to ask him about it, with my old tongue, would never have been able to have a serious conversation about our feelings. The new tongue had changed all that.

"Is everything all right?" I asked him.

He looked up from his fingernails. He seemed surprised to see me there.

"Of course," he said. "Everything's fine. Just tired."

We said no more about it. But I felt as if I had done something wrong. He no longer laughed when I made mistakes. At first, I thought this was because I no longer made them. But soon I couldn't shake the feeling that all I was capable of was mistakes. And Thöre no longer had any patience for them.

I guess, with my new tongue, I should have known better.

I return to my old life, my old apartment, my old Berlin. But with the new tongue in my head, everything is different.

I know I have been back to my flat. I have had to wash clothes, pick up documents for work, make sure nothing is mouldering in the fridge. But when I move around it now, it feels like trespassing.

I try to reconnect with the other transplants from work, to revive the old friendships I had neglected during my time with Thöre. We go to a bar in the east. It is vaguely familiar, but the memory is dim. We settle at a table in the corner and talk in English. The language hangs in the air around us like haze, making us feel safe and invisible. As if to the Germans present we were nothing but the faintest of shimmers on the farthest horizon.

The lawyer is there. It is the first time I have seen her since Thöre and I broke up. She is the partner of one of Thöre's friends, Elke. A slight brunette whose family ties to Bavarian aristocracy show through in the imperious way in which she ignores me. When I speak, she does not look at me. The others exchange looks. I wonder if I am saying something offensive, but no one interrupts, so I persevere. As the conversation goes on, and empty glasses crowd the table, one of them finally asks: "When did you start speaking like that?"

"Like what?"

"Like that. Your English is weird, now. It's as if you can't really speak it. And your accent. You don't sound like you any more."

You seem like a different person now.

"Who do I sound like?"

"You sound like you're from Hamburg," the lawyer says.

"But I'm not," I say. "I'm from..."

I sit there, dumb. The tongue in my head lolls lifeless. I try to remember but the word is not there, only *Kauderwelsch*, burning brand-hot, turning my cheeks crimson.

"I didn't mean to offend you," the man says.

"Don't worry," I say. 'It's yesterday's snow."

I hear it, then. The words sound wrong; the voice is not mine. The table seems to move off into the distance. The room is spinning, or I am. Nothing is solid. I excuse myself, telling them the *Weissbier* has gone to my head, and dive into the night air.

The Soviet high-rises tower above me. Headlights cast long shadows along their faces as I try to find a train station. I walk. Time slips away. I do not recognise these streets; they were not part of me and Thöre. And now I am lost. In this city I thought I knew.

I hold my hand out in the road and a car stops. I climb into the taxi. As it drives to my flat, I look out the window, trying desperately to recognise just one building on the other side of the glass. But nothing looks the same. When the driver stops and asks for the fare, I ask if he's sure we're there.

"Positive," he tells me as he takes the money. "Hey, are you from Hamburg? My brother lives there."

I tell him to keep the change.

I thought I would feel safer back in the apartment, doors locked, curtains drawn. But I still can't shake the feeling that the person who lives there is going to come back, that they will demand that I leave and go back to my own home. But where is that? Where am I from?

Without Thöre, I have nothing to do on the train out to the Grunewald except watch, through the window, as the city recedes. The forest slowly wins back its space. As the train approaches the stop for the clinic, I notice a building in the distance, red-roofed, surrounded by trees in neat rows. It is familiar, somehow, though I am sure I have never been there.

The doctor places my tongue in clamps, the long root of muscle drying in the air, and runs his fingers along the small bumps where the gills of the tongue have closed shut.

"Excellent," he says. "Barely a scar. How are you finding it, any problems?"

"No," I say. "It seems to be working fine. I speak German, now. No problems."

"And faultlessly, too, I have to say. Your boyfriend must be pleased. Is he working today?"

"No," I reply. Then: "Yes. I mean, yes, he's working, but no, he's not my boyfriend. Not any more."

"I'm sorry to hear that," he says. His eyes are wet, glistening with sympathy in the clinic lights. It is strange to see the man that way. He looks like a little boy. And yet, he doesn't seem surprised.

"Does this happen a lot?" I ask.

"It is a danger," he says. "But most of the time, no. It depends, you know? On the people. The new tongue helps people speak, that's all. Sometimes it's a blessing, and in other cases..." He shrugs. "Sometimes, post-transplant, things just fall apart. Your guess is as good as mine why. They just do."

"Doctor," I say. I hesitate, not wanting to offend him. I put my hands on my knees and look down at them as I speak. "I'm sorry, doctor, but I want you to give me my old tongue back."

He puts his hands over mine.

"I'm sorry," he says. "But I can't."

"But it's mine," I say. "It's *my* tongue."

"When you give up your tongue," he says, "you give it up. You can't go back to it. It's a problem of auto-immunity: you can take in a new tongue, if it's managed properly. But your body remembers the old one, and if you try to put it back in, as if it were something new, you would confuse your defences. Your body would try to destroy it."

"What have you done with it?"

The doctor hesitates.

"I can't really tell you," he says. "There are issues of... confidentiality."

"Doctor," I say, "it's my tongue. I don't think you'll be breaking confidentiality if you tell me where it is."

"That's the thing," the doctor says. "It's not your tongue any more."

"What do you mean?"

"Perhaps..." he says. "Perhaps it would be better if I showed you."

We had gone to a restaurant on Charlottenstraße for my birthday. Thöre picked German wines, regional specialities, laid all of Germany out on a table for me. The soft lights of the restaurant made everything gleam and blur.

A taxi back, and we were walking unsteadily up the stairs to Thöre's place, bodies soft and lush with wine. Thöre pressed me against the wall of the stairwell, then pressed a box into my hands, his swallowing mine. Then lip to ear, he whispered: "One last gift."

The box was black, its join sealed with a disc of red wax and the imprint of a 'T'. A key wrapped in red crêpe, small bow around its waist, nestled on a mound of grey silk. Next to it lay a strand of snowdrops.

"A key?" I asked. Chapter 2: The Home.

"Aye," he said. The sound of the word, made strange by his mouth, was almost musical: as if the affirmation were carried away by it, the vowel now a note, fading, *legato*, as Thöre plucked the key from its swaddling and placed it in my hand. Little teeth of metal dug into my palm.

I turned the key in the lock. Thöre stood behind me, his hands on my shoulders, watching, seeing from just above my eye-level, his own home open to me with the swing of a door. I knew what to expect: a minimalist art print in a black frame, a concrete vase with three plastic lilies, dust on their mouths, and a glass sphere for percolating coffee. Yet for some reason, opened with a key that was my own, it seemed different. As if by some sleight of hand the room behind this door had vanished, replaced by another through subterfuge and shifting compartments.

Thöre swept me off my feet. Literally. One arm buckled the hinge of my knees, so that I fell back and into the other. The key in my hand flew up in the air.

It took me over an hour to find it again the next morning. When I locked the door behind me on the way to work, I wondered whether the same apartment would greet me that evening, or if each turn of key would always make things feel new. A new apartment, a new Thöre. A new me.

The doctor punches a code into the wall. His hands are sheathed in latex gloves, powder blue. There is a brief sigh as the door swells open at the press of a hand. They seem so small, in those gloves. Like the hands of a child.

There is darkness before us. Then fluorescent lights shudder, flicker, race along, until off in the distance, the corridor is nothing but light. The doctor leads me down the corridor, explaining that normally this area is out of bounds, but that he wanted me to understand how it worked. We walk by glass boxes in airtight recesses. In each one, a stub of muscle glistens.

"Where do you get them?" I ask.

"Donations," he replies. "Donations. The tongue you have, now, for example, was donated by the family of someone who had recently passed. Originally from Hamburg, I believe."

He stops in front of a case. The tongue inside seems impossibly small. I imagine it must have belonged to some sort of animal.

"This is your tongue," he says.

I look at it. I look at it the way an animal looks at its reflection, recognising there something strangely familiar and at once completely other. How had I never seen it before, its swell, the lumps at the root, those bumps on its surface, like a secret written in Braille? Is the new tongue like this? Are all tongues the same? Even on the way through this room filled with them, I had only noticed their pinkness, their wetness, how fat they seemed, lying there disused.

"Unfortunately, it already has a buyer. A politician. Tongues like yours fetch a premium," he says.

"What do you mean like mine?" I ask.

"People whose mother tongue is English," he says. I am alarmed by the mistake. It feels dangerous. Like a trap about to spring shut.

"But it's not," I tell him. "English isn't my mother tongue."

He is visibly unsettled.

"But that's what your boyfriend wrote on the application form. Mother tongue: English."

"No," I say, realising that in the time Thóre and I had been together he had never asked me. "He was wrong. English isn't my mother tongue."

"Oh," he says, crestfallen. "Do you have any proof?"

"What kind of proof would I have? Look, wouldn't you get in trouble if you sold him my tongue, knowing full well that, proof or not, there's still a danger that it's not worth the 'premium'."

He sighs. "I'll tell him the situation and see what he says. He might still want it. But if not, it's yours for the standard price."

"Does this mean I can have my tongue back?" I ask.

"Yes and no," he says cautiously. "As I said, we can't put the tongue back in your head. But we can give you it back, I suppose. If the buyer no longer wants it. You'd have to buy it, of course. And take care of it. It has to be kept cool and moist. When people purchase the tongues as gifts, we supply a glass box. Technically there's no reason that it couldn't be kept in one long-term."

"Please."

The word hangs in the air for a moment, in that room of quiet tongues. I hear the rawness in it, how desperate I must sound to him. I wonder if the tongues hear it too.

The doctor nods.

We make the necessary arrangements. I fill in paperwork, declaring that I will take responsibility for the tongue, that it will be gifted to Thóre on a date to be confirmed. The doctor signs off on the lie. After the paperwork is filed, I ask him why he is helping me.

"Let us just say that I have a certain amount of sympathy for your situation," he says. He sticks his tongue out on its side: along its underbelly I see faint arcs, like the closed slits of gills. "The marriage didn't last long after. Like I said, sometimes things just fall apart."

The doctor shakes my hand at the entrance. His hand seems bigger to touch, almost gargantuan. Yet it fits perfectly into mine, as if made of a piece. I turn to leave but stop, unable to shake something.

"One thing," I ask. "Do you keep the tongues until they find a new owner?"

"We try," he says. "But some tongues aren't as popular. We keep them as long as we can, but if we can't find an owner, we have to get rid of them."

"What do you do with them?"

"Well," he says. "You'll have noticed this clinic is in the Grunewald. There's a reason for that. If we can't find a new home for a tongue, they get processed into fertiliser. It's quite interesting, actually: the composition of the tongue, all the things that go into making it, produce a fertiliser that makes things grow almost twice as fast as normal. We sell it to a small paper mill nearby. Maybe you saw it on the way in, it has a red roof?"

"A paper mill?" I ask. An image flashes in my memory of a house with a red roof. It feels as if I had lived there, once.

"Yes," he says. "It's owned by a pretty famous publishing company. They make language textbooks. *Die Gabe der Zungen.* Maybe you've heard of them?"

That night in my apartment, I count tongues in my head, but can't sleep. Each time I close my eyes I see them: all the tongues no one wanted, falling between blades, their pink meat turned to slurry, poured on to saplings. The slim frames shake with the weight of the tongues. The leaves are slick with them. From little acorns, mighty oaks. Then with an axe, down they go. Cut and pulped, pressed, printed. And the people carry them with them as they walk, under arms, wrapped in brown paper, just as I had done – the last of someone's tongue.

I get up to fetch a glass of water. The apartment is quiet, still. Peaceful. I am growing used to its space, the hush of the cars below the window. The feeling that someone might come in at any minute has lessened.

I pour ice cubes from the freezer into a glass then fill it from the tap. Stopping for a moment, I go back and take something out of the refrigerator. Seated at the kitchen counter, the clink of the ice fills the quiet space, as I watch my warm fingerprints fade from the chilled surface of a glass box.

It lies there, under glass. My tongue. The one I can't put back in my head. It is strange to have it there, that I should be the one to keep it. It belongs to me, but at the same time, it doesn't. I can't shake the feeling that I am only keeping it safe for a time, that it is something held only until it can be passed over. Like a gift. Is this how Thöre had felt, safekeeping the tongue that now moves in my head?

A car's headlights drift through the window. Shadows dance along the walls of the apartment. Beyond the glass, Berlin glitters in the night.

He is out there, somewhere. Thöre. I will never see him again. I am sure of it. A wall has lifted itself between us, something not uncommon in this city. Our lives take place on either side of it. Any conversation would happen only through the bricks. Perhaps he has already found someone else. Perhaps he will buy them a tongue; gift it to them in a box of red crêpe, in that apartment where he had once given me a box sealed with a gold ribbon.

I still have a key. I could open that door, step between the walls, and enter. But each turn of the key, something changes. The Thöre in that room is a stranger. I do not speak the language he speaks. Though we share a tongue, now.

Under glass, a long slab of muscle. Pink, glistening. *Eine Zunge*. A gift, kept for the time being. One day, I will give it to someone. I will say the words: *Ich liebe dich*. And they will not know what to say. But, perhaps, they will respond. Somehow. In another language. One of slightest touches, of tender embraces – of hands, and lips, and tongues. One day. *Eines Tages*.

Velocity

Steph Swainston

My brother had driven his lap of honour slowly, savouring the rising applause, waving his golden wreath at the crowd. The cheering of thirty thousand people in the hippodrome had swollen like an avalanche and ebbed away, and then the vast muttering and rustling of thousands of conversations began, as everyone in the crowd stood up, turned around, remarking to each other, and dropped all their refreshment boxes. They shuffled among the litter like fallen leaves, along the marble stands, into the tunnels that funnelled them into the vomitorium, down the great steps and out into Micawater town, leaving the tiered benches empty.

I closed the tower window and watched, through the grease smeared on it, where so many noses and palms had pressed, the old spiders' webs in the corners, clogged with dust and husks of flies. The last few spectators lingered by the tunnel archway, poking over the flapping posters pasted there, idly commenting on them. One of them tried to peel off a poster of my brother, and managed it all the way around, but the glue had stuck in the middle. It tore, leaving a hole, and Gyr's torso and chariot faring plastered to the stone. They rolled up his face, arms and horses anyway, and meandered out through the arch.

One or two cleaners, high on the tiers, started sweeping the paper debris. My brothers emerged from the royal box and bounded down to the side of the racetrack, leant over the marble barrier, and Gyr trotted his chariot alongside.

His horses were covered in blood and foam. They tossed their heads and pawed, and Gyr halted his lightweight chariot at the wall, leant out, with one hand braced on the wall top, and showed Peregrine and Besra his victory wreath. He tilted it left and right, and the sun caught it, and gleamed.

I rested my forehead on the glass for a second. Straightened up, and sighed, looking through the hazy, round patch of grease my forehead had left, to my brothers joshing and bantering below. Then I turned and limped down the stairs of the observation tower, through the carceres stinking of hay and horse sweat, fear and determination, through the open gates of the starting block, and across the sandy track to Gyr.

He glanced over his shoulder. His reins were tied on their bright brass loops.

"Oh, here's the lightning bolt!" he cried.

Besra sniggered.

Gyr gave him the wreath to free his hands, and turned round to me in the chariot. "What are you doing here? Shouldn't you be away sunning yourself on the Emperor?"

I said, "I've got leave for the weekend. This is my home, too."

Besra shuffled his feet and said, "The town's ours but the track's Gyr's."

Peregrine said, "Brothers, no. Give Saker the respect he deserves."

I said, "I came from the Front, we're fighting hard. I only have two days' leave before I need to return to Oscen. You could be more welcoming."

"You could have congratulated him," said Besra.

"I missed it," I said. "I only saw your honour lap."

"He missed it," Besra scoffed. "He's too good for us, like you said."

"I'm away at the Front because I'm *fighting*."

Gyr tapped the inside coving with his heel. "One of San's pet immortals. His super-soldiers, aren't you special, Saker? Little brother, suddenly all high-and-mighty? You used to fit in a light-weight. Now you'd need to tow a great big cart behind, to carry your swollen head."

I was stung to the quick. "I'm saving your wretched hide!"

"The whole court thinks you're snubbing them," said Besra. He was thrumming one of the jewelled peacock-feathers of the wreath. The garland wasn't gold at all, or the plume would have bent. It was nothing but gilded bronze. That's all we can afford, since the Insects came.

"Give me that!" said Gyr. He settled it on his head. "I hope you realise Besra's passed you in age now. You're becoming a younger brother all the time... I hope it gives you pause for thought because it freaks the fuck out of us."

"I'm sorry if you're envious," I replied – but that was the wrong thing to say. Gyr, with victory in his eyes and the dust drying on his naked chest, glanced at Besra, and both of them sneered.

"*I'm* the star!" Gyr said. "Didn't you hear the cheering? Why would I be envious of *you*?"

"I don't think that's what Saker means," said Peregrine quickly.

"Yes, it damn well is," I said.

Gyr surveyed with great contempt the longbow on my shoulder and quiver of arrows at my hip. "You think you're above us mortals. Even above the undisputed hero of the races. You with your peasant's weapon." He glanced to the sweat-dark backs of his four horses, their docked and ribboned tails. "This is the real champion's sport!"

Chariot racing is our greatest obsession, the nation's passion, and Gyr is the highest-lauded hero in all Awia. His plaudits eclipsed mine of the archery field, and the vale of battle. The roar of the crowd for him drowned out the trickle they reserved for me, because people would rather be entertained than saved.

But Gyr couldn't stand the fact that his little brother with the humble longbow had won immortality, and he had not. At the Games, five years ago, when I became the immortal Archer, he had galloped up to the Emperor, and offered to hold races to discover the best charioteer, which he knew he would win. He thought that, since he could prove himself the best, the Emperor would make him an immortal Charioteer, to join him in the struggle against the Insects. But the Emperor had rejected him, for you cannot pit chariots against the swarm. Gyr was so accustomed to being glorified that he'd taken the rejection as a personal affront.

The thick grooves embossed in the skin of his waist were returning to normal, where he'd wrapped the reins around his body, over the muscles of his washboard stomach, leaving his hand free to wield the whip. Red fillet straps held back his curly blond hair, on which the perspiration was drying, and the gold locks were beginning to shimmer. He showed off his slender legs with tight leggings tucked into the tops of his boots, the right toe scuffed where he'd hooked it inside the faring to lean out. Gyr is gilded youth, an Awian prince; he knows the value of everything and the meaning of nothing.

"Insects think chariots are fast food," I said aloud.

"What?" said Peregrine.

"He thinks he's too good for the court." Gyr twirled his whip.

"You never see Mother," said Besra. "You never put in an appearance."

"But I'm here now," I said.

"Very well!" Gyr cried. "Then cut a figure worth a prince, in a real man's sport. Race me tomorrow. Three laps in the midday meet."

Peregrine and Besra exchanged glances. Peregrine spoke up, with the crown prince's authority he could, occasionally, muster. "Lightning has already proven himself at Bitterdale. He still walks with a limp. You shouldn't race a wounded man."

"'Lightning'," Gyr chuckled. "Go on, Saker, can you command the lightning? Zap Besra. Call down a bolt of fire, and zap him in the head."

"It's just a name," I said.

"That's all you've got! Immortals giving themselves airs with daft names! A label doesn't make a man. *Action* does!"

"I'll do it," I said. I slipped the bow off my shoulder and rested the horn tip on my boot toe. The grip felt comfortable in my palm. "But aren't all the places drawn?"

Gyr let his look of triumph float over the massive, empty hippodrome, over the forty tiers of marble seats, across the straights of the oval track that shrank us, but not him, into insignificance, at the carceres starting block with its five gates open. The compressed sand around us had been pounded and shelled-up by hooves, darker beneath, with the wheels' shallow ruts and long skids flattening it out, down at the turn.

The Sphendone turn curves round, where lane discipline ends, and two attendants down there were picking up bits of the Green chariot and sponging blood off the marble barrier.

I swallowed. "I used to race Blue."

"Well, tough. Blue is spoken for. You're white."

"I want the third gate."

Gyr gave Besra a smug look, "Listen to him! We drew this morning. I'm in the third gate."

"Then give me the fourth."

"The first is empty."

"I want the fourth."

He shrugged, as if it didn't matter. "You've got the fourth. Tell Abishai. Get the word out. See you tomorrow – in the starting box." He stared at me, until I turned and left. As I passed through the arch he was still chatting to Peregrine and Besra, and when I reached the street I looked back, through the tunnel, across the racetrack and the spina, and up the far lane he was cantering his horses, out of the turn we call the Sphendone, the sling, for the speed of its dangerous curve. He poised, statuesque, in the chariot, with ruby studs on its gleaming chassis, and blood on its wheels.

In the bath-house of the palace that night, I sat on the blue-tiled step of the hottest pool, in the clouds of steam. Martyn's breasts pressed softly into my back as she knelt behind me, pouring water over my hair and wings from a silver jug. The steam drifted around us, concealing us from any searching eyes or disapproving glares.

She said, "You shouldn't have come to see me, even the battlefield is safer than here."

"I didn't come to *see* you, I came to take you away. Why –?"

"Shh –" she breathed in my ear, placed a finger on my lips, "Not now..."

She leaned back, stroked my left wing. "Go to the starting block early and check for sabotage. Turn the chariot over and look at the axle. I've heard that sometimes Gyr's groom loosens a link in the horses' bits... They say he killed Larus."

"I know," I said.

"I don't think you'll have any sleep tonight at all."

The reins were tight in my hand and my palm was sweating. Beside me, the marble column with its cool, grey grain. Ahead, the gates of gold filigree, fret-cut patterns, almost diaphanous, and through them I saw the length of the track and the stands above it packed with crowds. Thousands were roaring!

Their noise distant. In another reality. The reins slipped a little through my hand. Sweat darkens the leather.

My horses are aligned in the tight box. A column either side separates me from the Green chariot on my left, and, on my right, Gyr standing tall in the Red one. Around me, the small sounds of tension. Concentration. The moment gels, and I force myself to breathe slowly. I calm my heartbeat. Green's axle sighs as he shifts his weight.

My four white horses are still. I glance down at their matching rumps. Their long backs slick under the white tack straps. I feel nauseous, push it into the pit of my stomach. The horses, the chariot, myself, are one being, waiting. I can't smell their rank sawdust. I focus through the gates, on the track, and the position a hundred yards hence I must capture when they fly open.

Being in four puts me too close to the central spina, and Green on my left will be crammed against it. If I make it out ahead of him, he won't recover. But Gyr has a clear run down the straight. I have to go hell for leather to beat him into the first turn.

I glanced sidelong at him. Eyes slipped right, turned my head slightly. He's looking directly at me, smiling with malice. See his gold hair, grey eyes, broken nose. The mole that lifts his lip. I alter my grip on the rein straps. I've wound their heavy bulk around my waist, tight, with just enough slack, I can guide them with my right hand.

He knows he's going to win. He's on home ground. The hippodrome is the palm of his hand, and I don't know these horses. He knows every inch of the track, every single trick. Those studs gemming his battered crimson chariot are one for every victory.

He gave me The Look.

I sneer and face forward, return to marking the point ten yards ahead I must reach first, get central position, command. The gates don't reach the ground. They'll all flick wide together when Abishai throws the lever. And now he's approaching, solemnly, under the weight of the crowd's attention. He passes out of view behind the column and I know he's reached the wall.

I take deep breaths. There's absolute silence. The fountain on the spina stops. The shadows of the monuments along that central reservation have shrunk back beneath them. The palace clock begins to chime. In the royal box mother stands up.

Her handkerchief hangs white from her hand. The horses sense the tension. They brace. I draw a breath to shout.

She lets go the handkerchief.

The gates spring open.

Ha!

We leap forward, the glare and heat and sense of space belts me across the eyes. Gyr thunders past on my right and suddenly he's a length ahead.

His red silk shirt is billowing between crossed straps. All I can see is his back. My horses are plunging like surf. Dead ahead of their noses, the rear of Gyr's chariot, his knees bent and streamers flying. I have the sensation that my horses are in control, not me, then I surge back over them, yelling, and I've totally lost the position I needed. I steer right, come abreast of Gyr on my left with the horses charging shoulder to shoulder, knees lifting, hooves pounding, manes stringing out, and our wheels and tops of our farings match. We're leaning forward equally, my lungs are burning from yelling, the reins in my hand thrumming, my right arm lashing the horses. The floor's transmitting every hoof strike – and his face is a snarl of screaming. The crowd are on their feet and we're so close I'm urged to punch him, and we're neck and neck all down the straight, flashed past the façade of the royal box, and already I'm preparing myself for the turn.

My true love Martyn is in that box.

She's watching!

I screamed at the horses, *Ha! Ha! Ha!* Gyr leant out to balance, flashed round the Sphendone turn with a wing spread wide, was away. Green didn't have the mettle to tackle it at this speed; struggled with his courage. Lost it. Slowed. I shot ahead of his horses' back legs, forelegs, noses, the shadow of the high hippodrome arches cut across the track. We hurtled into it,the turnpost came up, and the wall dead ahead.

Suddenly the crowd was all around me, towering above, in the Sphendone seats. Up came the post. I gripped the left rein, slacked the right, threw my weight to the left side of the chariot, smacked the faring with my thigh, threw out my left wing and my feather tips brushed the turnpost. My left wheel dug in the rut Gyr's had made, the right slipped, I thudded down my weight, both wheels bit, and I straightened out of the turn and screamed up into full speed in the tracks of my brother's wheels. He was two lengths ahead, his wings clenched tight and packed sand hurling off the hooves.

A gold dolphin on the turnpost bowed, and a bell must have rung but the air was solid noise. Behind me, Green and Blue made the turn simultaneously, forcing Blue so wide he nearly scraped the wall.

Ha! Ha! Yelling my lungs raw like bellows, I slipped rein to the horses – they bowed their heads and yanked the leather through my palm – I felt the burn, clamped them. That's enough. So the four lowered their heads, forelegs flashing out under their chins, and showered sand off the wheels, at full charge down the straight.

Gyr's still a length ahead! The pounding of our eight sets of hooves. His strong voice screaming. His crimson-silver streamers flashing. The multi-coloured crowd rushing past. All these people in Gyr's scarlet, yelling! One fat man leaning over the barrier, a fake wreath on his head!

Thundering past the familiar markers on the spina. Past the fountain. Past the ancient obelisk from the Pentadrica. The snake sculpture from

Lazulai. Murrelet's bronze statue of Princess Gerygone shipwrecked, rescued by mermaids. I've got to reach Gyr before we pass the Morenzian iron wolf, I've got to get abreast of him on the inside, or I won't beat him into the turn.

No chance.

He was ready for it. He was starting to stretch his left wing.

"You bastards! *Come on!*" I yelled at my stallions. They couldn't charge faster. Foam whipped from their open mouths, flew past me, stuck to my faring. Barely in control, we hurtled down the straight.

I'm gaining on him!

The feathers of my brother's left wing had brushed that turnpost so often they'd worn down. He had to cut in front of me. He bent his knees further. So did I.

The starting block angled ahead of us, the gates wide open, the towers either side, the gigantic gold Quadriga with rearing steeds on the roof. The sun striped through their outstretched legs. Their driver is our grandfather as a young man, the Eagle standard in his hand. In the shadow of the wall, there's Abishai by the gates' lever, fists clenched, his mouth open in a yell of love for Gyr.

Everyone's roaring for Gyr. It's deafening! No one's cheering for me. Not one in a hundred thousand!

Only Martyn.

Martyn will be rooting for me. But I can't hear her!

This is the easy turn. Gyr zipped into it, put a length between us, allowed himself wide, sliding, and his horses seemed to go sideways over the churned ground. He straightened up and was away down the straight.

He flicked both wings at me without looking round, leant over the faring, over the axle, and urged his horses faster, the wheels a blur, ripping up the sand.

I whipped round the turn. Every bump and rut coming up through my feet, every jolt, and the reins rived so tight they tugged me forward, as my horses saw free ground ahead of them and lunged.

Slick turn!

Inch by inch, I closed the ground between us. Came up behind him. Slipped into my lane inside his left quarter. I'll rip his feathers out!

Green took the turn too fast and swung out on our right. Blue was nowhere.

I gained. There's blood on his horses' muzzles. Did he give them too fast a start?

Coming up to Martyn's box already. The air buzzing. There she is, waving her hands high!

As we passed her, I caught him. He pulled wide. I charged up on his inside.

Just me and Gyr out ahead now. Just white and red – yelling first to reach the turn. Now I was on his inside lane. He glanced over, at my horses coming up. Steered left, and started to push me against the central wall. The marble rushed past. My wheel hub half a metre from it. My horses wouldn't let themselves be run into it, they veered away, towards him. I let my spoked wheel encroach on his. The iron rims nearly touched – he screamed in fury, started giving ground back into the centre. He screeched at his horses – found a burst of speed and pulled directly ahead of me. Suddenly, I was looking at his broad back and the step of his chariot.

He slowed into the Sphendone curve. Damn it! Stuck behind him, I had to slow down, too, and he suddenly sped up, slung round and was away up the straight. My horses slipped sideways, slowing too much and mashed the trodden sand all the way around the curve, sliding into the long middle lane, too far from the turning post – too close to the wall.

I wrestled them out of the curve, straightened them up, more so, accelerated down the straight. Gyr was hugging the inner lane. I came up on his right. The crowd was going wild.

Now I can push *him* into the wall. I steered my horses left, more and more. He looked straight ahead, scourging the whip. My left horse's pounding shoulder started to press his right horse. Our wheel hubs an inch apart.

He shrieked. "You fuck your cousin!"

"You fuck your mare!"

"Incest!"

"*Mortal!*"

I kept him against the wall, faster towards the easy carceres' turn.

Our wheels matched pace. Two sets of horses galloping as eight abreast. His against the wall resisted, their knees lifting, nearly tangling. If he spread a wing the wall would snatch it.

His face was furious. "I'll stuff you in the starting box!"

"I'll smash you against the post!"

The starting block shadow grew closer. Closer. I brought him in too fast, timed it, fell back and left him. I drifted right, coursed round the bend. The hard marble arches swept past on my right, way too close. I saw the straw on the ground inside them. The springs on every open gate. Abishai flattened himself against the wall.

My brother struggled. He loosed reins, skidded right, his horses plunging sideways over the peaked ground. They couldn't find grip, the prints and ruts deeper here, bits of straw in them. The ground too churned up, too soft.

The weight of his chariot swung it like a pendulum and his horses began to fall.

The crowd gasped.

Gyr pulled left so tightly his right wheel left the ground. I saw it stop, mid-air. He flapped once, stomped down the floor with his right foot. The wheel hit the sand and bit.

We roared out of the curve simultaneously and plunged down the straight neck and neck.

Now Gyr was still in the middle lane and I was wide, racing along the barrier with the crowd towering above me. The smooth stone wall grey, with deep scrapes, rushed by as a smear.

His fist tightened on the reins. No! *My move!* My grip under the vibrating left rein, I squeezed it, pulled them left.

We hurtled side by side, past the crowd, past Martyn, the people torrenting past, faces above us, mouths open wide.

I kept him against the spina all the way. He was shrieking on tip-toes, flogging his horses' heads. I controlled him. I stuck to him. He whipped the air around my eyes. But I wouldn't peel away.

Madly he started lashing and screaming his horses faster. Started accelerating – into a manic charge – right up against the wall. His chariot faring started to slide ahead of mine. His horses' noses free, then their forelegs – then I was looking at his back, abreast of my horses.

He can't!

The turn's coming up!

I started letting him go. No! I won't! Out of my mind, I started lashing my horses faster too. Faster, faster! I'll keep him against the wall. No matter what happens!

We should be slowing now!

We can't go into the turn this fast!

He tried to wrestle right. His strength against the horses'. His shoulders stood out like a bow.

The Sphendone turn raced towards us. His expression hard, jaw clenched. Too fast! We're going too fast!

We should be starting the turn!

Solid wall ahead of us!

He's going to break our necks!

He doesn't care!

His nerve held. Mine broke. I peeled away, leaning into the curve, leaving him closest to the post. Then he pulled away too, deliberately. He swung out, forced me right. Away from the turnpost, pushed me across the lanes, towards the wall. I fought back. He kept sliding me into it! The high wall streaked past on my right, its ascending curve ahead of me like a dead end.

Gyr leant his backside on the chariot faring, hooked his boot toe under its opposite lip and leant out, completely horizontal. Disappeared round the turn on one wheel, the other high in the air.

Sand hurled off it, spattered in my face.

My own speed was pulling me with uncontrollable force into the ascending curve of the wall. I saw it coming up, and I knew I couldn't pull out.

I'm going to crash. There's nothing I can do. But with all my strength I fought the inevitable, dragging the reins for seconds, my muscles rock hard, my arms, chest, stomach screaming. Tension slapped the reins. Can't pull them out of it! Can't pull away!

I twisted my body. The curved wall rushed in. My right horse baulked at it, tangled his forelegs into the other three. I grabbed the faring front, braced myself for the impact. We charged into the wall.

My two right horses hit the stone full gallop. The impact smashed me into the air. My feet left the deck. As I flew up, I saw their necks buckling, heads thrown back over their shoulders. Their hooves scraped high against the wall, rumps down. Crack! The sound of snapping spines. The sheer force propelled me over the faring but I hung on – landed stomach on it, winded. My soles smacked down, on the chariot deck.

My right wheel was mowing to matchwood against the marble. The faring screeching along, showering sparks over me. The left wheel dug in, the floor suddenly vertical. My grip white on the faring – with a mighty snap I felt the axle break. The two left horses were still going at full speed – yanked my left arm out straight, breaking my fingers. Snatched at my waist, pulled me round – I let the reins go, then the two left horses fell, sprawling and kicking. The chariot flipped left, the left wheel came off, bounced high, ahead of me, twice, and smashed itself to splinters on the ascending curve of the wall.

I saw a flash of the turnpost, the sand filled my vision, I struck the hard ground full length and the coving of the chariot axed down in front of my eyes.

Everything went dark.

Quiet.

I'm underneath it.

Around me, its bronze walls tugged along, grating the sand and cutting deeper into it as the horses struggled. Then stopped. I lay, on my back, the roar of the crowd muted and tinny. Distant. The chariot floor flat, gritty metal, inches above my nose. My left shoulder raged in agony, my left fingers numb, ripped by the reins. They didn't seem to be in the right place. And I couldn't feel my right leg at all.

That's wrong. My whole body can't fit into the chariot.

Hmm.

My leg must be sticking out.

Hooves thundered past and I heard the chime as the last dolphin nose-dived. Two more sets of hooves and whirring wheels, air rushed by for each. The crowd gave a roar of horror – then erupted in triumph. Their applause crescendoed to an ultimate frenzy. Gyr must have reached the finish line.

It kept the same hysterical level as I... I began drifting into unconsciousness, in the dark of my chariot's upturned shell, and it's strange... I shouldn't be able to sleep when my shoulder's in so much pain. It didn't seem fitting... but I felt content, and... I faded between midnight-blue layers, deep into sleep... and was roused, irritably, by a vibration and a drumming.

I must be in bed, damn it, I must have overslept, and they're parading the troops. Martyn will be coming in to wake me. She's so zestful; she ducks through the tent flap, laughing at my sleepy-face. She crawls onto the bed and teases me with kisses.

The bedsheets slipped on my chest, and I tried to get up... but something was pressing down on me.

It was the chariot floor. The drumming is the pounding hooves of my brother taking his victory lap. As he passed me, he slowed to a walk.

I heard his wheels, and I thought he was going to stop.

He didn't stop. He drove by slowly, and the hoof falls ebbed away. He'd be drinking in the adoration of the crowd tiered into the sky, gazing up at their cheering faces, their fists punching the air. He'd have stripped off his shirt, driving with his bare torso shining. Urging the crowd into ecstasy. Brandishing his wreath in one hand, his proud horses dripping foam. The way he always did.

Sounds gusted. My shoulder flamed. A loud man was calling for bets on the three p.m. race. Then muffled voices, and the chassis around me tugged left and right, scraping into the sand. They were cutting my horses off the shaft.

A commanding voice hallooed, inside. "Are you awake?" It was Rayne, the Doctor.

"I've broken my shoulder," I gasped.

"Argh! You're the *Archer!* You *need* your shoulder!"

A chink of light appeared along the rim of the chassis. Bunches of fingertips appeared, bent up around it and, with a flash of bright daylight they hefted the thing off me and twisted it away.

"You fool," said Rayne. Above me, her face blocked the sun. I blinked, cast an arm over my eyes. She crouched down by my leg. I blinked against my sleeve, suddenly terrified. *What was wrong with my leg? Was it still there?*

I writhed to see it, feeling sand in the nape of my neck. Smelling blood, the sweat-stink of my horses, and a sudden waft of grilled lamb kebabs and fragrant spices from the stalls. Rayne held me down firmly. "Your shoulder's only sprained. But your leg – damn! Your leg is *very* broken. Very, very, very! It's a comminuted fracture."

She helped me sit up. My shin had been crushed in a line, straight across, where the top of the faring had smashed it into the ground. It had severed the soft leather of my boot, and the skin beneath, which had pulled away – and all I could see was a wide, red gash, brimming with blood like a newly-breached well. The sand all around us was soaked scarlet with it.

Rayne scowled at me. Her arm, at my back, held me upright. "I'll have to cut your boot off."

I vomited into my lap.

She barked at her stretcher-bearers. "Stop staring after Gyr! Worship your hero in your own time! You have to lift Lightning."

I wiped my mouth with the back of my good hand and squinted through the blazing sun, at her face – her tanned cheeks padded and criss-crossed with wrinkles. Rayne is nearly eighty, but woe betide anyone who considers her old. Vertical lines of concern bunched up between her brows – her eyes full of disapproval and alarm.

Immediately above us, people packed the curved seats of the Sphendone. Every row, from ringside up to the colonnade, and more spectators were pushing along the bleachers to join them, staring down at us. Lads were craning over the barrier like human tassels, pointing in awe at the enormous mess of tangled hooves, shaft, tack, haft and chariot embedded in the end of its ten-metre furrow of deep-ploughed sand.

You pay more for seats in the Sphendone. They give the best view of the carnage, but being ringside puts you close to danger. A couple of men were collecting pieces of my left wheel that had landed among them, and were chucking them over the boundary wall, down to the track.

The impact had killed my right pair of horses. Abishai was kneeling by the other two, sawing through their throats with his sword. Blood spattered their velveteen muzzles, and the sand-dusted domes of their eyes began to glaze.

Rayne snapped, "*Why* did you race Gyr?"

I groaned.

"You *knew* he'd try to break your neck!"

My leg didn't hurt. I couldn't tell why.

Her aides dragged me onto the stretcher. As they raised it, I saw down the straight and, through the gap between the turn post and the bronze mermaid, I glimpsed another stretcher team carrying away the limp body of the Blue driver, whose chariot adhered in a mangled mess to the central spina.

Gyr had murdered him.

The stretcher lifted, and its rough canvas obscured my view. Rayne walked alongside, her hand on my chest. "The mortals are packed with envy," she said. "And Gyr's no different! ...We immortals confuse them. Five years is enough for everyone to see we haven't aged. That immortality wasn't a hoax on San's part. They know *they've* aged! We should look different too, but we don't! So of course they hate us! Maybe that hate will turn to awe... given enough time. But for now Gyr thinks you're still his little brother!"

"My leg..."

"You might lose it! Then what, Lightning? If I have to amputate, chances are you'll lose your next Challenge, and you'll lose your immortality. Well! It's been nice knowing you!"

"But Martyn..."

"Sh! Not here."

We entered the tunnel. The dazzling sky became the masonry of the archway ceiling. Peaceful shade, then out again into the striking sun, and we continued to the palace.

"We don't belong in the mortals' world any more," she said. "Stick with the Emperor, at the Front or in his Castle. Not in Teale's court, where Gyr can bait you."

"But honour..."

"Stuff honour! Lightning, you have to *live*! For the good of the world. Gyr will be thrilled he's hurt you so badly that you might lose your immortality."

"I'll shoot him!" I said.

Rayne sighed. "You won't, because you're eternal now and you've sworn to protect them. It's going to be a harder task than I thought."

The stretcher bearers jolted me up the steps fronting the palace. Their sandal soles slapped on the hot, dusty mosaic. Then there was a sudden cool dimness, and the smell of pale, waxed oak. We had passed into the hall, under a flash of vine-green frescoed ceiling, and reached my bedroom, on the ground floor.

They raised me high, laid me on the bed. I had spent a year here, recuperating after Bitterdale, and the battle tumulted through my mind, as the sapphire-silk canopy filled my gaze – and the pain came on.

My whole leg was raw fire, a solid blaze – but it must still be attached, because I felt the fragments of bone scraping against each other, and the smuts of racetrack dirt floating on the surface of my skin, against the hairs. I was running with sweat, the dust washing off me and, with the blood, it was soaking into my back. My white silk shirt, pulled out between its straps to billow, now clung sopping-wet to me, like a second skin.

I struggled to see my leg, but Rayne pressed my chest and pushed me down. All I could see was her brown, age-withered hand, and my pectoral muscles hard beneath the translucent-wet silk.

She began unbuckling the straps crossed over them.

"Martyn!" I cried.

"She knows," Rayne said, soothingly. "She saw it. When you crashed, her hands flew to her mouth. Besra laughed, and she slapped him." Rayne bent to tighten a tourniquet below my knee. "It's a poor way to keep your love a secret."

But everyone knows! I thought, in a fever. Who can keep a secret in the palace?

"She tried to run to you. She'd have dashed between the chariots. She would have tried to lift it on her own! But Peregrine grabbed her." The Doctor began sponging the blood from my leg. "She struggled, but he calmed her. Your mother was watching, and so was hers – watching very closely indeed. So she composed herself, and left with Peregrine, though she looked very pale."

A great heartache started pulling, like a hook in my chest. How thick is its rope and how broad is the point! The searing agony in my leg was nothing compared to the intensity of my desire for Martyn.

"It smashed your bone to smithereens," Rayne said. She ran her expert hands over my calf. Tears were trickling from the corners of my eyes, I kicked and spread my wings, shivering them. I would not scream in front of mortals.

Dirt mottled my arms, thickening every hair, turning my skin brown. Rayne sponged the dust, blood and stinging salt away from my eyes, and my hair, running wet, suddenly stretched freezing cold on the pillow. I raised my hand with its dislocated fingers, trying to comprehend how the reins had twisted them.

The door opened and closed.

"At last!" said Rayne. "Well done!"

A servant had come in, bearing a golden cup. Her head was bowed, and covered with a scarf. She came up to the bedside, raised her face and smiled at me mischievously. It was Martyn.

She said, "It was the only way we could think of, to get me past your brothers and the Queen."

At the sound of her voice my heart swelled, and courage sprang up within me. Martyn's green eyes glittered. She clasped my hand and squeezed it. "I love you," she said. "We'll make Gyr pay." She helped me curl my hand around the cup. My fingers sank into the hollows between the embossed figures – I tilted it to my lips and watched the wine elongate towards me, glistening like a ruby in an arch of gold. It tasted of port and liquorice. It seemed to coat my throat, and I began to feel warm inside, high up, within the chevron of my ribs.

Martyn took the cup. "It's opium, my love. Sleep now. Don't fight it. Rayne will set your leg and I'll be here, all the time. I won't move from your side."

The Doctor nodded approvingly and busied herself, cutting my white boot away from my skin. I could feel her tugging my leg, gently tussling, and the fragments of bone jostled and scraped within the muscle, my calf rubbing this way and that on the bed. The pain had become just numb discomfort, but my mind was churning.

Why wouldn't Martyn marry me? What was wrong with me? What was wrong with her, with the whole situation? I struggled inside my mind, writhing and kicking. How could she not understand? Or what was I missing? It was simple: I came to take her to the Castle, so we could marry and the Emperor could make her immortal. I'd assumed she would rush to be with me, and I could carry her away, overwhelmed with excitement, bursting with pleasure.

But she declined me. Why? I sank like a stone into waves of confusion and dread. She mustn't really love me, but she *says* she does, and she's here *now*. So she must! And, even if she didn't, what sort of person would decline the chance to become immortal? *I don't know why!* I thrashed, terrified of losing her: ripped from my chest.

How could she be so mistaken? What was going on in her mind? It must be different from mine. Too different. I thought I knew how she thinks, but she was forcing me to admit I had no idea. All I'd ever thought was wrong. I thought I'd known her well – but I didn't, really. Did I? Anguish rose inside me, and chariot wheels sped by, knifing the sand.

I let loose a tortured howl.

She pressed my hand.

I groaned and sweated, under the waves of torment, the dark red colour you see with your eyes closed. I can't face the centuries without you, Martyn. Without you, I can't be complete. I'll be only half a man, forever. I tried to be calm. She must be testing me. I can feel her hand. She must love me in return. I struggled behind squeezed eyelids, trying to recapture the last time we'd been together. Searching for any signs of hidden meaning. I'd read our intimacy rightly, hadn't I? I must have! There is so much love!

The last moment we had snatched together: away from my mother's spies, I had stolen away to the belvedere. Martyn found my note and rode out beyond the woods. She opened the glass door and came in, exhilarated from the ride, her shirt of lemon silk half-unbuttoned and the straps beneath showing. I lay on the couch, growing harder while she caressed me.

And no, we shouldn't do this, but no-one else seems alive but us. How we love our senses! We love to fuck and ride, we love each other's bodies, we feast and drink. We embrace life!

How else can we Awians laugh in the face of death?

Oh, my love!

And then her face became Gyr's face, floating below the sapphire canopy and sneering at me, and turned into Insect mandibles, gaping. We are in the starting box, I have the reins in hand, and I turn to look at Gyr poised in the chariot beside me – and he has an Insect's head. His sculpted body and his head is that of a giant Insect, chitin shining, compound eyes staring, antennae brushing the rafters, and his jeering mandibles open wide, and he strikes and bites my hip.

My arm is itching. I glance down and scratch it. The skin peels open under my fingernails, and underneath, shining black, is smooth Insect chitin. I can't stop scratching, it peels away further, revealing more chitin, my skin sloughs off, tough bristles emerge here and there – my skin falls away, my whole arm is a spindly Insect's leg. I look at my hands holding the reins and they are Insect's claws.

Martyn drops the handkerchief, the gates spring wide, we burst away. Now I'm human again and hurtling with a human Gyr down the straight. He speeds ahead, I'm whipping and yelling, and the reins start to vibrate in my hand. The chariot is shaking and juddering. There shouldn't be this much movement! The bit rings fly apart – out of the horses' mouths – the reins snake into the air, thick white straps with gold bosses, they fall to the streaking ground, trailing, wrap around the wheels. The horses' heads are free, they charge out of control! The rings linking their harnesses to the shaft begin to widen, opening up, sabotaged cut metal shining. They fly off! The horses charge away. The shaft bites into the sand. Its joint on the front of my chariot buckles, my chariot halts abruptly and I am flung into the air, onto the freezing mud of Bitterdale. My body mangled and broken. The Blue chariot driven by a corpse drives over me, bowling me over, my body crushed and spilling. My mouth is full of sand, I taste it, acrid, grinding on my molars. I moan and spit but my neck and back is broken, I can't crawl. I lie under the black Bitterdale sky, in the seeping mud of the battlefield, surrounded by the screams of the dying. I run out of strength, lay staring glassy at the piled night clouds, and I die. The moon, larger than normal, drifts out from their silver edge. My gaze sets. I see it, but I do not know, for I am dead.

My two soldier brothers, Lanner and Amur, are crouching beside me, peering into my face, but I do not see them, for I am dead. They pick me up, my nose and vision to the horse hair, and gallop me back to the palace. I am lowered on a bier, on silken ropes, into the tomb, smelling of myrrh and wood amber, but I do not know, for I am dead.

Martyn stands above me at the mouth of the tomb. She is crying into the handkerchief that starts the races, and above and beyond her bowed head is the pink coral marble ceiling of the family mausoleum. Martyn draws back, weeping, and the great tomb slab crashes into place, and all is black, and I begin to rot.

I leap up, through the tombstone, across the room, and plunge my face in the washbowl. I grab the pitcher and pour water over my head. Its chill strikes my scalp. Agony blazes in my leg and I drop to my knees, clutching the stand. My pulse is racing! I'm panting!

My heart is hammering so hard it's standing out from my chest!

"Saker!" Martyn appeared beside me, took my arm and led me back to the bed. "Broken leg, remember?"

"The race!" I cried.

My leg was hard and heavy. It was in a plaster cast. I lay on the bed and it locked out straight, with atrocious pain.

"Sh! Sh! Nobody could have pulled out of that curve. Nobody. Gyr slammed you into the wall – we all saw it."

The sunrise, behind her, was backlighting her stacks of gold-red hair. It shone like marvellous bronze; her whole outline was singing.

"I had a bad dream," I said. "The hippodrome..."

"Oh." She bent and kissed my cheek. She smelt soft, of black pepper and nectarine, and her lips brushed the folds of my ear as she whispered, "It'll fade."

"Ah... I don't know..."

"Gyr is a scourge on the earth. Let me kiss you properly." She wriggled onto the bed and kissed me, palm holding my cheek, entwined my tongue with hers. I held her soft breasts. The great strength of my love for her seemed to lift my body, and my pain began to ebb away.

She pulled at my lip with her cupid's bow mouth, bit my lip gently, kissed them and drew away. "Saker," she told me. "Rayne is right. You don't belong here any more."

She was looking into my eyes so tenderly I saw her very soul, and I knew, that behind all her propaganda of energy and excitement, she was just as afraid as everyone else, of what I had become. "You must be really angry with Gyr."

"No..." Strangely enough, I wasn't.

"Do you remember the crash?"

"Yes."

"...*What* do you remember?"

"*Martyn!*" I laughed. "Everything went dark."

She nodded, thoughtfully. "After he did it, he was waving at the crowd. He even slowed down. He was grinning like mad, and they were cheering back – as if he'd done something clever. He let the Blue catch up," she said. "And he drove him straight into the Spina. Did you hear the crowd howling?"

My stomach knotted. Was this monster really my brother?

"But why do they love him so much?" I said. "And why do they hate me?"

"You had your accolade after Bitterdale," she said. "That was a year ago. It's over." Her fingers, as light as feathers, thoughtfully traced the edge of the plaster cast, and then began creeping up my thigh.

I said, "But if it wasn't for me, none of this would exist. By now, everyone in the crowd would be dead or fled to Hacilith. The whole of Awia would be the Insects' nest. The town and the hippodrome would be buried deep inside it."

"I know," she nodded. "I know, you saved us, but their gratitude fades very quickly. It ebbs away. You're the Archer. Just like Rayne keeps saying, they're envious of you, Lightning. Their envy erodes their gratitude even more – and what have you done for them since?"

"I've been recovering from being savaged by an Insect!"

"Ha! People are hungry for entertainment. Especially since they've had such a narrow escape, they want a blow-out party."

"But they're still at risk," I said, bewildered. The Insects hadn't gone away. They were seething like a solid tide, the edge of their mass at Oscen, a hundred miles north of here. We had to stop them before they swarmed back across the river.

Martyn stroked my hip, the opposite side from my Bitterdale scars. "The Insects are out of sight and out of mind. You pushed them out of Micawater, Saker. You did it, but people will never stop and think. As soon as the crisis is over, they return to life as normal, as if nothing's changed... with an emphasis on partying, while they still can."

"But we have to prepare!"

"Oh, Saker. People want light relief and Gyr's ready to give them the thrills they crave. He indulges them with cake and circuses, and they love him. So it's his manor now."

We were quiet for a while.

She had opened the balcony windows wide, and a gentle breeze was billowing their gauze drapes into the room. For a long time we held each other, motionless, with the sheets rucked around us, and the sun splintered pale gold rose over the horizon.

Martyn stretched her auburn wings. She was the only worthwhile thing in the world.

"Please marry me," I begged. "Come with me to the Castle, and I'll make you immortal."

"Marrying your first cousin..." she murmured. "What an example that would be, for all time..." She reached out and touched my throat. "Lightning, it's against the law. The Queen would be furious. It's the last thing the Emperor wants... And what would the public say...? You must be above all reproach. You must be immaculate, to deflect the jealous talk, the people who would undermine you. You must give them no ammunition." She laughed with soft bitterness. "Set yourself above, and apart from everyone, like a star... at the zenith. Shining without the faintest stain of blame, for evermore... Ha. I wish you understood what a tough task 'evermore' will be..."

She kissed me. "Look at you, all broken already! Five years and your body's already ruined. Clinging to a position never works, my love. Where will you end? In what year? How far will you make it, into the future, before the Insects get you? Will you live to be a hundred? Two hundred, even? ...Oh, my love. Why did you have to become immortal? It's wrecked everything."

I loved her so passionately it hurt. I could wait for her, but we were changing in different ways, growing apart. The racing tempo of time was tearing me away from her – with ever-increasing velocity. She didn't know how little time she had. She shouldn't tarry and waste it... but like every mortal, she does.

I kissed her, and lost myself in the soft silk of her sparkling hair, the taste of her lips. She suddenly pulled away and yelped.

Gyr strode into the room. He screwed up his face in derision. Very tall and assured, he paced right up to the side of the bed and sneered down at Martyn and me.

"What are you doing here?" Martyn snapped.

He tilted his head on one side. "Cousins in bed together?"

"He's wounded. I embraced him," she said, assertively. "No one else has bothered!"

"Not so much heartening him as foreplay! You were kissing, like the lovers you are."

"Were you spying?" she demanded.

"For hours!"

"Why?" I snarled.

Martyn was glaring at him. "Were you planning to cut his throat as he slept, like you killed his poor horses?"

Gyr didn't deign to reply; he did not so much as look at her. He said, "Saker, mother is disgusted with you. Peregrine is revolted with you."

"I *fight*. All you do is drive round and round in your little cart."

He laughed, and spun the handle of his whip, so its thin end lashed the air above his shoulder. "At least I *can* drive, without smashing myself to bits! Everyone's laughing at you, Saker – it's such a shame you're missing it. Everyone thinks it's hilarious that a great immortal can't drive. You're not used to losing, are you? It must have been a shock! From the top of the world – to the dirt of the track! Lightning tumbles to earth, ha ha ha!"

"Get out!" I said.

"Make me! You've only been on your feet for a few months, now here you are, abed again! Are you injuring yourself on purpose, to be with *her*? Will the Emperor have patience to wait, now his Archer's always malingering? He has a problem, doesn't he? All his immortals are good at only one thing each, and they're crap at everything else! If you practised as much with the bow as you do with your dick, you wouldn't have got our little brothers killed at Bitterdale."

"How dare you!"

"You were lying among the dead. They went back for you. Mother blames you, you know. Lanner and Amur carried you from the field, returned to the battle, and the last Insects killed them. Everyone remarks upon it. And upon your absence, too: how you spend your time fucking like a rabbit –" he jerked his thumb at Martyn "– with that slut."

He tapped the butt of his whip on my plaster cast, then trailed it up my body – the skin of my stomach – prodded me in the middle of my chest – lifted the whip butt up, to under my jaw – and Martyn punched him squarely in the balls.

Gyr dropped to the floor, clutching his groin. "Argh!"

"Fuck you!" said Martyn.

"...*Bitch!*"

"*Worm!*"

He gasped, couldn't breathe. Couldn't say anything else. The skin of his face went mottled red and sickly yellow, shining with sweat. Damn him! He writhed there. He was just a pathetic baby. Full of mortal concerns – driven by them – and they no longer meant anything to me. For the first time, I realised that the rivalry of princes is the squabbling of babes – and I became truly immortal. The centuries stretched out ahead of me; I was walking towards them, gaining in stature and strength. I could see clearly now, that the threads of their petty cares are nothing but the tangle of a repulsive game.

Disgust knotted my stomach. It forced me to stand, off the bed, not heeding Martyn's cry. I didn't even notice the flare of pain. I grabbed Gyr's chest. Glorying in my strength I seized two handfuls of his rich, white tunic, and dragged him across the floor. He braced his legs and resisted. I spanned my biceps like a bow, and with ease I picked him up bodily. I carried him between the gusting drapes to the balcony, and hurled him off the parapet.

He fell the height of the terrace to the bushes below. Disappeared into them, and all I could see were his two legs sticking out, kicking.

"Also-ran!" I called. "You make me sick!"

Martyn joined me, laughing, and I laughed too. She leant her head on my shoulder, her arm close around my waist. I couldn't accept the possibility I was going to leave her behind. I couldn't stand to grow away from her, in time and place. I kept my weight from my broken leg and, hugging together, we watched Gyr floundering in the bush of Donaise thorn.

"Martyn, please come marry me," I said, softly. "We'll be together, forever."

"I love you," she said. "So I'll try."

Now I lean on the self-same balcony, and look out over the grounds of my palace, one and a half thousand years later, and I am alone.

As I surface from the memory of my lover and my brother, that bright morning in the summer of 625, the Insect-ravaged landscape before me disappears. The vista of bare soil and trees stripped to naked trunks, standing like thick, white staves, becomes a beautiful panorama of lush, green lawns, and well- tended woods of walnut and beech. Fallow deer graze the shadows of their margins, and Micawater lake glistens, lying calmly like a cast of jewels.

My palace grounds, I love so much, overlay my memory, fifteen hundred years old but just as real, of the churned swamp and river of Martyn's day, the corpses scattered on the bank, their armour dulled with mud. Antennae and Insect legs loop out from the trodden, puddled clay and silt, and the sky above resounds with the screams of the dying.

I can flick back and forth between my vivid memory of that wasteland, and the flourishing gardens of today. And, because I still live, the sun-drenched hippodrome, the battlefield, the crunch of dewy sand under the chariots' wheels, are somehow still alive, as well.

In my mind, vivid, all-encompassing, as if they're happening in this instant. I live in my memories... but the bushes below the balcony have gone, and Gyr's legs have gone, too. Roses are planted where that thorn bush once grew. The horizon, where I stood on the brink of Bitterdale against the Insects, is no longer a bleak curve of empty earth against the sky, but wheatfields with farms, a statue on a column to commemorate my younger brothers, who lie there forever as part of the earth.

And now, at the distance of time, I realise my mistake. Marriage between cousins is not the immovable object Martyn thought it was. Things that seem impossible, totally insurmountable, become unimportant, with time. We set the rules. If we brave the initial outcry, the world will soon come to accept us. But she, for all her daring, feared truly rebelling. So she over-complicated the question, when in reality it was a simple choice. She preferred to be left behind. She was trapped, by convention, and couldn't escape... acquiesced to die rather than to marry me. Her fear of what other people may think... so influential, that it made her care more about convention than she cared for me. A few days after the race she asked mother for permission to marry me. Queen Teale forbade her, and she submitted, and that became her excuse to conform.

And time passed. I was fighting at the Front, and one day a letter arrived that she had married the Steward of Donaise.

Gyr became king, and I was no longer able to visit the palace, while Martyn raised a family. Her children grew up and had children of their own; she aged, and died, and now she lies in the family tomb, beside my parents, beside hers. Perhaps she was not the person I thought she was, nor the person I thought I wanted. But I'll never stop searching for her, forever, and Rayne still calls me a fool.

The palace is mine now, and it stands empty. I'm sure it seems cold and desolate to you, but for me it echoes and throngs with tangs of memories, sudden shouts in attic shafts of bright sunlight, snatches of music in the corridors around the hall. Reverberations of laughter, from a thousand years ago.

I think I hear the footsteps of her children as they run in the hall. Gyr strides through that door with a sneer on his face. My memories are recorded in the fabric of the stone and the grain of the polished wood; I knew it well when I was young. Down there on the terrace, that corner of the fountain always seems more significant than the others, because when my leg was healing I paused there on my crutches to rest, and Martyn kissed me in full view.

Don't feel trapped in an impossible situation, like she did. Don't let it be a prison around you. Yes, the walls seem unbreakable, but you built them. Take a step back. Breathe out. Realise it is simple. The solution has been there all the time.

Relinquish your set beliefs, allow them to fall away, and the walls will fall, too. Step forward. See! The prison has gone! You can walk out of it. You have escaped. Do what you will.

And now the clock is chiming six p.m., the sky is louring grey, and quietly, down in the Great Hall, dinner is being served. Jant and Simoon have come to visit, so I have guests, and I won't eat alone as I normally do.

The wind skittered the stiff first leaves of autumn across the terrace... and they sounded like my chariot wheels, crunching the sand of the Sphendone. They blew through its spokes, and I shuddered. I clasped my coat close about me, pushed through the thick drapes of the balcony, and went down to dinner.

Counting the Pennies

Rhys Hughes

"Count the pennies and the pounds will look after themselves," is what my grandma always told me when I was quite small.

I have never forgotten that advice, though I never acted on it until recently. I had come home from the office in a dejected mood. My boss had fired me for some little mistake I'd made. So I was without a job.

I threw the envelope containing my final week's wages down on the table, but my aim was poor and it slid off and burst on the floor. It had been overstuffed with notes but I knew they wouldn't last long. The cost of living had become very expensive in the past few years. I sighed and sat down.

The chair scraped on the bare floorboards and I knew I wouldn't be able to afford that luxury carpet I had been saving for.

My coat felt heavy and I wondered why, then I remembered.

The pockets were full of small change.

I dipped my hands like the grabs of mechanical diggers into my pockets and drew out fistfuls of pennies. I deposited them on the tabletop and stared at them. Should I start counting them? I guess I ought to.

I would have to live a frugal life until I found a new job.

Waste not, want not, so they say.

I began counting the pennies. One, two, three, four...

You know how it is done.

And I found myself wondering if the pounds would really look after themselves if I continued counting these pennies, and thinking this thought made me lose count and I had to start again, because counting pennies is such a boring thing to do that it's easy to become distracted by anything at all.

I counted and my mind wandered again. I had to start a third time. My mind kept wandering. A fourth, fifth, sixth time...

You know how it happens.

I had probably counted more pennies than the total number of pennies on the table top, but some I had counted more than once and others not at all, so the total sum would be wrong. I had to do it properly. I took a deep breath and concentrated on the task before me. I was determined.

I counted them with a frown, with tightly-pressed lips.

But when I was halfway done I noticed something peculiar out of the corner of my eye. The notes on the floor were rustling. There was no draught inside the house, the windows were tightly shut. Yet they were moving and emerging from the burst envelope, undulating like freshwater eels.

I stopped counting and they went quiet. I started again.

They began moving again.

It was most strange!

I was curious about what might happen if I kept counting, so that's what I did, and the notes, mainly twenty pound and ten pound notes with a few fivers mixed in, now began to wriggle more skilfully, with confidence and purpose. It was as if they were learning how to ambulate across my floor.

I watched them furtively as they left the room through the open door. My instinct was to forget about the pennies and run after them. I was in absolutely no position to lose that much cash, but I also knew that they couldn't escape the house. So I relaxed somewhat and I kept counting and the experiment proceeded, because that's what it had become, a clever scientific experiment.

Hadn't it? Sure it had.

Then I cursed, because I had lost my count again and had to start all over from the beginning. One, two, three, four...

As I counted, I was aware that some of the notes had returned to the room but they were folded in an unusual way. They were twisted around one end and it seemed they were clutching objects that at first I was unable to discern properly. But I soon had a chance to see for myself what they were.

The table I was sitting at was quite a low one, but there were suitcases piled around it in such a way that they formed steps to the top. The reason for this is that I live alone and I'm an untidy and chaotic person. I often put things not where they are supposed to go. The notes began to climb the steps.

I watched them but didn't stop counting because it was my counting that powered them. I was counting the pennies and the pounds were looking after themselves, just as my grandma had insisted they would. Exactly *how* they were looking after themselves wasn't known. Not yet, at any rate. Be patient.

That's what I told myself with a part of my mind while another part kept counting the pennies. I watched the notes unfold themselves and then they placed down on the table a few nuts and bolts and screws and items like that. They had clearly been into the storeroom at the back of the kitchen.

That's where I kept the bits of hardware I'd accumulated over the years. Half-dead batteries, copper wire, nails, broken corkscrews, pieces of metal that have no purpose I can recall, cogs and levers from old clocks, the usual junk that a man is supposed to possess for those occasions when something needs to be fixed. As I counted and kept watching, the other notes trooped in.

They climbed onto the table too and the first set of notes went off again to fetch a few more odds and ends. They were very busy and watching them was like watching ants, flattened valuable ants without legs. Then I realised that they were constructing something on the table in front of me.

Before long the shape of the notes changed. It seemed they had learned the art of origami all by themselves and now they were folded into little animals that ran, crept, lurched and hopped across the carpet.

As a result, the depositing of raw materials on the tabletop went faster and more smoothly and the construction of the machine also accelerated. I kept counting the pennies because otherwise all this activity would cease and I was eager to find out what the finished machine would be like.

But counting was a monotonous task or rather it was hypnotic, and I soon fell into a trance and this trance turned into a doze, and I nodded off, still mumbling numbers in my sleep, "One, two, three, four..."

Something cold touched my forehead and startled me awake.

It was one of the pennies.

My head had fallen forward and come to rest on the table top and the penny was now stuck in the middle of my brow like a third eye. I brushed it off impatiently, blinked, struggled to focus on my surroundings.

The machine was ready.

I saw at once what it was and what it was doing.

An automatic counting device!

It was counting the pennies. Counting them much faster and more adroitly than I had been able to do. I looked around but the notes had vanished. I got up and left the room with a sinking feeling in my guts.

The front door was open.

My money had escaped from the house.

"Oh Grandma!" I wailed. "Why did you ever put that idea about counting pennies into my mind?" Because it was clear that counting pennies is how pounds obtain the energy to move and be sentient.

And now the automatic counting machine was providing them with the necessary life force much more effectively than I had done with my manual counting. In fact it had saturated the notes with so much extra energy they had been able to unlock and open the front door without help.

What else were they capable of, I wondered?

Perhaps I ought to destroy the machine. But it occurred to me that if I did that my money would stop dead in its tracks wherever it happened to be. Then it would surely be picked up by some random passer-by and pocketed. If I left the machine on, there was a chance the notes would return to me.

It whirred and hummed and counted the scattered pennies.

And I went out for a walk.

Actually I had to go to the bank and inform them that I had lost my job and that I wanted to withdraw all my savings. It seemed to me that I could deposit my money in another bank with higher interest rates. I had to take every measure, however small, to get the maximum benefit from my remaining funds. A thrifty life in the near future was a given. I headed to the town centre.

The receptionist in the bank gave me a puzzled look.

"But you simply don't have any savings here," she told me, as she checked on her computer, "so I can't give you anything."

"How is that possible?"

"Your account stands at precisely zero."

"But I haven't made any withdrawals for weeks!"

She shook her head sadly. "The notes in your account just got up and walked out of the bank this morning. When I tried to stop them they folded themselves into origami cheetahs."

"The fastest land animal in the world!" I cried.

I had no choice but to leave the bank empty handed, my confidence deflated and my pockets collapsed flat against my trousers. Cheetahs, yes, and cheaters too! I went for a melancholy stroll around the park. I kept an eye open for the notes because they might have returned to the wild.

They might be hiding among the leaves, yes indeed.

But I saw only squirrels.

And birds. Neither of which I can spend.

After an hour or so, I went back home. I left the automatic counting machine on. It was my only link to my missing money. I realised that the faster the machine counts, the more energy the notes will have, so I took away all the coins but one.

It is very easy to count just one coin. That's a task that can be done extremely quickly. The counting machine doesn't need to stare too hard at the coins with its prehensile eye on a stalk, nor does it need to uncurl more than one finger from its counting hand.

Now the absent notes will be moving so rapidly and with such force they must be a blur that nobody can snatch. That's how I made them safe from opportunistic thieves.

I hope they will all come back to me, those mischievous notes, after they have enjoyed their fling.

I guess that if they do, some will be folded into origami men and others into expensive origami suits for them to wear and a few into fast origami cars they can drive recklessly.

This is what I am doing right now, sitting up late, waiting.

The penny-counting machine is relentless.

It counts the pennies.

One, one, one, one, one, one.

Somewhere the pounds are looking after themselves.

She was a fine woman.

But Grandma has a lot to answer for!

The Councillor's Visit

Beth Goddard

Karen was folding clothes when the doorbell rang. Jumpers, to be precise, in the methodical manner she'd been taught as a Saturday girl at M&S. Sleeves neatly tucked inside the two halves of the jumper as it was folded horizontally. She added the last jumper to the pile on the end of the bed before going downstairs.

She had hoped that whoever it was would have given up and left by the time she got there. But through the frosted glass she could see the outline of someone, waiting.

Whoever it was, she couldn't really be bothered talking. They didn't get friends turning up unannounced often, and their family lived over in Leeds – a safe distance. Karen couldn't face small talk with a neighbour. Or even worse, the prospect of having to ask someone she knew vaguely in for tea. She remembered a story she'd heard on a radio phone-in once, where a husband and wife opened the door to a total stranger. He'd claimed to know them both well and so they'd invited him in for a coffee, each presuming that the other recognised him. They'd sat him awkwardly in the living room, and after whispered discussions in the kitchen, they established neither of them knew him from Adam. On the phone-in it had transpired that a long time previously, after befriending the man on holiday, they'd extended an invite to visit – if he were ever in the area. And so he'd turned up. Years later. She had been horrified by the thought of it at the time. Had actually gasped at the radio. It had obviously stuck in her mind as she could remember the feeling of panic lodged in her throat as she had listened. She must have heard it a while ago now, though.

She sighed and opened the door. A man, who looked vaguely familiar, was standing there. Could he be an old holiday acquaintance as well, one she'd long forgotten? No, Karen, she told herself. This was the kind of madness that came from spending the day indoors by yourself. Putting two and two together to make five. Besides, they didn't make that sort of friend on holiday. She would never extend an invite like that to someone they barely knew. She doubted James would either. He was only slightly less antisocial than her.

God, maybe it was an old fling, like in that Helen Dunmore novel. What was it called again? She had a momentary feeling of panic and counted through a short list of exes in her head. No, this man was at least fifteen years older than her. Her love life had never been that adventurous, not even before she'd met James.

"Good morning. Can I help?" She tried to sound as breezy and normal as possible. She really ought to go and work in a cafe tomorrow or something. No more sitting at the dining table with her laptop. All this time at home was beginning to do things to her brain.

"Good morning, Mrs Smith," The man smiled. "I'm Malcolm Farrar. Your new councillor."

He knew her name then. And he'd said his name as if she should recognise it. She accepted the outstretched hand and shook it.

He had a solid, dependable handshake.

"Hello. How can I help?"

"Well," he looked hopeful. "I was wondering, is James in?"

"Ah, he isn't, I'm afraid."

A pause.

"Well, you might not be aware, but James joined us recently. It's party policy to welcome all new members into the fold as it were. I was hoping to chat to him about how he might be able to support our work in the area."

This was the worst of all imagined scenarios. Someone Karen would have to make small talk to, who she would have to speak to again. Someone she couldn't fob off.

Following the referendum six weeks ago, they'd both vowed to be more political. They'd felt so betrayed by the whole thing. In the first few days afterwards, they couldn't even walk past people in the street without guessing which way they had voted. James had even got into an argument with someone in the barbers when he'd overheard them crowing about the difference the referendum would make, "How we'd get our country back." Karen was barely speaking to her parents. They'd both decided they had to do something. It was people like them doing nothing that had got them into this mess in the first place. Karen had written angry letters to her MP and James, always more the community type, had joined the local branch of the Lib Dems.

She smiled and opened the door more widely. She was already

starting to feel guilty at how grudging she felt about speaking to him, even having opened the door.

"Well, if you don't mind waiting a minute or so, he'll be back shortly. You'd best come in."

"That's very kind of you."

He followed her in through the door and she noticed with some relief that he bent to take his shoes off in the porch. They were well worn but highly polished, a deep brown leather. She imagined you could probably see your face reflected in them if you looked close enough. What you would expect a man like Malcolm to wear.

"Just follow me this way."

She took him into the front room and gestured at the sofa.

"You can wait for him here."

Malcolm perched on the edge of the sofa, and pulled a small notebook from his blazer pocket. His clothes were as predictable as his shoes. A tweed jacket. A woollen jumper over a shirt and tie. All that he was missing were some elbow pads.

"Can I get you a drink while you wait?" She felt conscious that he could hear her, judging him. He looked so stiff-backed and uncomfortable and she wanted him to feel less awkward. How many of these visits did he have to make, she wondered? How many evenings did he spend trudging around town in those shoes?

"Oh, yes, a tea would be lovely, thank you."

"How do you take it?" She moved towards the doorway.

"Just a touch of milk please, and no sugar."

She backed out into the corridor and towards the kitchen, saying louder now, "Congratulations on your appointment by the way! You must be very pleased!"

She heard a muffled response and carried on filling the kettle, then wiped her hands on a tea towel and looked at the clock. She hoped James would be home soon.

She could still hear him talking. "Well, that is great," she shouted at what seemed an appropriate pause. She set up a tray with the teapot, a jug of milk and a plate with a couple of shortbread biscuits on. She wanted him to remember her as being kind. It was absurd really. She'd never met this man before and now it mattered that he thought she was hospitable when he turned up on her doorstep unannounced. Maybe James would be a councillor one day, though, and she'd have to go to dinners at the liberal club with Malcolm and all the rest. Christmas meals, fundraising, sending in gifts for the tombola at the summer fete.

Humming, she picked up the tray and walked in the hall. Malcolm had stopped talking and the door to the living room was now only ajar. She kicked it open with her slipper.

"Jesus Christ!" She dropped the tray and the teapot bounced once before smashing against the wall. It sprayed the carpet, rug, wall and side of the sofa with tea and spattered Karen's leg. She could feel the warmth and wetness of the tea spreading through the gauzy cotton of her trousers. Karen thought of a TV advert she'd seen once for washable paint. She'd probably need to buy some after this.

She sank to her knees in front of Malcolm. "What the fuck happened to you?" She was whimpering, gasping with fear now.

He was still perched on the edge of the sofa out of politeness. Still wearing the green jumper. The shirt and tie, the jacket. His feet still looked absurd in those threadbare socks. But now he did not move. His hand was raised in gesticulation, his mouth wide open. But he was still and unmoving. His skin had taken on a curious sheen. The patina he'd acquired made him look like one of those ill-advised pieces of public art; a statue sitting on benches in the middle of a shopping precinct. She bent over him and felt for a pulse. Nothing. Not a glimmer. What the fuck was she supposed to do now?

"Mr Farrar? Are you okay?" She touched his shoulder gently and was surprised by how cold it was. There was a faint murmur from his throat. She leant in closer.

"MR FARRAR?" What was it you were supposed to do? Chest compressions? She remembered something about using the same rhythm as Stayin' Alive, and started humming. An absurd vision of the Gibb brothers in flares popped into her mind. If she could just get him on the floor, or at least on his side on the sofa, she might be able to do something.

"Now I don't know if you can hear me, Mr Farrar, but I'm just going to move you sideways". She attempted to lever him downwards, putting her arm under his, which was still raised in the air. Despite a monumental effort, where she pushed against him with all of her weight and with her feet braced against the rug, he did not move even an inch. She tried a second time. How could such a slight man be so heavy? No matter how much she bent against him or yanked his arm towards her, she couldn't move him at all.

"Well, that's not going to work."

She sank back into the floor in front of him and stared. His face was glistening and something strange was happening to his eyes. Although still open, they looked more like well-worn marbles now, smooth and opaque. His pupils were fading and his irises were leaching colour into the whites around them. She frowned. What was that on his cheek? A smear of pale green. Like copper oxide.

You always wonder how you will react in this type of situation, she thought. Karen was now discovering how she would: By sitting in front of the fossilised figure on the sofa, paralysed by shock. Staring in disbelief whilst she sobbed.

In the distance she heard the door slamming.

"Hi sweetheart, how was your day?"

"James!" she said, and struggled to her feet.

James came into the living room. Karen heard the crunch of shards of teapot under the heel of his shoe.

"What on Earth…?" He dashed to the sofa. "Is that Malcolm, the councillor? What's he doing here? What happened?" He bent down in front of the man on the sofa and just as Karen had done, tried to shake his shoulder. "Malcolm? MALCOLM!" He felt for a pulse and shook his head. He crouched in front of Karen. "What the fuck has happened? He's – I mean what has happened to him?"

The tears had started in earnest now and all her words came at once. "He came to see you and I said he could come in and wait. Apparently they always come and visit new members. I suppose he wanted to check you out and see what you would do for them. All I did was go to make him a drink and then I came back in and he was –" She raised her hands and then shrugged, unable to find words to describe this part of the encounter. "Like this."

They stood and stared at him. To anyone looking in at the window, it must have seemed as though they were both listening intently to whatever Malcolm was saying. His arm still extended in gesticulation.

"Is this some kind of joke, Karen?" said James. "I know you're not finding things easy but –" He stopped, seeing the way Karen was looking at him. "I just don't understand what's happened!"

"This is what happened." She said in a more neutral tone now. "I left the room and when I came back," She hesitated. "When I came back, he'd turned into this. Like he's made of bronze."

"Look," James said. "He doesn't even look like – well he doesn't even look like he's ever been alive now."

James was right. Malcolm was no longer just statuesque. He *was* a statue. Karen touched him gently on the cheek. It was smooth and cool, soothing even. As she drew her hand away, she noticed a spot on the top of his head more golden and polished than the rest. As if people patted him on the head for luck as they passed.

James was regaining his composure. "Look, you sit down whilst we think about what to do. I'll make us some tea."

Karen perched on the sofa next to Malcolm. She looked at his open mouth. He looked as though he had been declaiming some important point about successfully revoking parking charges or securing funding to repair the pothole-ridden road on Market Street. Karen remembered standing in the kitchen and wishing him away whilst she heard him talk down the hallway. Was it her fault in some way? Rubbish, she thought. She didn't have magical powers. This wasn't a fairytale.

James came back in, carrying two mugs. "We'll have to keep him here for now while we think about what to do. I mean, if we go and tell someone… No one will believe us! But someone will report him lost at some point so we'll have to do something."

And so that was how it started. They sat on the sofa drinking their tea whilst shafts of afternoon sunlight lit the room. One caught the tip of Malcolm's outstretched finger in a spot of gold. He sat between them, feet pinioned to the ground like railway sleepers, whilst they thought about what to do.

For the first week or two it was strange. They thought about how to report it, how to explain the story without one of them being sectioned or arrested. Every idea they had sounded too ridiculous, too implausible. At first, Karen wouldn't go in the living room whilst she was working at home alone. One day James came home and got out a hammer and chisel from the shed. "I'm going to try moving him, at least." Karen had been making dinner in the kitchen. After half an hour of hammering, she had gone in the front room to find James sitting back on the floor, exhausted, surrounded by splinters of floorboard.

After a fortnight of working from home, she took to leaving the door ajar. She'd pop her head round the door on her way to the kitchen to check he was still there.

After a month or so they realised he had not been reported missing. James heard that Malcolm, who lived alone, had told another party member he was going abroad to see his daughter soon after his appointment.

They worried again about what to do, and James thought they could write a letter from Malcolm, resigning his duties, declaring that he wasn't coming back. That would be the end of it. But how could they get the right postmark? Best just not to get involved, they decided. Best just to keep their heads down and carry on as they were. Except now they had Malcolm, of course.

They got used to him in the end. They'd ask his opinion about politicians on TV, offer him a cup of tea when they were making a brew. At Christmas they'd wrap him in tinsel and fairy lights to try and cheer him up a bit.

They'd invited him in and now he sat, rooted to the floor in the middle of their living room. He'd never leave.

Yard Dog

Tade Thompson

I thought he was a Fed at first.

Okay, no, I didn't, but in hindsight I should have. The second time he turned up at Saucy Sue's, everybody noticed him on account of his height and his clothes which were righteous. I'm the only one who saw him arrive the night before. He was furtive, dressed in… I don't know what, man. He wore shoes and pants that even the Salvation Army would turn down. The height was there, but he was such a dark cat that, without the flash of jewellery, he faded into the background. I played percussion, that first night. Al played the horn, some shit he'd cribbed off watching Dizzie in St Louis. Saucy Sue's was a gangster's joint, but many of the jazz clubs were back then, and a Fed or two or an undercover cop wasn't out of the ordinary. He was a yard dog that first night, and every other night he came in, that's the name that stuck in my head, even before he started playing.

Al and I were filling-in. The usual percussion and horn guys were dope sick trying to kick a habit, and the manager, a cat called Layton, literally plucked us out of the crowd. That was the beginning of a six-month gig, sweet, and I cut my teeth for later in my career. Nothing like playing six nights a week to hone your discipline.

Yard Dog was at the back, watching, smoking some hand-rolled stuff that I thought had some reefer mixed-in, but when the cops stopped us one time and checked, it was only tobacco. But. It wasn't that simple. Motherfucker switched that shit, I'm sure, because I remember he blew the smoke in my face when I was talking shit one time. I saw things, but considering what happened later, a few hallucinations were nothing to make noise about. Yard Dog was like six-six if he was an inch. Broad shoulders, narrow hips, athletic looking, but stooped, bringing himself down to Earth, Al would say. First night, he didn't say nothing, just watched, smoked and left.

Second night, he was waiting when we packed up for the night, and he said, "That was real cool." He walked away before I could respond.

We had a singer then, called herself Shonda, voice would break an angel's heart. She took her sweet time watching him walk away. Difficult not to, I suppose. Yard Dog was visible, noticeable, even before he opened his mouth. Why, then, had nobody seen him on that first night? I think that was down to him, down to how much he wanted to be seen.

Sue's had audience nights every two weeks or so, usually when the band was fatigued or someone was sick or talking to their P.O. Those nights, Al and me would kick back with some drinks and listen to some hopped-up or drunk motherfuckers trying to hold a tune. Though we always refused, one or two of them always asked to try our instruments, and Al had to smack a persistent cat once. Al wasn't big like Yard Dog, but he was fierce, fast, and experienced. He'd been in plenty of fights, and loved to talk about either music or beating a person down. I remember a cat they used to call Captain, before our time, just got out of prison. Captain stole Al's reefer and sat on the stoop of the Patterson Hotel, smoking, all hotsy totsy. Al takes a mouthful of coffin varnish, walks up to Captain, spits the liquor in his face, kicks him in the bongos, *lights him on fire*, and only trillies because of a pounder who ran up. But fuck Captain, he was unhep.

On this night, some drunk guy was playing Armstrongs, but sadder than a map, depressing everyone. Sue's doesn't waste time with inferior entertainment. You could be high until you're touching God's toenails, nobody would care as long as you played well. But if you blew shit, your survival time was the five minutes it takes Benny to get from the door, through the crowd, to the stage. Open night is no excuse for bad jazz. So, shitty drunk guy was out and Yard was next. He went up there and put his lips to it. I can't tell you what he played because I don't remember, but I do know that the note was clear and high and piercing. Not a soul spoke. Not a soul *could* speak because whatever Yard played made everybody blow their wigs, man, bible.

I was unaware of any other person in that room. Yard himself disappeared and everything was that note, that sound, that fucking horn. I don't know how long it lasted, but when he stopped he was staring down at the floor. There was silence and I know I was crying. Shit, everyone in Saucy Sue's was crying: pimps, prostitutes, hustlers, every single one. It seemed it was silent for hours but it couldn't have been more than a minute or two, then people started clapping and whooping. Yard calmly picked up his instrument and walked off the stage. No other blower would go up there because how do you follow that? Understand, I'm not talking about skill here. Yard could beat it out, but what I'm talking about here is magic.

One other thing, something curious: all the drinks in the house went bitter that night. When people got their emotions together, they found themselves thirsty, and they drank. And spat everything out. There was nothing worth drinking or listening to. The drug fiends even said there was no dragon to chase. All intoxicants would not intoxicate. It was the damnedest thing.

I tell you, that night? Any woman or man would have dropped their drawers for him, but Yard left.

Next night, he's back, leaning against the wall, cool as ever. Better dressed, but his name stuck. He carried his horn everywhere.

Gossip blossomed like hopheads in a flophouse. Where did he live? Where was he from? Where did he train? He wasn't some tender motherfucker on leave from Julliard. Choir boy from church, maybe? Many jazz guys got their chops blowing Amazing Grace. What kind of horn was that anyway? One of those English Bessons? A Higham? The fire of speculation burned and would continue to burn until the next open night. Shonda took a fancy to him and preened to get his attention. It worked. You should know that Al and Shonda used to be a thing, and now they're... well, I don't know, I can't say not a thing, but they still have business.

Shonda did go on a date with Yard, but that was after Shed came along.

Shed wasn't his name. We called him that for reasons you'll understand in a minute. Never did catch what he called himself, and by the time we met him later, there was no need to call him anything but scary. Shed turns up during this godawful argument between Saucy's and the supplier about that booze that went bad. This was unnecessary because, for one thing, the booze was fine until Yard blew. Secondly, it wasn't just the liquor that went off. The water, the milk, the orange juice, anything you can chuck down your neck had been bitterified.

Unlike Yard, Shed was small. Not ugly, but plain. You never saw a person more uncomfortable in human skin. Shed moved like the Devil hisself was walking behind him, prodding him with a pitchfork: spurts of speed, then uncertain shuffling, then fast again, always looking surprised when he made a few steps. Speaking of skin, he was one of those brothers minted so dark, he seemed navy blue. He, at first, couldn't be heard over the shouts. Then, when noticed, his language seemed so garbled that they thought him a foreigner, which, I suppose, he was. Nobody saw him come in.

"Negro, what do you want?" Sue said. "Speak slowly and in English, fool,"

You need to know that Sue herself was a formidable woman, not to be fucked with. Not just that she was big, nearly six feet tall and with the attitude of a drill-sergeant. She had backing, if you know what I mean. There were shadowy people who owned the bar lined up behind her, folks who don't declare to the IRS, and who pounders and snatchers ignore because it's impossible to convict. This was not unusual, and you need to remember the times for what they were. This was when luminaries like Cab Calloway and Dizzy Gillespie got into a knife fight back in 1941. What I'm saying is, nobody was to be fucked with back then, not even refined motherfuckers like Earl Hines. You didn't start nothing, you didn't mess with anybody. Nobody worth listening to, anyway.

Shed just smiled into her face and spoke slowly. In English.

"Please, have you seen my brother, thank you?"

"What?"

Shed said it slower and louder. "Please. Have you. Seen my. BROTHER. Thank you."

"I don't know you or your brother. How did you get in, anyway? We're not open. Get the fuck out of here."

The way I heard it, Shed just smiled at her and went to use the john, but never came back out. Hours later when tempers had cooled somewhat, Sue got curious about him, had one of the men check the bathroom. They found his raggedy clothes, a trail of blood, strips of skin, meat and other fluids leading from the door to one of the stalls. Al said it was like he had shed his skin, which is how come we called him Shed. It wasn't till later that we figured he was looking for Yard. Over the next few days we didn't see Shed, but knew he was all over the place because people kept talking about this guy asking questions and finding crumpled clothes and any combination of skin and flesh, no bones. It was the weirdest thing, but it was a stunt of some kind, right? Like in '53 when those dumbasses shaved and dyed a rhesus monkey green, then blowtorched the asphalt, calling it an alien landing.

Yard was hanging out with us a lot, at rehearsals, whenever we were kicking back, or sometimes at Dizzy's house on Seventh Avenue in Harlem. He met Miles and Monk. Charlie Parker was usually too high to remember meeting him. One night Shonda finally convinces Yard to go yam with him at some fancy place. She was really insistent, and they left us. I noticed Al watching and I first thought he was jealous. I was worried he was going to attack Yard, but that's not what happened.

He said we had to go too. I'm not too proud of this part, but Al and I used to run together. We weren't making much money as musicians and we did take drugs. Pretty much everybody in the scene did back then. Al did some burglaries and I went along sometimes. Not trying to say he had to twist my arm, you understand. I wasn't willing, but not exactly unwilling either.

Al took us to Yard's place that night. Don't ask me how he found out where the guy lived, but he must have followed him. He said he was working with Shonda and we'd have to split the take. No lock can resist Al, and when we got in he went about the business of finding valuables. I saw the horn case. I'd like to say there was some magnetic pull or that the thing called to me, or something that would absolve me. Fact is, I was just curious. The case was unremarkable and opened easily. The horn itself gleamed. I could not tell who made it, and there was no brand, serial number or trademark anywhere. That was itself strange. Brass wasn't cheap, and all the good ones had serial numbers. Next thing I know, it's in my hands, and then... well, it's on my lips. I blew.

Later, Shonda told me at that very moment Yard looked up, alarmed, and stood to leave the restaurant without so much as a see-ya-later. Al said he dropped the cash he had scavenged and clasped his hands to his ears to shut the sound out. I didn't know any of this at the time 'cos I heard nothing, even thought it was broken. It wasn't. What happened is the room started to glow, orange, like a coal fire at first, then a hurricane of colour swirling around me, but detached from the origins. Blues, maroons, greens, swirling like ghosts. The walls, though still there, became immaterial, or invisible. Everything clear as one of those engineering drawings, leached of colour. I saw the night sky, and the clouds ignited with a yellow-red flame, and rolled back in all directions. The stars... most of them winked out in an instant, but dozens of them started falling to Earth. Then I heard a great wind blowing, and from far away, a voice.

In the blackness of that sky-which-was-no-longer-a-sky I sensed something stirring, something meant to be in slumber, something malevolent and implacable.

"Stop," said Yard, and I came to myself again.

Al was gone, and the building was on fire around me, hot wind howling past my ears, putting my heart in a ferment. Yard acted as if nothing was amiss. He took the horn, cleaned it, then placed it in the case. After he had sealed it, he turned to me, shook his head and offered a hand. I swear, with the building coming down around us, backdrafts and flashovers everywhere, nothing harmed us. He walked us calmly out of the building where Al was waiting with his hands wrapped up.

Later, he told me he tried to lift me, to get me out of the building, but I was hot. He said he got burned from touching me. Al is full of shit at the best of times, and he probably touched a banister, but so much crazy stuff was going on that I was willing to believe him.

About that time, Shed came doddering down the middle of the road. He left a trail of blood and shredded skin.

Yard's shoulders slumped when he saw Shed.

"Brother," he said.

"This... sound is not for listen on Earth, brother. Not for listen. You know this." Shed's words were still mangled, but we understood him. He turned to me. "Why this one's face glowed, please?"

"He blew the trumpet," said Yard. "It will be fine. It was for a short time only."

"Who are you people?" asked Al, a quaver in his voice that I ain't never heard out of him before right then.

Shed smirked.

Yard said, "We are two of the seven motherfuckers whose job it is to fuck this reality up when the time comes."

"But not time yet, and my brother, he knows it," said Shed.

"I wanted to play, that's all. No harm done." Yard seemed petulant, like the younger of the two.

Skin dropped off Shed, and the more he lost his covering, the clearer his speech became. "Yeah, I'm gonna disagree with that. I heard you all the way from home and I was sent to bring you and the trumpet back. You're not even supposed to have it." He came to me and touched my face. "You'll be all right. Get some sleep. And stop stealing shit."

With that, the flesh of his face slid off, revealing the bone underneath. His jaw fell along with the muscle, leaving his tongue lolling like a prick. He looked at Yard. "I can never do these human bodies as well as you do. Take off the vessel. Let's go home."

Al and I disagreed on what happened next, but I'm telling the story, so I'll give you my version. They fell into their clothes and shrivelled up. Yard, Shed and the horn, gone. We kicked their clothes into the fire, even though Yard had some fine threads. By the time the cops and the actual Feds turned up we were long gone.

That's almost the end of the story. This shit happened in 1944, maybe '45. You don't have to believe me. Shonda spent a lot of time searching for who or what they might be, got entangled with some tinfoil-wearing motherfuckers for a while. She said she had to know, like it was some itch in her brain that she had to scratch or something. I don't know about that. I do know that I have not been sick a day since I touched that horn, and I am now ninety-five. I still have all my own teeth and I've outlived two wives. I kicked the cocaine, made some minor waves in bebop and what came after. Al is still alive, and he was older than me to start with. I'd say we look about forty. Shonda is still alive. She and Al are still on again, off again, or makeups-to-breakups as I think the kids say these days. Nobody who was in Saucy Sue's the night Yard played died young. That trumpet did something to us all.

When I sleep, and I don't sleep much, but when I do, I dream of that thing out there beyond the sky, that thing stirring, waiting to wreak havoc. In some versions a taloned, scaled arm reaches out of the abyss and hands me a horn. I wake up screaming. Then I have to go outside and look at the stars and the moon or even just the clouds, night air on my face.

Then I am fine.

Dark Shells

Aliya Whiteley

There's a feeling amongst the villagers that I should stop talking to the river.
Rivers and voices have much in common. They rise and fall, swell
with energy, diminish to a trickle. They travel. They never stay still, even
when they seem caught in an endless repeating. Mum repeated herself
often, near her end, but every time the words were new to her. I realised,
after, that they had been new to me, too, bringing fresh emotion every
time although for different reasons.

And so on we travel through our lives, like water riding the land.

Water is water, she used to say, back when her eyes were light and I
was a young girl. I used to complain about having to take a bath after
her. Well, now I know that each piece of water is a drop. A drop of liquid,
or a lurch in the stomach. Jolting awake from falling far in a bad dream.

"Could you talk a little more about life during the war, instead?" says
the young man with a tape recorder.

"1940s?" I ask.

"Yes, around that time. It's 1988 now," he adds.

"I'm aware of what year it is, thank you."

He has the good grace to look ashamed.

"Nothing much changes over the years here, anyway." I gesture with
my hand around the large, shabby lounge of the home for the elderly
where the council saw fit to put me. The other residents are watching
television, or nodding to themselves. I'm certain I don't belong here. "I
just worked the land, along with my parents. Essential labour. I don't
even remember it much."

"Really?" He sounds disappointed.

"This is Lincolnshire, not London."

"There are a lot of airfields around here. Did you see any planes?"

He's quite a pleasant young man, really, and I like a bit of company.
I pretend to think, and then say, "Oh yes! There was that time when the
sky was filled with those big bombers. The noise of them, it was so loud,
I covered my ears with my hands. I remember now."

Next thing I'll be claiming I was up in the sky with them. Still, it does the trick, and he goes away satisfied, promising to return. I could tell him about the flooding next time. Five of my relatives have drowned, in the past. What a miserable way to go.

The river used to burst its banks. That's clear in my mind. The rain, spattering, and then the swelling, the speed of the flow, and the houses along its banks put out sandbags on their doorsteps. Ruskington is a large village, based entirely around the River Slea. It flows right through the centre, past the church, past the grocers, then the butchers, the bakery, that fish and chip shop that's too greasy for my tastes, the carpet shop Bill and I own – no, wait, that's closed down, and the little cafe, that's gone too. The village is in a bad state. So many shops are dark shells, now. Their grey, cobwebbed windows watch me; I can feel them at my back when I sit on the bench and feed the ducks.

But the bench is very cold today. I have an audience, as usual. A few villagers are gathered, staring at me with disapproval. How did I get here? I have no memory of leaving the house. Yet here I am, and soon the bread is gone and the ducks desert me, and it's obvious I'm talking to the river because a woman is coming out of her shop and saying, "Here again? Come on in the warm and I'll get you a tea while I phone the home."

"Hold on while I finish up," I tell her, and I speak my private thoughts in one long breath, murmuring, because the river hears me well enough at any volume. "All right, lovely, two sugars please, dear." I could walk home, but why bother when I could get tea and a lift? Besides, whenever I walk home across the fields my shoes get muddy and there's somebody else living in my house.

Tea is not what it used to be. Thick, brown tea: what happened to that? I used to start and end the day on it – tea as punctuation, my full stop to break up this long sentence that rolls on without pause, without meaning. I could drain a cup of such tea, but in the absence of that I sip the pleasant young man says, "Do you mind if we try something different?"

"Where did you come from?" I say. I was by the river. At least here, sitting in my comfortable chair, nobody is glowering at me.

He turns on his tape recorder; I watch how he does it, two fingers on the red button and the black button at the same time.

"What would you like to hear about this time?"

"Tell me a memory of feeling happy. In the village. A joyous occasion."

"Did you know," I say, relieved to find some facts still come to me, "that Ruskington is mentioned in the Domesday Book? It was called

Rischintone which means *farmstead where rushes grow*. The people then were short and they died young. They were an ugly bunch, too. My family were amongst the first here. We go all the way back."

"Well, I'm surprised you can remember that far," he says, and his cheeky grin is a shock. It moves me, I'm like a rusty old waterwheel trying to turn; it's the flirtation, of course, that's what it is. Dad used to say *a smile can work wonders* and he was right. He was not a clever man, but he said good things to me. I wish he could still talk.

"Dad's farmworkers had a party after each harvest," I say. To be smiled at, to be held in someone's warm eyes. "There was dancing. I'd had my hair cut short, had seen it in a magazine. And there was a new dressmaker in the village, moved here from down south, and she'd make these miniskirts if you had the money. I got her to make me a red one, and I thought I was very daring. But to get across the fields I had to put on wellies. Wellies, and a miniskirt! Music was pouring across the fields, the sound of the Twist bouncing over the empty troughs of dirt that had held the sugar beet. I had my other shoes in a bag; I couldn't wait to get there. The mud sucked at my boots the whole way."

"And you were happy?"

"We were all happy. It was a good way to live: the crops coming in, the demand for sugar was growing as more and more people got a sweet tooth, wanted cakes and biscuits and bags of sugar."

"So your family grew beet for sugar?"

"We did. Had done for generations. There was a factory at Bardney that bought up all we could grow. Then the factory went under." To go into what happened next is not so happy. Dad's face. His eyes, as I changed: dark shells. Losing the farm. Mum turning to drink, to drown out the disapproval of those silent villagers.

"And how was the party?" says the young man.

I'm not ready to tell him that. "Did you know a lot of the farmers don't use hedges around here to separate the fields? We use ditches, but you can't see them as you walk along; it looks like all the land is joined together, owned by nobody. Or by one great big all-knowing farmer, I should say."

"You're religious?" he asks me.

That's far too difficult a question to answer. "No more than the next person," I tell him, and we move on to the next topic, but his words sink into me. So I'm not surprised to find myself in the graveyard at All Saints Church, next to the bridge on the way out of the village, with a handful of bread stolen from the kitchen. I am a collection of these moments, now – these appearances in places with no interlinking journeys between them. My memory no longer flows. I am a series of drops.

There are no ducks in sight. I throw the crumbs anyway, and spend a while telling the river about my memories of All Saints. The day I wore white and the days I wore black. The water washes the words away, and my mum and dad are with me. At least they smile and do not stare.

This time it's the butcher who comes out and says, "Well, you should be an escapologist, shouldn't you? Come on."

"I don't know why you don't want me to talk to it," I say. "It can't tell anyone."

"Whispering to the water, are you?" he says.

Yes, that's it – water whispering. I see a painting in my mind, from that time Bill took me to London. We were just married, and we spent the morning in a gallery. Ophelia, with flowers, in the rushes, floating. Her river was nothing like the River Slea, or the ditch water. Both are heavy with mud from the fields; when you fall in there's not a speck of pale skin left in sight.

London was an experience. The Thames was a grand sight, and that's a different sort of river again. We walked along the South Bank, after seeing that picture. I was crying; I had told him everything. He said, "We can be happy. You must promise you'll try to be happy, that you'll forget about it, not waste any more time and words on it, it's just a thing, a problem with your mind, no more than that," and it was one of the very few times he named it, my unhappiness, and let it take up a moment of his time.

"I'll try," I told him, "but it's a part of me. Of my family."

"We could move away. There's nobody down here to see, is there? None of your relatives, living or dead."

But I said no. I couldn't leave them. And so I left my chance of happiness – our chance of happiness – behind.

Enough of happy. I'm sick of happy. The prison of it a weight on my lungs: the thing I should be aiming to feel, and make others feel. It's a relief when the pleasant young man asks me instead, "Can you remember a time in the village when you were sad?"

Is this a new session, or the same one? I don't know. The river has moved on. "You want all the stories, don't you?"

"It's for a local history project," he says.

216

"Oh yes, I remember. So what will you do with this tape of yours?" I lean forward and tap the recorder.

"It'll go into an archive along with all the other memories. There'll be an exhibition in Sleaford Museum."

So I'm just one of many. Just a drop in the ocean of old people, muttering on about tea and dances and the war and how things were so much better then. Let there be some truth amongst the flood of their thoughts. Let me speak it, here, although the meaning has moved on.

"It happened in the summer," I say. "The murder."

He is all attention. I see it in his face. "The murder?" he says.

"He was the travelling type, working the fields up and down the county, taking work where he could find it. The villagers had been warned against him. There had been some trouble, rumours that he…" I lower my voice, "he liked it rough, beg your pardon. Had hit a girl. These rumours don't just follow after people. They chase them, catch them up. But she wouldn't listen."

"What happened?"

"He didn't turn up for work, and she didn't come home, and people put two and two together and thought they'd run off, away. I went out across the fields, in my wellies, in my miniskirt, walking until I was right on top of the ditch. I found her there. Her lovely white skin, muddied. She was face up, floating in the water, flowers surrounding her. Her eyes were dark shells. She was so beautiful."

"She was…?"

"Marks on her throat, nearly as red as my skirt, from where he held her down."

"He held her down?" he repeats.

"You're like a record with a scratch, you," I tell him, annoyed. "That's what I said."

"Did the police look into it?"

I shrug. "I don't know. I only know about her. I saw her. It was the first time I saw one, you see."

"That's shocking. That's terrible." He is agog. I've given him what he wanted. "What was her name? The woman's name?"

"Anna. Anna Pigott."

He frowns at me. Then he reaches forward and turns off the tape recorder. "That's your name," he says.

"That's right. And it's my great-aunt's name, too. We've got a lot in

217

common. The gift of my family. She was my first, and so many others came after her, all frowning at me, all wanting me to see them, bear witness to them." I clap my hand over my mouth. I shouldn't say so much.

'Well,' he says. 'Well. Perhaps it's about time I was going. You must be tired."

Water can be clear and true and cold, or it can be muddied and thick and smelly. Sometimes, just like time, it can hardly move at all.

Later, just after Bill bought the carpet shop and both Mum and Dad had been put in the All Saints graveyard, he said, *Don't tell me about them, I don't want to hear it, to picture them around us still*, and I tried so hard to never mention how they stood beside me, how they smiled at me and watched me as I slept. I tried to never talk to them directly. Bill didn't like me going out to the ducks and giving my memories to the river instead. But it had to come out of me somehow, in words, in water.

He said, "We should not have children, Anna. We should end this thing, here." And I begged him, but he was strong. Stronger than me.

Bill was a good husband, though, all in all.

I'm sitting on the bench in the heart of the village. Here they are, standing before me, and their eyes are dark shells. With them I see my grandparents, and their parents, and more. So many of the Pigotts. And the first one who came to me – my Great-Aunt Anna, still muddied, still so sad. Soon I will become one of them, but there will be no new Pigotts with the gift to see me. Perhaps it will mean the end of the village. Perhaps the river will dry up for good. Or perhaps everything will simply trickle on, as it has for a thousand years before, while we Pigotts silently seethe on the banks of the Slea.

I feel so guilty. I'm not meant to open my mouth about them at all, not to anyone, not even to the river. That's what Bill said.

"I'm sorry," I tell him, lifting my chin to the cold white sky. How strange it is, talking to someone who is not there – to thin air. The villagers will think me touched. "I had to tell someone."

"Tell someone what?" says the woman from the bakery, disapproval dripping from her voice. She sighs, and says, "They just can't keep you still, can they?" She'll take me inside now, and give me a cup of tea. I hope she brews it for a little longer; you might say tea is always the same but I say it doesn't matter how often you drink a cup down. It's like the past. Each drop tastes a little different, every time.

Coruvorn

Reggie Oliver

It is three years ago now since Dennis Marchbanks became a god. Of course he did not know this immediately; the realisation came upon him slowly as such things do and he was decently reluctant to believe it in the beginning. Dennis would have been the first to admit that he is an unlikely god. Do I believe it? Well, that is unimportant; I must simply record what happened, as far as I can.

Dennis and I had been contemporaries at the same Oxford college. We had both read classical 'Mods and Greats', and belonged to the same dining clubs and societies. Dennis was highly intelligent, but not very imaginative and, though conventional in most of his attitudes, he liked the company of unconventional and artistic people; hence, I suppose, our friendship.

I graduated from Oxford with a modest second and went into literary journalism while Dennis who had got a first in 'Greats' stayed on to take a law degree and studied for the bar. In time he became an eminent Q.C, dealing mainly with commercial cases, hence a rich one. We kept up with each other through college reunions and I would often see him at the first nights of plays when I became a drama critic. We occasionally dined together at Brummell's in St James' of which we were both members. I would not say that our friendship was really close, let alone intense, but it was of long standing and invariably cordial. We were able to share confidences from time to time, partly because our worlds did not impinge on each other's too much. Dennis was unmarried and, though he had met my wife once or twice, he had never visited my home.

One Friday night we happened to meet and have dinner at Brummell's. (My wife, incidentally, was away visiting relatives in Yorkshire for the weekend in case you are wondering if I had callously abandoned her for this still exclusively male preserve.) We ate together at the long table in the Coffee Room. There were several others dining at the table but they were down at the far end, so we could be fairly sure of not being overheard or interrupted. Dennis was not quite his usual genial self and I asked him what was the matter.

He told me that he had just lost a case in the appeal court. He had been representing Centaur, the online retailers, whom their employees on zero hours contracts were suing for better rights and conditions. Centaur and therefore Dennis had lost both in the High Court and on appeal. Representing the workers on both occasions was Dame Maggie Standish Q.C, the well-known human rights lawyer and campaigner.

"No, Jack, it's not what you think," said Dennis, taking note of my raised eyebrow. "It was not being bested by a woman or anything like that that irks. As a matter of fact, I think she probably had the better case. Their Lordships certainly thought so. It was the way she treated me. She obviously saw me just as some sort of boss's lackey, a – what is the term they use? – a 'lickspittle'? But, dammit everyone needs legal representation, even criminals, even bosses. It's a human right, after all."

"No doubt Centaur paid you well."

"Well, yes. If you want the best you have to pay for it. But that's not the point. There is such a thing as professional courtesy, professional respect. As far as she was concerned, I was 'less than the dust beneath her chariot wheels'. I think she sees herself as some sort of champion of virtue and anyone who opposes her must therefore be contemptible." There was a pause. "But I am sure she is a genuinely good and highly principled person."

I smiled at his reluctant gesture of magnanimity and he, eventually, smiled back.

"Just unbelievably arrogant," he added in an undertone. We both laughed. Dennis was not without a capacity to see the funny side of himself. We moved on to more benign topics, and though he relaxed a little, I could tell there was still something on his mind.

After dinner Dennis asked me back for a drink at his apartment in Albany, that exclusive and discreet domain of the wealthy and well-connected off Piccadilly. The usual procedure at Brummell's was to have after dinner drinks in the little snug under the stairs at the club, so I sensed that Dennis was anxious to confide in absolute privacy. I just hoped it was not to be any more railing against Dame Maggie Standish Q.C.

We took a cab to The Albany. I would have been glad to walk, but Dennis was never an exerciser and thirty years or so of doing well for himself had expanded his figure considerably. He was, like me, in his mid fifties. He had a pleasant round face and thinning sandy hair and, if I had been asked about him at the time, I would have said he was the epitome of contented prosperity and success. He was, as he had put it to me once, 'not a man of strong urges where human relationships are concerned', so bachelorhood suited him.

We were silent in the cab, and, when we arrived at Albany, barely a word was spoken until we had seated ourselves with a large brandy apiece in armchairs on either side of the fireplace in his drawing room. Coming to Dennis's Albany 'set' was like stepping back in time a hundred years or more. The lighting was subdued, the furniture antique but comfortable. Georgian silver gleamed on the sideboard and a faint lustre of gold emanated from the tooled backs of Dennis's antiquarian book collection. An illuminated glass-fronted cabinet glowed with a small but impeccable collection of *famille verte* porcelain. Family portraits hung on the walls, a couple dating back to the 18th century, and one to the 17th. The atmosphere was steeped in wealthy, cultured bachelordom.

"Do you dream a lot, Jack?" asked Dennis when we were settled and had taken our first sip. I was a little taken aback: it was not a familiar conversational gambit of his.

"Yes. No more than most, I suppose."

"I hardly do at all. Or if I do, I remember practically nothing of my dreams when I wake up. At least, I used not to. It all changed a couple of weeks ago. But then, I am not at all sure if it's a dream I am talking about."

He then began to tell me his story. One night, he had returned to the Albany rather later than usual, having attended one of those legal banquets in Lincoln's Inn. He had given a speech – "rather a good one, though I say so myself" – and was feeling exhausted from his efforts. He could barely remember undressing and getting into bed, but once in bed he fell into a deep state of unconsciousness of this world.

"I found myself in what I can only describe as *another* world. I was walking on a hillside towards evening. The sun was setting and I carried a long staff and wore a blue hooded cloak. The landscape was clothed in peace and the colours were deep umbers and greens and azures, such as you see in a landscape by Claude or Poussin. You may think this all sounds very dreamlike, but it wasn't. It was as vivid as you and I in this room now, if anything more vivid, and, unlike a dream world, it was utterly solid and consistent.

"One thing that appears in retrospect most curious, though not at the time, was that I seemed to see myself standing on that hillside and yet be inside the person on the hill simultaneously. It could be compared to being in a TV studio and being aware of yourself on a TV monitor at the same time, except that I *was* the monitor if you see what I mean. There was no effort involved in this double perception, no sense of a 'divided self': quite the contrary."

The image of himself that he saw was different to the one he presented to me. He saw not a plump, middle aged lawyer but a tall gaunt figure in a long blue cloak with a hood, carrying a staff. He was shod in boots of soft leather and underneath his cloak he wore a closely fitting tunic of dark violet velvet. As he walked, the earth seemed to give way slightly under his feet. "It was like," he said, "walking on water, though naturally that is something I have never actually done, but it's how I imagine walking on water to feel like."

Dennis's descriptions of his experiences were full of these precise and pedantic qualifications. At times it was like listening to Henry James at his most delicate and tentative, so I shall continue in third person précis.

The sun was sinking, salmon pink, below the horizon, as he walked down the hill towards a cottage from whose roof came an aromatic plume of grey blue smoke. The feelings he had were those of immense calm coupled with that of purpose, though to what end? That he could not say, though he tried to at considerable length.

The cottage, perched on the hillside, was surrounded by a small garden fenced and gated. Dennis opened the gate and went up to the door on which he knocked with his staff. He noted that the lintel was only just high enough to let him in without his having to bow his head.

The door was opened by a pleasant-looking elderly woman in a brown, homespun dress who welcomed him into a low whitewashed room. Beside an open fire sat an old man, white haired but still hale. When he saw Dennis, he rose, greeted him and told him that he was most welcome under his roof.

Dennis tried to convey to me the extraordinary gratification he felt on being received so courteously. His whole being was suffused with benevolence towards this elderly couple and with this goodwill came a sense of power. The old couple – they were husband and wife – asked him to share their simple meal. Dennis told me that he had rarely tasted anything so austerely delicious. It almost persuaded him to eat less elaborately in future, to order only one plain dish at Brummell's, even to try his hand at cooking for himself occasionally. I took these raptures on the simple life with the scepticism that they perhaps deserved, but he was on fire with enthusiasm when he spoke.

One incident of interest and importance occurred at the end of his stay with these good people. They had finished the meal and the woman of the house was offering to make up a bed for him. Dennis politely refused their kind offer. He told me that he felt not tired in the least. A kind of calm energy was passing through him.

As he was explaining his need to set forth again and his gratitude for their kindness, he noticed a small niche in the wall beside the fireplace. It would appear to be some sort of shrine. In it was a lighted candle and a small figure of a cloaked man bearing a staff, carved in wood. It had been carefully painted in muted bluish colours. The image struck him as vaguely familiar.

"Who is this?" he asked.

"That is our God," said the woman, touching her forehead with her right index finger and bowing to the statuette. "It is Coruvorn, the Wanderer, Lord of the Hills."

At that moment, Dennis told me, he knew that he himself was Coruvorn, and that the image that they were worshipping was an image of himself. "It appeared at the time," he said, "the most natural thing in the world. It was only later and on reflection that the implications seemed rather problematic."

He turned towards the elderly couple, a golden light shone from him and they fell on their knees in adoration.

"This made me feel slightly awkward," Dennis told me, "because, while I seemed perfectly confident that I was – or rather *am* – a god, I was still conscious of being myself, that is Dennis Marchbanks. It's a complicated business. Since then, I have been subject to these visions almost every night. Time is different over there and weeks, months even seem to pass during the time that I am asleep in this world."

I asked him why he was confiding all this in me.

"I couldn't think of anyone else. You are the only person I know who might remotely understand. You are literary, after all: artistic, imaginative. You've even had a novel published."

"I gave you a copy, if you remember."

"Yes, I know. I actually read it. It's really not at all bad, in its way.

That's why I thought you might be sympathetic."

"To tell the truth, I don't know what to make of what you've told me."

"That's all right. As long as you don't dismiss it out of hand."

"'I am a man; I count nothing human alien to me.'"

"Nor nothing divine too, I hope!" He smiled rather complacently at this little joke.

"But isn't there some more 'professional' advice you could seek?"

"Not really. I wanted a lay person. Someone without an idealogical axe to grind; someone with no real metaphysical opinions of their own. As you know, I am a Catholic, so this is very disturbing for me. I can't exactly go to confession at the Oratory and tell Father O'Hare that I'm a sort of god. He'd be most offended. We've been friends for ages. I might even be excommunicated."

"Surely an exaggeration."

"Perhaps, but it would be very embarrassing for us both."

"Why not go and see a shrink?"

"Well, you know my views about psychiatrists." I didn't. Dennis had a habit of assuming you knew all about his habits and opinions, most of which, it must be admitted, were extremely predictable. "They'd say it was all due to a mother fixation, or being taken off the breast too early or nonsense like that. It's no such thing. I'm perfectly sane. It's just a – a phenomenon, I suppose. I am an eminent Q.C in this life and a god in another."

I don't think Dennis was a vain man but he was one of those people who, thanks to a trouble-free passage through public school to Oxford and beyond, had a calm and confident sense of his own worth and place in the world. A friend of mine once said of Dennis that he had in life 'to take the smooth with the smooth'. But everyone has their own particular struggles and difficulties which most of us don't appreciate, being preoccupied with our own. And I suppose you could regard being a god in another life as a peculiar problem: Dennis certainly did.

It was very late, but I asked Dennis to go on with his story.

Dennis, or rather Coruvorn, raised his hand in benediction and then pointed to the figurine in the shrine. It was turned on an instant from wood into gold except for the blue cloak was now of pure lapis lazuli. The ancient couple gazed at their new treasure in delighted astonishment. The next moment, Coruvorn was standing on the hillside in the moonlight. The moon was full and low, a pale peach colour. It was beginning to sink below a dun coloured belt of trees before Coruvorn stretched out his hand and raised it a few inches to see it better, then he let it fall into its original position. The Earth gave a little shudder, but otherwise there was no disturbance.

Coruvorn took to the air and floated over hills, forests and cities. He visited many homes, answered many prayers, righted many wrongs until he descended once more upon a hillside and stretched himself under a great oak.

"The next moment I was in Albany again in my own bed. My alarm was ringing and I was due for a conference in chambers in an hour. My experience hadn't exhausted me: in fact I felt thoroughly refreshed." He looked at his watch. "Good grief! It's two in the morning! You'd better come back tomorrow and I'll tell you the rest. It's a Saturday. Would you be free for lunch?"

During the course of that weekend Dennis told me much more about his life as a God. Some of it was not that interesting in the way that other people's dreams are always less enthralling than your own. He seemed to spend his time wandering his world dispensing arbitrary and unsystematic benevolence and receiving homage in turn. Not everyone in his world believed in Coruvorn, but he seemed to bear no grudge against the unbelievers. If his acts of random kindness favoured those who acknowledged his existence that was only to be expected. I thought it was genuinely magnanimous of him that he expected no servitude towards him, nor even credence.

I asked him if he regarded himself as omnipotent in his world. Dennis pondered this, genuinely intrigued by my question.

"Well, I suppose in theory, yes," he said. "That business with the moon for example. But I don't exercise it. I want people to be free to worship me or not as the case may be. I must be adored by free spirits or there would be no point in being a god. The same, *mutatis mutandis*, I suppose applies to human relationships."

I agreed that this applied to human relationships as well.

"I see myself, I suppose, as a tutelary deity in the old classical sense. One who stands guard over his people and his planet."

"So you don't command a galaxy, or a universe?"

"Well, I don't think so. I may do, of course, but that understanding has not been vouchsafed me." I found his complacency rather irritating and was beginning to feel that it was my duty to puncture his illusion. Because that was what it was, make no mistake about it. At least, I suppose so. You must judge for yourselves.

I asked him for details of his planet and its people. Did they all speak the same language? Were they all of the same race? In what state of technological and political development did they exist? Were their animals and plants similar to ours? In this way I was hoping to convince him, and myself, that the world over which he presided was simply the product of his rather infertile imagination.

In a way, I was proved right. The world that he described could have been dreamt up by him. Its culture and state of technological development was a mixture of classical and medieval, its language was a version of Latin that Dennis was well equipped to understand. There were cities and city states and kings. There was no established religion, but in small shrines on hillsides or in homes, people paid homage to Coruvorn, the Wanderer, Lord of the Hills. Libations of wine were poured to him and small cakes, not dissimilar to the *madeleines* so beloved of Proust, were placed before his statue in the shrines.

The flora and fauna were similar to those in our world except that in his certain beasts existed which we regard as mythical. There were centaurs, hippogryphs and unicorns. There were also dragons, fire-breathing flying reptiles, but they were no bigger than ostriches and easily tamed.

The world of men and women on his planet was, according to him, peaceable and mercantile. The city states and petty kingdoms rarely had disputes, so there were no wars to speak of. If a crisis threatened between two powers Coruvorn always contrived to have it stopped before it went too far. There was no printing and though there were some books in manuscript, literature was mostly disseminated orally, consisting in long epics or shorter lyrical pieces sung to the accompaniment of an instrument resembling a lyre. The visual arts were on the whole decorative and abstract.

It all sounded very conventional and a little dull, just the sort of world that Dennis's rather staid imagination might have created. When I pointed this out to Dennis, he nodded as if he had considered this already.

"Yes, of course," he said, "I am quite aware that it might well be what you call an illusion, or is *delusion* the word you are looking for? But what exactly do you mean by delusion? If I were to say to you that I was a jar of marmalade, then you could quite easily say I was deluded. I am self-evidently not made of glass and filled with boiled-up Seville oranges; I am not an inanimate object. But when it comes to my experiences as Coruvorn, to which I have access mostly at night in some kind of trance-like state, you cannot either prove or disprove their reality. They might appear to *you* to be just a dream, but they are quite unlike any dream I have ever had. They seem to me to be real. Now of course it might be possible that I am suffering from an acute mental illness, but you must admit that I show no signs of it, other perhaps than my so-called 'delusion'. I don't drink to excess; I certainly don't take drugs or imbibe strange herbal concoctions. I am at the top of my profession. You see? You might just as well apply the C. S. Lewis argument to me. You remember... Jesus claimed to be the son of God. To do so one must either be a lunatic, a knave or the real thing. He was self-evidently not the first two; ergo he must have been the latter."

"There are flaws in that argument. In the first place –"

"But I am not really claiming to be a god; merely that I have experience of godhead."

"A distinction without a difference."

"Possibly. Possibly." He lapsed into deep thought and seemed to be no longer in need of my company, so I left him.

After that he would frequently phone me and tell me of his recent adventures as Coruvorn. I would occasionally take notes and once or twice recorded our conversations, even though what he had to say was not always very interesting. It was the concept that remained intriguing. I confess, I had thoughts of making my friend's strange aberration into a book or a series of articles.

According to Dennis, Coruvorn went about his business in his benign way, pardoning, resolving difficulties, often healing, generally looking after his planet. Dennis would occasionally ask my advice about whether he should intervene in some particular issue. I always told him that it was his decision: he was the god, after all, and ought to know better. On one occasion he contemplated resurrecting an infant girl from the dead for the sake of her distraught parents. After some discussion, we decided against it, but for what reason I forget. Then something of significance happened.

He rang me at six one morning. My wife to whom I had said nothing about Dennis, other than that he confided in me, expressed understandable irritation and went back to sleep. I went down stairs in a dressing gown and took the call in my study.

"What on Earth is all this about? Do you know what time it is?"

"Jack, I'm most terribly sorry about the early hour, but this is important. And time really has no absolute meaning where I have come from. I have just woken up, so to speak, or returned to this world might be a more accurate way of putting it, and I must tell you while it is still fresh in my mind."

Coruvorn had been, as was his wont, wandering the hills towards dusk. The sun was setting in its usual luxuriant way behind a belt of pale violet-coloured cloud into the gilded tops of an oak forest. A nightingale was singing in a nearby brake and a faithful rustic was turning his flock homewards towards lower and safer pastures. The god was surveying this gentle crepuscular scene with satisfaction when his eye caught a gleam of bright orange through the oak woods that crowned the hills.

Was it a fire? If it was, Coruvorn must hasten to contain it or warn his people in a dream to come and put it out. In an instant he had lifted himself above the trees in the guise of an eagle and was winging his way over the tree tops towards the blaze.

He alighted on the topmost branch of a great elm tree at the edge of a large clearing, roughly oval in shape. Almost in the centre was a great bonfire of felled logs and around it was grouped a large number of men and women standing very still and solemn. In front of the fire at one apex of the oval was a raised wooden platform upon which stood about a dozen women dressed in long white robes. One of the women, older than the rest, appeared to be their leader. She stood in the middle holding a banner which fluttered in the ripples of heat emanating from the fire. On it in silver thread was embroidered the figure of a winged woman holding a sword.

Coruvorn flew down from the branches and assumed the shape of an old man on the edge of the crowd. The white women on the platform began to sing and the congregation was enraptured.

"The words," said Dennis, "as far as I can remember went like this –" And he sang, somewhat tunelessly:

Hail, Thora, our Lady of Wind!
Harbinger of Change, bringer of Purity!
Blow through our hearts, cleanse us with your breath!

"The music sounded to me a little like one of those Soviet anthems that Shostakovich and Prokofiev were forced to produce, but I can't really put my finger on it."

While this chorus was being repeated countless times, according to Dennis, first by the ladies in white then by the congregation, Coruvorn moved among them, picking up their thoughts and murmured conversations. This was a new cult, apparently, that had sprung up and the people were worshipping a deity called Thora, Goddess of Wind.

"Thora, Goddess of Wind –?" I interjected. "Are you sure about this?"

"Yes, of course I'm sure –!" said Dennis irritably. "I was there, wasn't I? So there was another god being worshipped apart from me. It was rather strange that I wasn't aware of it until now, and really I wouldn't have minded... After all, I suppose, two gods are better than one. (Three even better, if you count the Trinity which you shouldn't really.) The trouble was, the chief priestess was requiring exclusive adulation for Thora. Thou shalt have no gods other than Thora, that sort of thing. And I found that her devotees were actually going round and destroying my shrines. Well, naturally this sort of thing has to stop, but I can't use force. Violence is simply not in my nature; besides I felt my powers subtly weakening. I still had plenty of devotees but they began to live in fear of these Thora fanatics who were taking over whole towns and cities, setting up their own political institutions and demanding exclusive allegiance to Thora. Severe penalties were being exacted from those who refused to comply. My faith went underground. I wanted, of course, to get in touch with this Thora but she proves elusive. Sometimes, standing on a hilltop, I felt her pass by in a gust of wind that nearly pushed me off my feet. I tried to stay her and speak to her but she ignored me. She must have known I was there but she would not stop. I am perfectly prepared to come to some sort of amicable arrangement with this goddess, but I am being swept aside. What am I to do?"

Never having faced a remotely comparable situation myself I was unable to help. When I tried to make a joke of it and told him that I was sure 'it would all blow over', he slammed down the phone.

I didn't hear from Dennis for almost a fortnight, and I must admit I was rather relieved. I had begun to feel responsible for him. Should I alert some authority – the Bar Council? The Law Society? – that one of their most distinguished QCs was off his head? If Dennis had severed all communication, then it was someone else's problem.

Not wishing to burden her too much I had given my wife Jane a heavily expurgated version of the facts, merely telling her that he was subject to some 'strange delusions' and unburdening them on me. Jane suggested I had nothing more to do with him. I sighed as a friend, I obeyed as a husband.

Then he rang again, at three o'clock one morning. Jane advised me to tell him to go to hell. I said I would do my best though I am not a great believer in hell and took the call in the study. Dennis was in a state of high excitement and spoke as if there had been no hiatus at all since our last conversation.

"Jack, I know who she is!"

"Who?"

"Thora, of course."

"Yes. You told me, the Goddess of Wind or something."

"No, no no! Don't be an idiot. I know who she is in *this* world. Just as Coruvorn has an identity here, namely me, so does Thora. You're not going to believe this."

"As you have strained my credulity to breaking point already, I don't think I am going to be that surprised."

"It's Dame Maggie Standish! You know, the Human Rights lawyer."

"Good grief! Really? How can you possibly know?"

"I just do. It would take too long to explain in detail. Suffice it to say that there exist things called astral corridors which link different worlds in space —"

"You mean like... black holes?"

"Yes, something like that. Please don't interrupt. Well, once on my planet I managed to catch sight of her goddess form as she streaked across the sky. Incidentally, the weather there has taken a marked turn for the worse since her arrival on the scene. Well, at once I set off in pursuit, hoping to have a conversation with her of some sort. She fled from me down an astral corridor but I was close behind. We travelled light years in a few Earthly seconds and several times I nearly caught her. The next moment I was standing, still in my divine form as Coruvorn, in a strange bedroom. I was just in time to see the faint silvery form of Thora fly through the open mouth of a sleeping female in the bed. There was enough light for me to see that the female in question was Dame Maggie Standish. The next moment I was in my own bed in Albany."

"I see."

"Well, now I know, I can do something about it."

"What do you propose?"

"I shall just have to confront Dame Maggie with what I know and then we can have a reasonable discussion about it all. One just hopes she will prove to be amenable."

"I'm not sure that's a good idea, Dennis. She could be tricky."

"Oh, I'm aware that this is not going to be easy. Maggie of course is a big cheese in the Labour Party and I, as you know, am a lifelong Conservative." I did not know, as a matter of fact, but I might have guessed. Coming as he did from an old Catholic family, his ancestors had probably been Tories since the days of the Old Pretender. "As you are aware, she almost certainly disapproves of me. You know how priggish and censorious these Socialists can be."

"All political zealots of any persuasion are prigs."

"Exactly. That's the problem. She's a zealot. I'm not and never have been."

"But what if she just says 'you're mad', and tells you to go to hell?"

"I can only hope that she has enough personal integrity not to do so."

"But what if –? What if you are simply mistaken about this whole business?"

"Jack, we have been into this. I know it's hard to believe, but I am not mistaken. I simply am not." The tone of his voice was, I have to admit, level and sane. He told me that he would be encountering her 'in the flesh', so to speak at a Law Society banquet in two days' time, and would 'beard her' there. I once again advised caution and rang off. There was nothing more I could do.

My next news of Dennis came via a short piece in the *Daily Telegraph*. Dame Maggie Standish had accused Dennis of sexual harassment and stalking and he was about to appear in court and probably 'bound over to keep the peace'. He was being investigated and in disgrace. I couldn't imagine what his state of mind was like but I felt guilty about him even though Jane insisted that I had done all I could.

I rang the Albany and was told that Dennis was recuperating at a private sanatorium in Kent called The Cloisters. The man who answered the telephone, an Albany concierge, also told me that I was one of the few people to whom he had been allowed to give this information. The very next day I drove over to The Cloisters.

It was a fine June day. If Dennis needed a refuge from his difficulties, he could have done worse than The Cloisters. Though the building itself, a red brick Edwardian sprawl attached to some monastic ruins – hence the name – was not very impressive, the grounds were extensive and serene. Smooth lawns fringed with deciduous woodland and views of the Kentish Weald beyond might have been vaguely reminiscent of his planet. A nurse showed me to the back lawn where I found him seated on a bench with a plaid rug over his knees contemplating the scenery.

I had expected to find a distraught wreck of a man, for Dennis's reversal of fortune had been dramatic, but it was not like that. Dennis had lost weight dramatically and he had a haggard look, but he was not in any obvious distress. He greeted me with warmth and said he was pleased to see me.

"How are you?" I asked lamely.

"Dying," he said cheerfully. "Inoperable cancer. I've had it for some time, apparently, but it's only just been diagnosed. And, no, that does not explain anything at all. The brain has not been infected."

"But you admit that you shouldn't have gone after Dame Maggie in that way?"

"Not at all. I have exposed her for what she is: a ruthless dissembler and a fraud."

"So you accused her to her face of being Thora, Goddess of Wind."

"It was not an accusation, more an assertion."

"Which she vigorously denied, no doubt."

"Not exactly. She told me I was off my head and should see a doctor."

"So why didn't you leave it at that? Why did you persist in harassing and stalking her?"

"Because I couldn't stop there. I had obviously rattled her. I was sure I could break down her defences and make her see sense."

"But you didn't. And now you are facing a trial and complete humiliation. I'm sorry; you're ill and I shouldn't be talking to you like this."

"That's quite all right. I know you mean well. As a matter of fact, this case will never go to court. I will either be dead or too sick to plead long before it comes to trial. I am going, as the Bible says, 'to my long home'. I shall be resurrected as Coruvorn, in my own world."

"And what about Dame Maggie?"

"I have exposed her. I have got her on the run. Mind you, I will have to rethink the whole of my religious position. I can't be quite as easy going as I was." To use an incorrigibly vulgar expression, from now on it has to be: *No longer Mr Nice God.*"

He seemed positively serene. Our conversation drifted pleasantly into other topics and though he responded amiably and intelligently I could tell that his mind was not fully on them. The things of this world were no longer his concern. I was relieved of guilt.

One morning, barely a week after that conversation, a doctor rang me from The Cloisters to tell me that Dennis had died in the night. She said it had been very sudden and unexpected, but it was more of a surprise to her than to me.

As it happened, that evening, in my capacity as literary editor of *The New Observer*, I was due to attend the launch party in the House of Commons for a book by Dame Maggie Standish entitled *Human Rights and Human Wrongs – the Future*. It sounded like one of those books which is destined to be more talked and written about than read; 'an important contribution to the debate' no doubt, but probably not a page turner. I had been debating whether to go but Dennis's death decided me.

I had not encountered Dame Maggie in the flesh before, though I had seen her countless times on television. I was impressed. The fluent and passionate address she gave before signing copies of her book received enthusiastic applause. It was some time before I could get to talk to her, but I managed it eventually.

She was a tall handsome woman and exuded a personality that was certainly forceful but not unattractive. I had been prepared to dislike her, for my friend's sake, but I could not do so. She had a way of fixing her full attention and considerable charm on whomever she was with. It may have been developed for professional purposes but it had a natural origin. I told her that I represented *The New Observer*, a journal for which she expressed courteous enthusiasm. When I casually mentioned my name I saw a slight bewilderment come into her eyes.

"You know Dennis Marchbanks, don't you?"

"How do you know?"

"He mentioned you to me once or twice in his ramblings to me. You're not going to ask me to drop my charges against him, are you?"

"No. There would be no point. He died last night."

"What! Good God! I didn't know that!" It seemed to me a slightly strange reaction.

"Why should you? I only just found out myself."

"Did he...? Was it suicide?"

"Cancer. He'd had it for some time."

"Ah..." She gave a sigh which I thought expressed relief but also a certain irritation.

"Well, that's very sad," she added in a flat voice. "If you'll excuse me –" and she left abruptly.

Two days later, Dame Maggie was standing outside the Royal Courts of Justice in the Strand talking to a film crew about her latest Human Rights case when a freak accident occurred. A sudden gust of wind blew up and must have dislodged one of the stone finials on the Gothic arches of the façade. It was a heavy piece of masonry and it fell some sixty feet onto Dame Maggie's head, killing her outright.

Dennis Marchbanks's memorial service at the Brompton Oratory under the direction of his confessor Father O'Hare, was a subdued business, but a surprising number of his colleagues were present. His recent aberrations went unmentioned in the eulogy. Death, both his and Dame Maggie's, would appear to have expunged those egregious embarrassments.

After the service, I approached Father O'Hare and asked if I could speak to him about Dennis. He invited me back for a cup of tea in his rooms at the Oratory, and it was to him that I first related all that Dennis had told me. To begin with, Father O'Hare seemed hurt that Dennis had confided in me rather than his true Father Confessor. When I told him that he had been fearful of offending an old friend, Father O'Hare softened a little.

"The poor foolish man!" he said. In the utterance of that phrase I caught for the first time a hint of O'Hare's Irish origins. "Did he think I hadn't heard things like that before? Did he really suppose I was so hidebound and censorious? In my time I've had to cope with much worse delusions from members of my flock. I had terrible trouble once with a young man who thought he was an egg. Well, you can imagine."

As it happens, I could not. "So you think it was just a delusion?"

"Oh, lord, yes! It was all a lot of nonsense." His tone was brisk, dismissive, almost irritable. "Mind you," added Father O'Hare after a long and thoughtful pause, "if one *must* have a god, one could do a lot worse than Dennis Marchbanks."

I was going to conclude there, but only last week I was informed that I had been left a small bequest in the will Dennis had made shortly before his death. I was touched. It consisted of several choice items from his antiquarian book collection, including a complete original set of *The Yellow Book*. There was one other item which was the reason why I had been informed so late, as there had been considerable difficulty in establishing its value for probate purposes. Several experts had been consulted and none could agree as to its date or origin.

Dennis had named it in the will simply as 'my gold and lapis lazuli figurine' and there was no mistaking it. It stands about six inches high, the figure of a tall gaunt man in solid gold holding a staff. He has on a cloak of brilliant deep blue, fashioned somehow out of pure lapis lazuli. The experts could agree only on one thing: it is a work of astonishing beauty.

Godziliad

Adam Roberts

Book 1
Godzilla's wrath, to Earth the direful spring
Of woes unnumber'd, heavenly goddess, sing!
What grudge could light the fierce atomic breath
That burnt so many citizens to death?
What move four mighty limbs to crush and tear
Whole city blocks and scatter them to air?
Vast anger that found voice and fuelled the roar
Of this whale-monkey-kind-of-ichthyosaur
Declare, O Muse! what woke such monstrous foe
And summon'd him from ocean bed below;
What stirred him from millennial slumbers deep
To swap-out slaughter for abyssal sleep?
What made this slug-a-seabed rise as killer?
Gods of ill, why made ye him, gods, iller?

The seagirt freighter *Eiko-maru*, bound
For Odo Island, stagger'd and was drowned;
Another ship – the *Bingo-maru* – sent
To search and save, like suffer'd sea-descent.
In vain the fisherman his reel-line wets;
The catch absents itself from trawling nets.
Come journalists upon the anxious scene
And peer with fear upon the glassy green.
Godzilla's name is muttered on the street;
In bars and homes *Godzilla* folk repeat.
A ritual dance t'appease the monstrous foe
Is staged upon the strand – strange fandango.
Grim whispers pass from ear to ear: years past,
Young girls were sacrificed to beast's repast.
No sacrifice averts the creature now:
Monstrous it comes, and monstrous is its *tāo*.

Adam Roberts

As storm-winds wrap the islands, an attack
Wrecks homes, kills livestock: all is maniac:
And having sent nine people to their graves
The beast sinks back again below the waves.

What first provoked this horror to arise,
To leave its depths and batten on the skies?
Say, Muse, what wickedness might cause such grief?
And thus mutate the creatures of the reef?
Atomic testing is the culprit here:
Atomic bombs pollute the atmosphere
Still through the waters sink particulate
Atomic poisons to divert our fate.
Man's bombs explode, and loud their fiery roar
Re-echoes and re-echoes shore to shore.
Far in the deep recesses of the main,
Where aged Ocean holds his watery reign,
The god-*kujira* hears. The waves divide;
And like a hill it heaves above the tide;
Beholds humanity on naked lands,
And thus the anger of its soul expands:

"Unkind mankind," the monster cries; "oh ye
"Un-sapient homos that abuse the sea,
"A cannon shell upon your bullet train
"I come, t'derail and hurl it in the main!
"To heap the shores with copious death, and bring
"Disaster dark from Tokio to Beijing.
"Let fall upon Japan's aye rising head
"The bloody-red dominion of the dead,
"Know now regret that e'er ye durst disgrace
"The boldest monster of the Ocean race."

Thus raging still, and moving his huge weight
Came stern Godzilla stedfast in his hate;
Nor mix'd with mercy, nor in council join'd;
For wasting wrath lay heavy on his mind:
In his black thoughts revenge and slaughter roll,

238

And scenes of blood rise dreadful in his soul.
He wades the breakers, breaking ships apace
And seventeen are sunk without a trace.

From Tokio comes Kyohei Yamane
To plumb this monstrous puzzle of the sea.
Great footprints, trilobites of greater size
Astonish his trained scientific eyes,
And all his scurrying activity
Points to but one cause: *radioactivity.*
To Tokio he returns with warnings dire
Of monsters bred in Science's quagmire:
But tis too late! *Godzilla*'s on the scene!
And looking lizard-tough and lizard-mean!
Full fifty metres tall, this vasty brute
Too huge to be a man-in-costume-suit:
Sublime in giant stature heel to nape
He stamps to shards the toylike urbanscape.

Man strives in vain to slay what God enlarges
Aye pooping out explosion-primed depth-charges.
Such ordnance monsters laugh to very scorn;
They cannot harm a beast of H-bombs born.
Mere gravel off his scaly skin they bounce
And panicked men *Gojira* mispronounce.
Yamane's daughter, Emiko, breaks off
Her old engagement to her former love,
Poor Serizawa, close but no cigar
Compared with her new love, young Ogata.

Japan's Protectors build a mighty fence
Of 30-metre heighth, and pass intense
Electric charge along its wires and bolts:
Full fifty thousand terrifying volts!
But to the beast this fence no stronger stood
Than gossamer or drifting cobwebs would.

"Japan, submit; nor dare my will withstand!

"But dread the power of this avenging hand:
"Th'united strength of all the Japanee
"In vain resists th'omnipotence of Me!"
The thunderer spoke, nor durst Japan reply;
A reverent horror silenced all the sky.
The city wrecked, with grief Emiko saw
Her motherland undone, the gods in awe;
The wretched quarrels of *Old Nature*'s state
And politicians lost in blank debate:
Let senior soldiers senseless strife employ,
T'attack the Ocean's Unit, th'Absolute Boy
Their pilots have their orders and comply,
And jet planes break the silence of the sky:
Roused to rage, they loose their missile load,
Launch the red lightning at the *Zilla's* god.
But all in vain the high explosive burns
The monster's skin each empty shell returns.
The army's rifles blaze like stutt'ring torches
But blithe Godzilla's atom breath still scorches.
Attempts to kill the beast with tanks all tank;
Soon Tokio's o'erdrawn at its *blood bank*.
The Wakō Clocktower, the National Diet
And Kachidoki Bridge fall to his riot.
Large loss of life, a city's heart destroyed:
Tis more than could be fixed by celluloid.

Emiko tells Ogata, spills the beans:
Of Ser'zawa's research and what it means.
An *Oxygen Destroyer* is her news
That works to break the O2 atoms loose,
Slays ocean life from whale to small crustacean
Consigning them to rot's asphyxiation.
They ship the Doom Device into the bay
To Serizawa's earnest heart's dismay:
Lest others copy his most dread design
He vows to sink down with it in the brine
End his own life in detonating death
Deprive Godzilla, and himself, of breath.

Close to the point where tidal swell turns round,
The chugging frigate hurries cross the sound.
Now *Zilla*, rising from the seas profound,
The *God* whose earthquakes rock the solid ground,
His shouts incessant leave Japan aghast,
And fire feeds fire from belching atom-blast.
While thus the monster mocks a world destroyed
The Oxygen Destroyer is deployed.
Amidst the tumult of this martial run,
Die Serizawa and the beast as one.
The man is lost, the seas his corpse en-grave
The monster sinks in death beneath the wave.

Loud then the grief for noble Serizawa!
And tears of sadness griméd faces scour.
Full of the pain that urged their burning breast,
The Tokio-ians themselves express'd.
Heart-piercing anguish struck th'assembled host,
But touch'd the breast of bold Emiko most
And those who rule the inviolable floods,
Whom mortals name the dread *Pacific gods*
Those beings whom the ciné future know
Add toil to toil, pile woe on up-piled woe:
As swift as wind, o'er Honshu's smoky isle,
The radioactive beams the skies defile
Through air, unseen, involved in darkness, glide,
To ev'ry chromosome and slip inside.
Fair Nippon trembles underneath the load;
Hush'd are her mountains, and her forests nod.
There on a fir, whose spiry branches rise
To join its summit to the neighbouring skies;
Dark in embowering shade, conceal'd from sight,
Sat Commerce like unto a bird of night.
"Ye think," quoth he, "*Godzilla* hath no equal?
"Prepare ye for *Godzilla 2: the Sequel.*"

Further Reading

Forty-one more interesting stories by British (or UK resident) authors, all first published in 2018:

- "Crooks Landing, By Scaffold" by G.V. Anderson (*Nightmare*)
- "The Lord's Prayer, From Memory" and "The King's Escape" by Jez Burrows (*Dictionary Stories*)
- "We All Know About Desire" by Regi Claire (*For Books' Sake*)
- "La Ténébreuse" by Storm Constantine (*The Alchemy Press Book of Horrors*)
- "The Giulia Effect" by Barbara Davies (*Making Monsters*)
- "Homebrew Wine Recipes for Favourable Effects, from the Regrettable Life of Mrs Poulman" by Matt Dovey (*Arsenika*)
- "Ain't That the Truth" by Bryn Fortey (*Compromising the Truth*)
- "The Species Assimilation Unit" by Mike Fox (*Cabinet of Heed*)
- "Sunflower seeds and supernatural beings" by Anita Goveas (*Willow Lit*)
- "The Thought Gatherers" by Victoria Haslam (*Mismatched Metacarpals*)
- "Counter Curse" by Cat Hellisen (*Learning How to Drown*)
- "A Little Star" by Verity Holloway (*Far Horizons*)
- "Ash" by Elizabeth Hopkinson (*Fairytalez*)
- "The Blitz of Din Barham" by Cameron Johnston (*Heroic Fantasy Quarterly*)
- "The Book of Mammon" by Michael Krawec (*Mismatched Metacarpals*)
- "Witness" by Kim Lakin-Smith (*Holding on by our Fingertips*)
- "The Hero of Aral Pass" by Mark Lawrence (*The Art of War*)
- "Channeling Aphrodite" by Rachel Lister (*Spelk*)
- "Ways to Wake" by Alison Littlewood (*Nightmare*)
- "Domestic Magic" by Kirsty Logan (*This Dreaming Isle*)
- "The Other Tiger" by Helen Marshall (*The Silent Garden*)
- "The Leonard Cohen Waltzing Society for Half-drunk Fuckwits" by Helen McClory (*Vol 1 Brooklyn*)

- "How the Mighty" by Daniel Micklethwaite (*Beneath Ceaseless Skies*)
- "How the Tree of Wishes Gained its Carapace of Plastic" by Jeannette Ng (*Not So Stories*)
- "How the Simurgh Won her Tail" by Ali Nouraei (*Not So Stories*)
- "Beyond the Border" by Benedict Patrick (*From the Shadows of the Owl Queen's Court*)
- "Meet the Family" by Charlotte Pratt (*EconoClash Review Vol 1*)
- "The Green-Hearted Girl" by Ella Risbridger (*Make More Noise*)
- "Blessed" by Geoff Ryman (*Fantasy & Science Fiction*)
- "Blocks" by George Sandison (*BFS Horizons*)
- "Small Town Stories" by Priya Sharma (*All The Fabulous Beasts*)
- "The Cocktail Party in Kensington Gets Out of Hand" by Robert Shearman (*This Dreaming Isle*)
- "The Vigil of Talos" by Huw Steer (*Making Monsters*)
- "Tales of the Immortals" by Steph Swainston (*Turning Point*)
- "Yiwu" by Lavie Tidhar (*Tor.com*)
- "The Pit King" by Ryan Vance (*F(r)iction Magazine*)
- "The Logicians" by James Warner (*Ninth Letter*)
- "Blood and Smoke, Vinegar and Ashes" by DP Watt (*The Silent Garden*)
- "The Palace of Force and Fire" by Ron Weighell (*The Silent Garden*)
- "Nox Una" by Marian Womack (*The Silent Garden*)
- "The Imprint of Leaves" by Elizabeth Xifaras (*The Cabinet of Heed*)

About the Contributors

RJ Barker is the author of The Wounded Kingdom trilogy, *Age, Blood* and *King of Assassins*, and his work has been shortlisted for The Kitschies Award, The David Gemmell Legend Awards, British Fantasy Society Best Newcomer and Best Novel and longlisted for *The Guardian*'s Not The Booker. RJ lives in Leeds with his wife, son, a bitey cat, far too many books, a lot of noisy music and some very particular home decor. You can contact RJ through his website http://www.RJBarker.com or find him messing about on twitter as @dedbutdrmng.

Malcolm Devlin's stories have appeared in *Interzone, Black Static* and *Shadows and Tall Trees* among others. His collection, *You Will Grow Into Them*, is published by Unsung Stories.

Born in India, **Harkiran Dhindsa** was raised in London and much of her fiction is set in this city. Her characters are often outsiders – out of kilter with the lives around them. Harkiran completed an MA with distinction in Creative Writing at City, University of London. Her stories have been shortlisted in the *Guardian* Short Story Competition and the Asham Award. Her unpublished novel was shortlisted in the SI Leeds Literary Prize and her writing then taken up for representation by Jonathan Clowes Literary Agency. "The Woman Who Turned to Soap" was first published in the debut edition of *The Good Journal* in 2018.

Jenni Fagan is an author, poet, screenwriter, essayist and a playwright. She has won awards from Arts Council England, Dewar Arts, and Scottish Screen, among others. She has twice been nominated for the Pushcart Prize, was shortlisted for the Dundee International Book Prize, the Desmond Elliott Prize and the James Tait Black Prize, and has recently written for BBC Radio 4, *The New York Times*, the *Independent*, and *Marie Claire*.

Lisa Fransson took seed in a forest in southern Sweden and was brought up on a diet of dark fairy tales and Norse mythology. As a teen she washed up on the shores of southern England where she now writes and breathes by the sea. Her short fiction has been published in *The Dark*

Mountain Project, The Dawntreader and *The Forgotten and The Fantastical 4*. She also has a children's picture book called *Älgpappan* that she wrote in her native Swedish. More information and contact details can be found on www.lisafransson.com.

Beth Goddard is a writer and former English teacher based in the North West of England. She has spent a lot of time talking about what makes good literature to students. Now she has more time for writing, Beth is discovering the difficulty of putting her advice into practice. As well as writing non-fiction articles specialising in education, she enjoys writing short stories and is currently working on her first novel.

Liam Hogan is a London based short story writer, the host of Liars' League, and a Ministry of Stories mentor. His story "Ana", appears in *Best of British Science Fiction 2016* (also from NewCon Press) and his twisted fantasy collection, *Happy Ending Not Guaranteed*, is published by Arachne Press. Http://happyendingnotguaranteed.blogspot.co.uk or tweet @LiamJHogan

Lizzie Hudson is a graduate of the English and Creative Writing programme at Goldsmiths, University of London and a member of the 2019 Northern Short Story Festival Academy. Her work has previously appeared in *Strix*, *Litro* and elsewhere.

Matthew Hughes writes fantasy and space opera, often in a Jack Vance mode. *Booklist* has called him Vance's "heir apparent." His short fiction has appeared in Asimov's, F&SF, Postscripts, Lightspeed, and Interzone, and bespoke anthologies including Songs of the Dying Earth, Rogues, Old Mars, and Old Venus, all edited by George R.R. Martin and Gardner Dozois. He has won the Arthur Ellis Award, and been shortlisted for the Aurora, Nebula, Philip K. Dick, Endeavour (twice), A.E. Van Vogt, and Derringer Awards. He is now self-publishing his backlist as ebooks and POD paperbacks. Learn more at http://www.matthewhughes.org

Rhys Hughes has lived in many countries. He currently shares his time between Britain and Kenya. His first book, *Worming the Harpy*, was published in 1995, and since that time he has published more than forty other books, eight hundred short stories and numerous articles, and his work has been translated into ten languages around the world. His fiction is generally fantastical, whimsical and inventive. His most recent book is *Mombasa Madrigal and Other African Escapades*. A lover of paradoxes, he incorporates them into his fiction as entertainingly as he can.

Kirsty Logan is the author of the novels *The Gloaming* and *The Gracekeepers*, short story collections *A Portable Shelter* and *The Rental Heart & Other Fairytales*, flash fiction chapbook *The Psychology of Animals Swallowed Alive*, and short memoir *The Old Asylum in the Woods at the Edge of the Town Where I Grew Up*. Her books won the Lambda Literary Award, Polari Prize, Saboteur Award, Scott Prize and Gavin Wallace Fellowship. Her work has been translated into Japanese and Spanish, recorded for radio and podcasts, exhibited in galleries and distributed from a vintage Wurlitzer cigarette machine. She lives in Glasgow with her wife.

Helen McClory's first story collection *On the Edges of Vision*, won the Saltire First Book of the Year 2015. Her second story collection, *Mayhem & Death*, was written for the lonely and published in March 2018. She also wrote *The Goldblum Variations*, a collection of microfictions on Jeff Goldblum. There is a moor and a cold sea in her heart.

Ian McDonald is an SF writer living in Northern Ireland, where the acronym SF has a rather different understanding. He lives just outside Belfast. His first niovel, *Desolation Road*, was published in 1988 and is still available as an ebook. His most recent publications are *Luna: Moon Rising*, the conclusion of the Luna trilogy (Gollancz, Tor) and the novella *Time Was*, from Tor.com.

Paul McQuade is a writer and translator originally from Glasgow, Scotland. He is the author of *Hometown Tales: Glasgow* (Orion, 2018), with Kirsty Logan, and the short story collection, *Between Tongues* (Cōnfingō, forthcoming). His work has been shortlisted for The White Review and Bridport Prizes and he is the recipient of Sceptre Prize for New Writing and the Austrian Cultural Forum Writing Prize.

Reggie Oliver is an actor, director, biographer, playwright, illustrator and award winning author of fiction. Published work includes six plays, three novels, and eight volumes of short stories, including *Mrs Midnight* (2011 winner of Children of the Night Award for best work of supernatural fiction). His stories have appeared in over seventy anthologies and three "selected" editions of his stories have been published: *Dramas from the Depths* (Centipede Press, 2010), *Shadow Plays* (Egaeus 2012), and *The Sea of Blood* (Dark Regions 2015). His most recent collection is *The Ballet of Dr. Caligari and Madder Mysteries* (Tartarus 2018/9), and *The Hauntings at Tankerton Park and How They Got Rid of Them* – a children's book with over 80 illustrations by the author. Recently his story "Flowers of the Sea" was included in the *Folio Book of Horror Stories* among such classic luminaries of the genre as Poe, Lovecraft and M. R. James.

Heather Parry is an Edinburgh-based writer and editor. She won the 2016 Bridge Award for an Emerging Writer and was awarded the Cove Park Emerging Writer Residency in 2017. Heather's work explores self-deception, transformation and identity. Her first novel is currently under consideration.

Ben Reynolds quit his job as a journalist in December 2016 to chase his creative writing dream and is working on his first novel, *The Last of Logan*, which is part grief memoir, part love letter to video games. "Mushroom Speed Boosts" is an adapted section from the book. His work has also appeared in @morestorgy and @EllipsisZine. He lives in Worcester Park in south-west London and has two children to feed, so also works as a freelance journalist and sub-editor.

Adam Roberts is Professor of 19th-century Literature and Culture at Royal Holloway University of London, and the author of eighteen novels, most recently the science fiction *By the Pricking of Her Thumb* (Gollancz 2018) and the historical fantasy, *The Black Prince* (Unbound 2018).

Priya Sharma's fiction has been published in various venues such as *Interzone, Black Static, Nightmare, The Dark* and *Tor*. She's been anthologised in many "Best ofs" from editors Ellen Datlow, Paula Guran, Jonathan Strahan, Steve Haynes and Johnny Mains. She's also been on many Locus' Recommended Reading Lists. *Fabulous Beasts* was a Shirley Jackson Award finalist and won a British Fantasy Award for Short Fiction. She is a Grand Judge for the Aeon Award, an annual writing competition run by *Albedo One*, Ireland's longest-running and foremost magazine of the Fantastic. Her collection *All the Fabulous Beasts* was released by Undertow Publications in 2018. Her website is www.priyasharmafiction.wordpress.com.

Steph Swainston started writing fiction at an early age for her own enlightenment and never quite stopped. Since 2004 she has written for other people's enjoyment too, and is author of the acclaimed 'Castle' series which includes the novels *The Year of Our War, No Present Like Time, The Modern World,* and *Fair Rebel.* She is currently recovering from breast cancer and is wondering where life will lead now. Hopefully it will involve more writing.

Tade Thompson lives and works in the South of England. He is the author of the *Rosewater* books, the *Molly Southbourne* books, and *Making Wolf,* as well as the short stories "The Apologists" and "Yard Dog", among others. He is a multiple winner of the Nommo Award, winner of the Kitchies' Golden Tentacle award, a John W. Campbell Award finalist, a Shirley Jackson Award finalist, a Theodore Sturgeon Award finalist, and a nominee for both the British Fantasy Award and the British Science Fiction Association Award. His background is in medicine, psychiatry and social anthropology. His hobbies include jazz, visual arts, martial arts, comics and pretending he will ever finish his TBR stack.

James Warner was born in Portsmouth and currently lives in San Francisco. His stories have appeared in *Interzone, ZYZZYVA, Ellery Queen's Mystery Magazine,* and elsewhere. He is sometimes seen busking in subway stations.

Aliya Whiteley was born in Devon in 1974, and currently lives in West Sussex, UK. She writes novels, short stories and non-fiction and has been published in places such as *The Guardian, Interzone, McSweeney's Internet Tendency, Black Static, Strange Horizons,* and anthologies such as Unsung Stories' *2084* and Lonely Planet's *Better than Fiction* I and II. She has been shortlisted for a Shirley Jackson Award, British Fantasy and British Science Fiction awards, the John W Campbell Award, and a James Tiptree Jr award. She also writes a regular column for *Interzone* and occasionally reviews films, books and TV at *Den of Geek.* Her latest novel,

The Loosening Skin, was published in the UK by Unsung Stories in November 2018.

~*~

Matty Long is an award-winning author and illustrator. He holds a first-class degree in Illustration and a Master's in Children's Book Illustration from the prestigious Cambridge School of Art. His debut picture book *Super Happy Magic Forest* was shortlisted for the prestigious Waterstones Children's Prize.

Jared Shurin has edited or co-edited over two dozen anthologies, including *The Djinn Falls in Love* and *The Outcast Hours* (with Mahvesh Murad), *The Lowest Heaven* (with Anne C. Perry) and *The Book of the Dead*. He has won some awards and lost many more. He's a certified BBQ judge.

More New Titles from NewCon Press

David Gullen – Shopocalypse

A Bonnie and Clyde for the Trump era, Josie and Novik embark on the ultimate roadtrip. In a near-future re-sculpted politically and geographically by climate change, they blaze a trail across the shopping malls of America in a printed intelligent car (stolen by accident), with a hundred and ninety million LSD-contaminated dollars in the trunk, buying shoes and cameras to change the world.

Kim Lakin-Smith – Rise

Charged with crimes against the state, Kali Titian (pilot, soldier, and engineer), is sentenced to Erbärmlich prison camp, where few survive for long. Here she encounters Mohab, the Speaker's son, and uncovers two ancient energy sources, which may just bring redemption to an oppressed people. The author of *Cyber Circus* returns with a dazzling tale of courage against the odds and the power of hope.

Simon Morden – Bright Morning Star

A ground-breaking take on first contact from scientist and novelist Simon Morden. Sent to Earth to explore, survey, collect samples and report back to its makers, an alien probe arrives in the middle of a warzone. Witnessing both the best and worst of humanity, the AI probe faces situations that go far beyond the parameters of its programming, and is forced to improvise, making decisions that may well reshape the future of a world.

Legends 3 – edited by Ian Whates

David Gemmell passed away in 2006, leaving behind a legacy of memorable characters, and thrilling tales. The *Legends* series of anthologies, of which this the third and almost certainly final volume, is intended to pay homage to one of fantasy fiction's greatest writers. Features a selection of dazzling stories written especially for the books by some of the finest fantasy authors around.

www.newconpress.co.uk

NewCon Press Novella Set 6: Blood and Blade

Four independent stand-alone novellas of sword play, sorcery, blood-drenched battles, noble deeds and fool-hardy endeavours, linked only by their shared cover art. Released summer 2019, in paperback, limited edition hardback, and as a slipcased set featuting all four novellas as signed hardbacks and **Duncan Kay**'s combined artwork as a wrap-around.

In **Edward Cox**'s *The Bone Shaker,* Sir Vladisal and her knights are lost within endless woodlands. Harried by demons, they seek the kidnapped son of their Duchess. **Gaie Sebold**

takes us on *A Hazardous Engagement*, wherein a wily gang of thieves are set an impossible task. Fortunately, they never know when to quit. In *Serpent Rose,* **Kari Sperring** takes us to the realm of Avalon and the intrigues surrounding some of the lesser known knights and characters of King Arthur's court,

while in **Gavin Smith**'s *Chivalry* we follow a young knight from the tourney fields to the battlefield, where he is forced to grow up rapidly as he faces challenges beyond his wildest imaginings.

Four stunning tales of epic fantasy at a smaller scale, by four outstanding authors

www.newconpress.co.uk

IMMANION PRESS
Purveyors of Speculative Fiction

Strindberg's Ghost Sonata & Other Uncollected Tales by Tanith Lee

This book is the first of three anthologies to be published by Immanion Press that will showcase some of Tanith Lee's most sought-after tales. Spanning the genres of horror and fantasy, upon vivid and mysterious worlds, the book includes a story that has never been published before – 'Iron City' – as well as two tales set in the Flat Earth mythos; 'The Pain of Glass' and 'The Origin of Snow', the latter of which only ever appeared briefly on the author's web site. This collection presents a jewel casket of twenty stories, and even to the most avid fan of Tanith Lee will contain gems they've not read before. ISBN 978-1-912815-00-5, £12.99, $18.99 pbk

The Lord of the Looking Glass by Fiona McGavin

The author has an extraordinary talent for taking genre tropes and turning them around into something completely new, playing deftly with topsy-turvy relationships between supernatural creatures and people of the real world. 'Post Garden Centre Blues' reveals an unusual relationship between taker and taken in a twist of the changeling myth. 'A Tale from the End of the World' takes the reader into her developing mythos of a post-apocalyptic world, which is bizarre, Gothic and steampunk all at once. 'Magpie' features a girl scavenging from the dead on a battlefield, whose callous greed invokes a dire curse. Following in the tradition of exemplary short story writers like Tanith Lee and Liz Williams, Fiona has a vivid style of writing that brings intriguing new visions to fantasy, horror and science fiction. ISBN: 978-1-907737-99-2, £11.99, $17.50 pbk

A Raven Bound with Lilies by Storm Constantine

The Wraeththu have captivated readers for three decades. This anthology of 15 tales collects all the published Wraeththu short stories into one volume, and also includes extra material, including the author's first explorations of the androgynous race. The tales range from the 'creation story' *Paragenesis*, through the bloody, brutal rise of the earliest tribes, and on into a future, where strange mutations are starting to emerge from hidden corners of the earth. ISBN: 978-1-907737-80-0 £11.99, $15.50 pbk

www.immanion-press.com
info@immanion-press.com